# MELISSA POULIOT

# SEARCH FOR SKY

The Rhiannon Series #4

By the author of the Number 1 Amazon Bestseller *Write About Me*

Published by MP Media (Vic) Pty Ltd in Australia, 22–2–22

978–0–9872355–7–2 (paperback)
B09NR21VYK (ASIN ebook Amazon)

A catalogue record for this book is available from the National Library of Australia.

Cover design Lara Walsh & Brent Occleshaw
Author photo Photos by Honey
Book formatting Jason Anderson, Polgarus Studio

This storyline and characters are fictional and not intended to represent any
individual or circumstance unless otherwise stated.

*The name Ulla is a girl's name of German, Scandinavian,*
*Norse origin meaning 'will, determination'.*
*It is short for Ursula in German-speaking countries.*

# ALSO BY MELISSA POULIOT

## FICTION

The Missing Annabelle Brown Series
*Write About Me (2013)*
*FOUND (2017)*

Detective Rhiannon McVee Series
*FIND ME (2014)*
*When You Find Me (2015)*
*You'll Never Find Me (2016)*
*Search for Sky (2022)*
*Lost Lucy (coming soon)*

## NON-FICTION

*Yellow Sunbird (unpublished memoir)*
*Yanga Track…Wanjab, Gadjin and Murnong*
*For Life…How We Got The Water Back*
*Project Hindmarsh, 10 Years and Beyond*
*A Pillar In Our Community, 25 Years of Wimmera Uniting Care*

*For my readers, who gave me the courage to*
*keep writing when the words wouldn't come.*

*And for Laura and her dedication to a glass half full life,*
*where every new day is a fresh start, even the bad days.*

This book is a work of fiction set in Australia in 1995, when Paul Keating is the Australian Prime Minister and Bill Clinton is the US President. *Braveheart* wins Best Picture and Mel Gibson wins Best Director at the Academy Awards. The most popular television shows are *Seinfeld* and *ER* and bestselling non-fiction books include *Men are from Mars, Women are from Venus* and Bryce Courtenay's *The Potato Factory*. *Toy Story*, which starts a new era in animated cinema, *Batman Forever* and *Apollo 13* are the top three box office successes. Australian cinema revolutionises the talking animal movie with the release of *Babe* which earns seven Oscar nominations and wins best visual effects.

On Australian television the ABC airs its television miniseries based on the relationship between Roger 'the Dodger' Rogerson and notorious criminal Arthur 'Neddy' Smith, and highlights widespread corruption in the NSW Police. The jury hands down a 'not guilty' verdict in the OJ Simpson trial for the murder of his ex-wife Nicole Brown Simpson and her friend Ronald Goldman.

Bryan Adams, Madonna, Michael Jackson, Maria Carey and Whitney Houston are among the top 10 musical artists and the most popular songs are *Gangsta's Paradise* from Coolio and *Kiss from a Rose* by Seal. Shania Twain establishes herself on the world stage with the release of her first number 1 hit *Any Man of Mine* on American country music charts dominated by Tim McGraw, Faith Hill, Trisha Yearwood, Alan Jackson and Brooks and Dunn. Closer to home, Gina Jeffreys wins Female Vocalist of the Year at the Tamworth Golden Guitar Awards, Lee Kernaghan's *Three Chain Road* is the top selling single and Graeme Connors scoops the awards with Song of the Year, Album of the Year and Male Vocalist of the Year with *Songs from the Homeland*.

Although official records weren't kept in 1995, the Australian Federal Police National Missing Persons Coordination Centre estimates around 30,000 people were reported missing. Many of those were found safe and well within a week. Others were also found, tragically for those left behind, deceased.

Of those fathers, daughters, brothers, sisters, cousins, sons, nieces, nephews, grandchildren, friends and valued community members who went missing in 1995, the national missing persons register lists twenty-one as still missing, leaving long, ambiguous decades of trauma in their wake. Their names are **Alan Thomas, Anthony Strong, Christopher Lane, Claus Schmahl, Daniel Sheppard, David Robinson, Edward Faulkner, Elizabeth Barlow, Frederick Bamboo, Geoffrey Rallings, Habtom Ghilagaber, Josephine Jennings, Kenneth Bethune, Koji Shiraishi, Leslie Hinton, Louise Brian, Richard Sajko, Roy Buhagiar, Shari Davison, Tamela Menzies and Wayne Pickett.**

There are many more missing people who aren't on official databases. This fictional story is inspired by these people and the many thousands of others who have still not come home.

## 1970

'I'M JUST NIPPING down to the chemist Lucy Lou, if you're a good girl and stay in your room, I'll bring you a special treat for a special girl.'

'Okay Mummy,' Lucy didn't argue. In her short three years, she had never argued.

'You are my golden child,' Mummy whispered as she kissed Lucy's hot forehead. Her temperature was still roaring. Last week they moved from Warracknabeal in western Victoria to the oldest tiny town in Queensland, a dazzling, glistening place overlooking brilliant blue oceans of the Great Barrier Reef.

She didn't know her neighbours, and had not had time to make new friends. She had no choice but to leave her little girl home alone to get more Panadol. She reassured herself, she'd only be gone a short time.

Lucy forced her eyes to stay open so she could admire her Mum's waving long hair and swinging bright red umbrella leave her room. 'Bye bye Mummy,' she whispered through her delirium.

A week later Lucy's temperature was finally gone, leaving her tiny body like an empty shell washed up on the sand, abandoned by its owner. Limp and lifeless during her fever, she hadn't had the energy to move off her bed and her sheets were putrid.

She whimpered softly, her matted mess of golden-brown hair over her face soaking first the sweat from her fever, then the tears she couldn't stop crying.

Something was wrong, terribly wrong. She was confused. Where was Mummy? Why didn't she come in and scoop her up in her soft, gentle arms and deliver the treat she'd promised if she was a good girl and stayed in her room?

She fell in and out of consciousness where dreams and reality were much the same. When the familiar sound of the front door opening broke through, she felt peace. Mummy was finally home.

The man came into the bedroom and gently lifted her out of the tangle of her urine and faeces-stained sheets.

It wasn't Mummy but that was okay. He smelt like her Mummy, so it wouldn't be long before she was back where she belonged, in the arms of the kind, beautiful, strong woman who was her whole world.

# 1

*14 February 1995*

'YOU LOOK BEAUTIFUL tonight,' Mac whispered as he moved Rhiannon around the dance floor during the wedding waltz. It wasn't exactly a waltz they were doing, more a shuffle, then a side-step, then a twirl.

'You've got two left feet,' she giggled.

'I can't dance and talk at the same time.'

She kissed him softly and snuggled close.

'Follow my lead,' she said, 'and you'll be fine. And you'd better let me do all the talking!'

'Mmm, what's new?'

'Hey!'

'You are known to be a bit of a talker.'

He stepped on her toes, again.

'Okay, you got that right. But you can seriously not step on my toes again or you'll break them with your big clodhopping, cowdy boots.'

He concentrated on the steps as she took him around the dance floor. When Randy Travis faded away at the end of *Forever and Ever, Amen*, Mac was quick to move back to their table.

'I guess I was lucky to get one dance out of you!'

At the wedding table they watched the newly married couple. Duncan had Rose on his hip and his other arm around Alice as they danced, looking blissfully content. The perfect family.

'I think Duncan must have had dance lessons,' Rhiannon commented. 'Maybe you should ask him for some pointers.'

Mac laced his fingers through hers under the table and leaned in to kiss her. 'And when might I need to do this, my beautiful bridesmaid?'

'Soon, very soon.'

Rhiannon pushed aside her reservations about their future while they sorted out their home location.

She felt certain they would marry, but when they did, she wanted to go home to him every night. With her working in Bourke and him living with his parents on their station near Cunnamulla around four hours away, that seemed impossible.

'Let's not get too carried away. Tonight it's all about Dunc and Alice, and I don't know about you, but I'm about ready to take off these heels and partay!'

'I thought it was kick up these heels?'

'Yeah, but my feet are bloody killing me!'

RHIANNON HATED SUNDAY nights, climbing into her little Mazda, which her dear Dad Bill would be pleased was still going strong, to face the long drive south, across the border, away from Mac.

She had company, her faithful Honey dog, who got excited no matter where they were going, as long as they were together. Honey helped, but she didn't replace the ache and loss.

They'd been mustering sheep all weekend and hardly had a private minute for themselves, making it even harder to leave.

'I love you,' he said softly as he gently moved his fingers through her hair, still damp from her shower and hanging loose around her shoulders.

'I love you too,' she replied, breathing him in.

'Better hit the road before the roos get too thick,' he said, not making any moves to let her go.

'Yeah, I should,' she replied, still hanging on tight.

'I hate this Rhee, I hate the goodbyes.'

'Me too, but hey, it's only fourteen sleeps and I'll see you again!'

'Fourteen sleeps, that's way too many.'

'I know. You'll be right though, crutching and all, you won't have a minute to scratch your arse, let alone miss me.'

'You're probably right, but I'll still miss you.'

The sting had gone out of the hot day and a slight breeze whispered around them as the sun sank lower towards to horizon. They continued their miss you, love you banter for another ten minutes before Rhiannon reluctantly pulled away. 'I've really gotta go, otherwise it will be dark by the time I get home, and I'd really like to get through that last stretch before the roos come in too thick.'

Mac stood at the back gate until her dust disappeared, wondering if his heart was still intact. He would give anything to wake up to her beautiful smiling face every morning. He'd even be happy to wake up beside her when she woke up on the grumpy side of the bed, he didn't care what side of the bed it was.

His Mum Rhonda, who everyone called Ronnie, watched from the back door, chook bucket in hand. She wondered if they'd ever get it together, with Rhiannon so focussed on her police career and Mac tied to their family property which she and Richard hoped to pass onto him, one day.

He turned as he heard the spring-loaded gauze door slam shut.

'How's it going mate? Want to help me feed the chooks?'

'G'day Mum, yeah, going alright.'

That was all he had to say on the matter.

'Got a busy couple of weeks ahead of us, hope the chooks are laying well. We're going to need your scrambled eggs for brekky to keep us going.'

'Lucky for you I've been saving the eggs, and lucky for you I shot the fox last week that was skulking around the chook pen. You'll be getting scrambled eggs, bacon, chops, sausages and tomatoes every morning.'

'I'm sure you're the reason we're never short on extras for crutching, they can't stay away from your cooking.'

'I love this this time of year, any excuse to get into the kitchen to feed the masses. I've been baking up a storm. The freezer is full of cakes and biscuits. I made your favourite walnut cake too.'

Mac laughed as he opened the gate for her. 'Mmm, not keen to share that with anyone!'

The chooks clucked around them, a couple jumping up impatiently for the bucket scraps.

'Hey,' Mac laughed. 'You pushy women, get back!'

It was just what he needed to snap him out of his sullen mood. He'd always loved his chooks, since he was a little boy he'd spend hours with them, watching their mindless peck peck peck and cluck cluck cluck.

He picked one up and snuggled it under his arm. Daphne. She was his favourite, even though she stopped laying six months ago. Her dark red feathers with black streaks were sleek and her giant feet put her at the top of the pecking order.

He sat on a giant tree stump in the middle of the pen with Daphne while Rhonda collected the eggs.

'What's today's haul Mum?'

'A dozen, a few eggs down. Pity Daphne isn't on the lay, she never skipped a beat.'

'Oh well,' Mac said, gently smoothing her feathers while she lay content in his arms. 'She's made her contribution, now she just needs to keep an eye on all the others and make sure they perform.'

'You and your chooks,' Mum laughed. 'You should have been a chook farmer, not a sheep farmer.'

'Maybe one day I will. I hear there's good money in chooks.'

Ronnie could see he was carrying the weight of the world on his young shoulders. 'It will work out, love,' she said as she kissed him on the top of his head.

She left him on the stump with Daphne to get started on dinner. Mac couldn't see it 'working out'. He couldn't see him and Rhiannon ever being able to live the way he wanted to, not when she was married to her job, and they lived so far apart. Every time he broached the subject of them settling down, Rhiannon would sidestep and change the subject.

His Mum's comment opened a tiny chink of an idea. Maybe he didn't have to be a sheep farmer forever, or even stay here forever? Mac shook his head and ran his fingers through his jet-black hair which was well overdue for a cut. It was too hard to think about now.

Daphne flapped her wings, impatient to get down and boss the others around.

Mac left his dreams in the chook pen to get ready for tomorrow, which was far easier to think about than finding a way to wake up next to Rhiannon every single day for the rest of his life.

**RONNIE'S WALNUT CAKE**
½ cup butter
1 cup white sugar
2 eggs (separated)
½ cup milk
1 teaspoon cinnamon
1 large cup SR flour
½ cup finely chopped walnuts

*Method*
Cream butter and sugar, add well-beaten egg yolks, then milk, cinnamon and flour. Lastly, fold through well-beaten egg whites with a wooden spoon. Bake on 180 degrees Celsius for 45 minutes. Ice with plain or lemon icing when cool.

# 2

'MCVEE.'

'Cassettari.'

'I've got news on one of your cases, Keely Johnson.'

Detective Senior Sergeant Andy Cassettari was Rhiannon's former boss from Kings Cross Police Station, where she had been stationed before transferring to Bourke to be closer to Mac and her Mum Jane after her Dad Bill died suddenly. At Kings Cross she had quickly worked her way up to the rank of Detective Senior Constable, but out here the Detective part meant very little.

Although three hundred and fifty kilometres still separated her from her cowboy and her incredible Mum, who had been running their property single-handedly since Bill died five years ago, it was better than a thousand kilometres.

'News' from Andy was always headlines. Everything else was just froth and bubbles.

'Spill.'

Andy paused, for a long time.

'You're enjoying this, aren't you?' Rhiannon said sarcastically.

Keely Johnson was one of Rhiannon's major obsessions; the teenager went missing soon after Rhiannon started working at the Cross in eighty-eight, straight out of the police academy and as green as the Granny Smith apples on her neighbour's tree.

'You're enjoying this aren't you?' Rhiannon said sarcastically, hoping Andy's big news was something solid, finally, that would lead them to Keely.

Seven years of searching, and still counting. They had several breakthroughs including a deathbed confession from a bikie gang leader of an eye-witness account of Keely climbing into a green EH Holden wagon.

After that trail went cold, Rhiannon stumbled upon another lead from an outback shearer, Jeremy, who grew fond of Keely after she found her way into a camp kitchen near Brewarrina. Jeremy had let her slip away, in the same EH Holden, one stormy night.

Rhiannon and Keely's sister Ashley ran into Jeremy in a Bourke pub while Ashley was on work experience under Rhiannon's supervision last year. Invigorated by the possibilities of one day finding her sister, as soon as she turned seventeen, Ashley enrolled into the police academy, champing at the bit to start her career.

The coincidences and degrees of separation seemed fictional and too good to be true but as Rhiannon explained to Andy, this was typical of outback life. Even with hundreds of kilometres between towns and stations, people seemed to always cross paths.

She used one of her favourite coincidence stories as an example. 'I ran into a government fella in a café in St George one day, we both went our separate ways then two days later we ran into each other in another café at Dirrinbandi, then a week later I saw him crossing the street in Bourke. I'd never laid eyes on this bloke before, but I can guarantee I'll be laying eyes on him again and again now, for years.'

Despite their best efforts, Jeremy's lead went cold. Keely slipped through their fingers yet again. More time passed. Keely's family grieved in *limbo land, that space in between*, holding onto hope she was alive while feeling helpless at not being able to find her.

'It's a long story but the first part is, I think we've discovered who S.K.Y. is.' Andy spelled out the letters.

Rhiannon shot out of her chair and paced around the desk within cord distance of the phone.

'Serious?'

Like a cassette on rewind, she went back to a warm October night last year when she sat under the stars beside a body roo shooters found buried in a remote paddock. To add to the mystery, the body's eyes were gouged out. It was clear a human had removed them as part of the killing ritual.

Stuck to a stick nearby was a bloodied piece of paper with the letters S.K.Y. scratched in biro. They had fingerprints off the stick and the paper but nobody to match them to.

The decomposed body still remained unidentified in the Glebe morgue. No identity for the body, no identity for the fingerprints of the killer. Rhiannon held the file at Bourke Police Station but Andy also had a copy – it wasn't standard procedure, but Rhiannon and Andy were far from *standard procedure* detectives.

Andy was her mentor; she was his prodigy. No matter where they were stationed, that would never change.

'I couldn't be more serious if I tried. It's taken some doing but we know who the girl with no eyes is.'

'Get out!'

'No, I will not get out, this is for real. Fair dinks as some might say.'

Rhiannon thought if she looked down at her chest she would see her heart beating, like in the Walt Disney cartoons.

'How? Who? How are they connected to Keely?'

'It's too much for a phone call. You're just going to have to wait a day until I get out to that shithole of a place you call home.'

'What? You can't friggin' do that to me. You can't call and tell me half the story, actually less than half, in fact, only one-eighth, then say you're not going to tell the rest until tomorrow. That's just plain cruel.'

'Sorry McVee, like I said, too much for a phone call. I'm leaving right now. See you in how long? Twenty-four hours?'

'You're soft if it takes you that long to drive from Kings Cross to Bourke Andy.'

'Who you calling soft?'

Rhiannon growled in frustration. 'Stop trying to change the subject. Are you sure you can't tell me now? At least give me a hint.'

'No. Absolutely not. Sit tight. I'll be there soon.'

'Watch for roos.'

'What? Roos?'

'You know, kangaroos. The things that go hop out here and rearrange your front bumper.'

Andy laughed. 'Aah, kangaroos. Yeah. Gotcha.'

'Bloody city slicker.'

'Bloody country bumpkin.'

Rhiannon stopped pacing, but her mind continued to fly in a trillion directions over who S.K.Y. was and what tomorrow would bring.

Andy indicated this was connected to Keely, meaning her other most pressing missing persons case Ayala Philips was still at a standstill. Ayala disappeared from her outback sheep station two years ago under a cloud of suspicion pointing to her sleazy husband Clive. Although they'd uncovered a bitterly unhappy marriage and were trying to bring him down for being part of an international paedophile ring, they were no closer to discovering *where the fuck* Ayala was.

Rhiannon reorganised her already organised desk. No surface, desk drawer, kitchen cupboard or filing cabinet at the Bourke Police Station was safe from her obsessive straightening. Their only reprieve would be when Detective Sergeant Andy Cassettari walked through the door.

# 3

BIANCA STOOD NEAR the hangar, waiting for the sound of the approaching small plane with her brother Red behind the controls. She had finally convinced him to take time off from his big city accounting job in Melbourne to visit home and put his accounting skills to good use in their family business.

The distant drone sent her stomach into a flutter. How was she going to ask him questions she didn't really want answers to? She had to be brave though if they had any hope of picking up the pieces their sick, damaged father, Clive, had left behind.

Clive's crumpled, shameful face flashed into her mind from the last time she saw him, when they faced off across a grey-blue laminated table with cold steel legs in Bourke Police Station's characterless interview room. A fizzing fluorescent light, just like an American cop movie, had given her a persistent eye tic.

Rhiannon was quietly standing in the corner when Clive admitted to molesting Red from when he was an innocent, little boy. If it wasn't for Rhiannon's presence Bianca may have leapt over the table and strangled Clive with her favourite Hermes silk scarf, a twenty-first birthday gift from Ayala.

Crafty, well-connected bastard that he was, he was now out on bail and living it up in one of their luxury apartments in Sydney. Bail conditions forced him to wear surveillance tracker and report to the Mosman Police Station at the same time every day. Still, he wasn't behind bars where Bianca believed he belonged – not only for the suspected murder of his wife but for his involvement in an international paedophile ring, and now, for the sins he'd committed against his own son.

Her brothers all voted for Bianca to become the overseer of the Philips' family business interests. Banks, electrical companies, government agencies and right down to sporting and other membership-based clubs had no clear systems in place for a family member to look after the missing person's affairs. While an investigation remained open, and a Coroner hadn't declared whether the missing person was formally deceased, simple things like wanting to access Ayala's bank accounts or property records weren't simple at all.

Although their Uncle Kenneth and Ayala's trusted lawyer tried to reassure her otherwise, she knew there was always a risk Clive would take the family's wealth away. If everything in her mother's shocking, heartbreaking diary she found hidden under the floorboards in her bedroom was to be believed, she wasn't taking any chances.

Uncle Kenneth was unable to help Bianca sort out the affairs because of ill health and recommended a younger lawyer he believed was a good match. Now Bianca was working with Michael Waters, who her brothers called Shiny Michael, to wade through the complications that ensued when someone went missing.

The wind picked up and she watched a whirly gig swirl along the immaculately graded red clay runway, wide enough and long enough for a small Qantas passenger plane.

Red brought the plane carefully in and stuck the perfect landing. Bianca closed her mouth to stop the red dust from coating her teeth, waving excitedly to the small head of carrot red hair through the windscreen.

Red waited for the dust to settle and the engines to cool before filling out his flight log and making sure everything was in order.

'Hey little Sis,' he said casually as he disembarked. They hugged awkwardly. Red always was an awkward hugger; now Bianca understood why.

Bianca helped him push the steps back up and lock the plane and they worked together to position it in the hangar next to a restored Yeoman Cropmaster, a single seat agricultural aircraft Clive painted bright yellow and used for taking visitors on joy flights over their expansive property of around two hundred and fifty thousand acres on the old scale.

'Have you heard from Dad?' Red got straight to the point as they walked over the battered-up Toyota Landcruiser that had been the station's workhorse for longer than Bianca could remember.

She started up the engine and headed towards the house, pretending she didn't hear him. She swerved to miss a kangaroo that jumped unexpectedly from behind a stand of mulga, and the crackle of a two-way conversation between their head station hand and young jackaroos still learning the ropes filled the cabin.

As they rattled over to the house they fell into a conversation about shearing and the upcoming cattle sale in Dubbo. Safe territory.

The new live-in housekeeper Clive insisted on Bianca having waited at the gate, her hand out to take Red's bag.

When Bianca told him she had a new housekeeper he imagined someone like the hideous ugly witch Nurse Matilda from the books on their childhood bookshelves. The woman who stood at his gate looked like she'd stepped off the front cover of a fashion magazine into the hot, dusty outback. Wavy blonde hair tumbled down her back, her naturally tanned skin was free of blemishes, not even one small freckle. She stood with perfect posture and grace to greet them.

When she said 'I take bag?' and flashed her pearly white teeth, Red was sure he'd died and gone to heaven. Claudia Schiffer's twin sister was standing at his front gate.

The large house swallowed Ulla, even her name was beautiful, while Red and Bianca washed up in the bathroom at the back entrance before heading to the kitchen. Ulla had the kitchen table laden with morning smoko, Swedish style.

'Geez, who's coming?'

Bianca laughed. 'You! Just like our smoko with scones, tea cake and Anzac biscuits, in Sweden they have 'fika breaks'.'

Red marvelled at the array. Chocolate balls, which looked like the rum balls Ayala would make in bulk at Christmas.

'Rum balls?'

'No, they're called Kokosballs, there's no rum in these ones. Not like Mum's, one of hers and we'd be over the limit!' Bianca and Red's laughter died quickly.

'Ulla puts a small amount of coffee in hers, they are delish.'

'What are these?' Red pointed to a plate of glistening sweet buns, still warm and giving off a cinnamon aroma that felt like a hug.

'Those are my favourites.' Bianca patted her stomach which was filling out thanks to Ulla ready to accommodate with a fika break every time she walked into the kitchen.

'Those are kanelbulle or kardemummabulle,' Ulla explained as she approached the table with the tea pot. 'Cinnamon buns. My great–grandmother's recipe, we learned as children, how do you say, it's given to the girls in the family?'

'Passed down through the generations?' Red couldn't help himself from blushing. He was never short of a woman on his arm, but Ulla unsettled him in a way he couldn't explain.

'Yes, that's it. Passed through the generations.'

Ulla's second language was English but she still stumbled over phrases in Australia. She got lost in conversations when too many colloquialisms ran together.

Red and Bianca sat down for their feast and Ulla made to slip away.

'You're not having a cuppa with us?' Bianca pulled out a chair for Ulla.

'No, you and Mr Red have lots to catch up on, I have washing to hang out. I leave you now.'

Bianca watched Red's face fall.

'She's pretty gorgeous isn't she?'

Red blushed again and reached for a warm bun, stuffing it into his mouth.

'She's nothing like all those flaky girls you've been hanging out with your whole dating life, so don't get any ideas.'

Bianca never understood why Red always went for girls who couldn't hold an intelligent conversation. Superficial types only interested in his family's status and wealth. Knowing what she knew now went some way towards explaining why he couldn't form meaningful relationships.

They moved on from the general chit chat to the impending court case for Clive, which Rhiannon and the Kings Cross Detective in charge of the case Andy Cassettari were stalling. Bianca explained to Red they were trying to find a witness for paedophile charges they wanted to lay, dependent on a key witness who had disappeared into the cracks of the pavement in the bustling tourist city of Phuket.

Ayala's diary Bianca had found hidden underneath the floorboards in her bedroom, supported the paedophile theory, but without Ayala to testify about the things she wrote in her diary, police needed something more concrete.

When Clive admitted to Bianca he'd molested Red as a young boy, she thought it was enough for Rhiannon to charge him then and there, lock him up and throw away the key.

However, apart from that one admission, which was not made in a recorded interview, he remained tight-lipped. Any attempt to get it 'on the record' resulted in him categorically denying ever saying it in the first place. His expensive lawyer had everyone so tangled up in legal jargon they had nowhere to go.

He sent letters weekly to Bianca, saying he had lied about Red, sticking firmly to a line he was so confused and traumatised since discovering Ayala had been trying to poison him. His rambling letters hinted at significant mental distress, squarely placing all blame on Ayala's shoulders.

'It is like a twisted Hollywood film plot, surely it can't be real,' Red mumbled.

'If they can at least get Clive behind bars on paedophile charges, and uncover his involvement in sourcing young men and boys for others based on a pattern of several of Clive's male business contacts being in Phuket at the same time, we might have a hope of getting him to confess where Mum is,' Bianca explained.

She left the words hanging, a strand of spider's web swinging precariously in a southerly spring wind. None of this was public knowledge but Rhiannon was keeping Bianca in the loop as much as she was able. Partly to reassure her they were doing everything they could, also so Bianca could keep an ear out for anything she might uncover as she picked up the pieces of her life.

At that moment the phone rang, a shrill interruption slicing through the web that would now need to be rebuilt from scratch.

Day disappeared into night. When Bianca eventually switched her bedside lamp off and went through her deep breathing routine to stop her mind from the circles it constantly ran, she thought she'd leave it alone. If police found the Phuket contact, that would be enough.

As she drifted into the sleep that only came when she was too exhausted to stay awake for one more second, she decided having Red here to help run the station was far more important than delving into that deep dark place where reality was worse than any news report or crime thriller.

RED WAS PRETTY good at keeping his mind organised. He had compartments; some never saw the light of day.

Out here, it was the silence that woke him. Living in a city that never slept meant he had noise around him every waking and sleeping moment. Here it was the silence, the absence of noise, he noticed most.

Pre-dawn, before the birds started chittering, it was more silent than ever. Had he been dreaming or was the shuffling sound when feet first hit timber floorboards before the creak and creepiness of tiptoes towards his room real?

He started to sweat. He knew every weak spot in the hallway between his parents' room and his. His heart thumped as he listened for another creak. His feet hung over the end of his childhood bed and he wondered why he hadn't just unpacked his things in one of the many guest rooms instead.

He was anticipating the next creak but his thumping heart was making it difficult to hear. He was eleven again.

'Red, you awake?'

'Mmmmmm...'

The warm familiar body of someone he loved. Someone he looked up to.

'I thought I heard you call out, thought you were having a bad dream,' Dad crooned while he stroked his back.

Red relaxed, it was just Dad coming in to say goodnight. But why was he staying? Why was he getting in under the blankets?

'It's a bit cold mate,' Dad whispered. 'I'll just tuck in here for a moment 'til you get back to sleep.'

Clive's hands didn't stop the whole time, rubbing, smoothing, softly, gently.

Red felt himself relax and drift back to the dreams of chasing sheep through the scrub on his motorbike.

How could he concentrate on the sheep when someone was pressing so hard up against him from behind, hurting him, making him cry? He tried to imagine he was still on the motorbike, but he could hardly breathe with Clive's hand over his mouth stopping him from calling out.

As he drifted in and out of consciousness he wondered if he had the strength to call his Mum. When he felt the sharp, excruciating pain, followed by a shameful feeling of something he couldn't understand, he knew he didn't. And he never would.

RED STUMBLED INTO the kitchen, his mouth dry since drifting back into a deep, dark sleep after his pre-dawn nightmare. He caught his breath at the sight of Ulla, drenched in the pure morning light coming through the large window over the sink.

'Morning,' he mumbled through sleepy dirt filled eyes.

'Good morning Mr Red,' Ulla replied in her sing-song voice that matched perfectly with her ethereal glow. Red had to concentrate to stop himself from going stupidly romantic.

'You like coffee Mr Red?'

She fussed around him, pulling out one of Ayala's expensive Danish-designed stools that sat neatly along one side of the central island bench where Bianca liked to linger over breakfast.

'Yeah.' He blushed, again, as her arm brushed against him while she settled him into his stool.

Ulla continued fussing, handling his Mum's expensive coffee machine, shipped from Italy, like a professional barista. Red sat dumbly in her presence.

'You like long black? Capp-you-cheen-o?' He smiled at the way she formed her words around her strong Swedish accent.

'Cappuccino please, and thank you. You don't have to make it.'

'Of course I make. That's why I'm here. To make for you. Cook for you. Clean for you. If you make, I have nothing to do. I don't like nothing to do. I like to do, do.'

He welcomed the loveliness she sprinkled around. He had been dreading coming home, where memories of Ayala were still so raw. He felt her everywhere and expected her to walk through the door at any moment, ruffling his hair and kissing him on the cheek on her way to her next task.

Ayala also never sat still, and whenever Red was home he sat in this very spot and accepted her lavishings of love delivered via cups of strong Italian coffee and home–baked delights you'd find in any French cafe.

Ulla filled the space neatly, and the stab of pain he was used to feeling every time he wondered if Mum was dead or alive, wasn't nearly so sharp.

Bianca came in from outside to join them, she'd been up early for her daily jog with her favourite kelpie Mags, followed by a cup of tea with the chooks. Mags was one of Maggie's pups; Ayala's dog Maggie who the police had dug up from the garden soon after Ayala's disappearance at Rhiannon's insistence that the freshly dug bed outside the kitchen window was suspicious.

'Hey big bro, decided to get up eventually?'

'Very funny little sister; you always were an early riser. Mad, crazy people who like to jog with the sparrows, can't see the point in it myself.'

'Looks like you could do with a few jogs along the airstrip yourself, getting a bit of office accountant paunch around your middle I can see!'

Bianca poked him gently around the waist, which he admitted had gotten a little squishier lately. He had stopped going to the gym after Ayala disappeared, seeking solace at the bar around the corner from his office six nights out of seven.

The only reason it wasn't seven is he had a Sunday night dinner arrangement with an old school mate, Shane, which they promised years ago never to break. He wasn't sure why they stuck to it, but he needed it more than ever. Now that his nightmares had come back, and he walked on tenterhooks waiting for someone to find out the secrets he'd lived with since he was eleven.

ONCE ULLA WAS satisfied both Bianca and Red had all the food and drinks they needed, she glided out of the room. Red watched, thinking she was a magical fairy, with invisible gentle wings carrying her around so gracefully, her feet didn't even touch the ground.

He pushed away his stupid romantic notions. He had never been like this before.

His infatuations with women were short-lived, a means to an end. Organised, clinical even. It was part of not letting anyone too close. He copped an ear bashing on more than one occasion for being insensitive, hard to reach.

Bianca shook him out of his troubled thoughts.

'How are you coping Red?'

'Pretty well, you?'

'I'm okay. Most days.' Red noticed Bianca's eyes mist over and quickly moved to smooth over the awkwardness of a bout of crying, something he avoided at all costs.

'I wonder where she is, you know? I wonder and wonder. It just goes in so many different directions. I can never land anywhere.'

'That's exactly how it is,' Bianca's eyes brightened with Red's description. It wasn't just her mind going in circles.

She paused, waiting for him to keep speaking. It was the first time he'd opened up to her since Clive's arrest and ensuing bail hearing. They tried hard to get on with their lives but she had borne the brunt by being here on the property, surrounded by memories of Ayala, in their family home.

It felt like they had more chance of finding a bush tic on a Persian cat than finding Ayala.

It was also the first time her and Red had been on their own without the other brothers. It was a completely different dynamic when the four of them were together. They were great mates and slipped easily into the relationships of their childhood with inhouse jokes, wrestles, competitions on who was the fastest, the strongest, the cleverest.

Jackson, the second eldest, moved home from the Northern Territory cattle station he'd been working on to step into Clive's 'boss man' shoes.

Known to everyone as 'Jack', he was practical, hands on and excellent at working out solutions for keeping the station running smoothly, organising staff, managing shearing and crutching, sheep and cattle sales, fuel trucks, water. He flew in and out like a busy bee and Bianca saw him at least once a week.

Lachlan or Lachie, the baby of the family, was in his final year of film school in Toowoomba. He came home regularly, slipping easily from behind a camera onto a horse and motorbike. Bianca believed he belonged in front of the camera and not behind it, with his father's black curly hair, olive skin and nutty brown eyes with extra-long lashes he inherited from Ayala.

Bianca, Jack and Lachie stuck to facts, figures, mustering, shearing, stock sales, manpower, water, breakdowns, fuel trucks and transport carriers. They all shed tears, both on their own and every once in a while when they were together, but Jack and Lachlan picked themselves up quickly, a quality Bianca appreciated because it helped her do the same.

Red had stayed away, citing major business clients needing his full attention. It was last week's Sunday night dinner with Shane that convinced him to come home.

After stepping into a support role and watching his childhood friend spiral deeper into himself, Shane gave it to him straight.

'You need to face up to this mate. It's bloody hard to watch. Bianca needs you, she's more important than the corporate dickheads you're giving all your time to. Put your brilliant accounting brain and knowledge to good purpose and help her wade through the legal and financial nightmare I'm sure she's struggling to sort out on her own.

'Your brothers are both stepping up, but not you. Full of excuses you are. It's not right.'

He knew Shane was right, but he also knew that facing up to Ayala being gone would involve facing up to what Clive had done. He'd buried it for so long, he didn't think he'd ever be able to say it out loud. Not to himself, and certainly not to Bianca.

'I miss her so much Bee. She was always there for us. Always. We used to have this monthly thing, every month she'd come to Melbourne, we'd go shopping and test out the latest restaurants she'd read in restaurant reviews in The Age. She'd clean the unit from top to toe until the place sparkled like a Christmas tree.

'I used to grumble, for the cleaning thing. I paid someone to do it so there was no need for her to get involved. She would tutt tutt the whole time, telling me to sack my cleaner because she was no good. It drove me mad.

'Now I'd give anything for her to come round into my personal space and polish my furniture, pick up my smelly washing from the corner and scrub my bathroom.'

'I know, I feel the same. Do you know how many times she tried to redecorate my bedroom while I was in boarding school? I yelled at her, you know?

'She was just trying to make it more grown up for me, but I wanted to stay stuck in my childhood. I really wish I hadn't yelled at her.'

Red's voice went soft. 'Me too. I want to take back every mean word I said to her face, every mean word I said behind her back. The diary, what she was going through with...'

Red choked up, unable to say the word Dad. '...with Clive, do you think it's true?'

Bianca choked on her words. 'I believe her. I believe her more than I believe him. We were so young when we left for boarding school. We spent so little time here, when you think about it. I just had no idea, we had no idea he was so cruel to her, so controlling. How could we? Their lives became so twisted, and wrong...'

Red felt like someone had pulled his heart out and was stomping all over it on the black granite benchtop in front of them.

Bianca drained the dregs of her coffee and wondered if she had the energy to make another. Red stared at his hands, soft, office worker hands, and wondered how many blisters he'd have after a week in the sheep yards.

'The shearing team will arrive later,' Bianca said.

'Yeah, things will get pretty busy today. What do you want me to do?'

'Would be good if you could go down to the sheds, have a look around, make sure everything's in order. Jack and the boys are very capable, but he'll appreciate an extra set of hands. He'll be happy to see you.'

'Ah yes, he'll be happy to have someone else to boss around!'

Jack, as the eldest boy, had always been in charge. Red and Lachie followed him faithfully around as kids, getting into all sorts of danger. Before they all turned ten they'd had at least one major bone broken from a motorbike trick gone wrong or falling off a horse.

'There is that, he will definitely enjoy bossing you around! I'll stay at the house with Ulla, we'll make sure we've got enough food, and drink, for the boys who are staying here. The shearers have got their own cook, but we've got about six here. Extra mouths to feed, extra thirsts to quench!'

Ulla returned to the kitchen, their laughter signalling it was safe.

'More coffee?'

'Thanks Ulla, I'm okay,' Bianca said. 'I'll just have halfa on the books, got a few quick phone calls, then I'll be back in the kitchen to help you with the baking, lunch and dinner prep.'

'The books?' Red raised an eyebrow.

'Yeah, the books. My least favourite thing. Looking forward to handing them over to you big brother, but I'll let you settle in a bit first.'

Bianca punched him playfully on the arm and he grabbed her in an arm lock. Ulla laughed. She loved when the brothers brought fun and frivolity into this house. Bianca was more serious by nature; her brothers brought out her playful side.

Ulla could instantly tell that Red, with his serious accountant face hiding deep dark secrets and a warm, kind heart, was Bianca's favourite.

'Mr Red you be careful,' Ulla laughed with them. 'I need help in this kitchen to feed all the hungry mouths. I don't think I can do it without Miss Bee.'

Red flashed a brilliant smile and moved towards her.

'Don't worry Miss Ulla, I've never been able to beat Bianca in a wrestle, not since we were kids. She's way too strong and wily for me.'

Ulla blushed, he was standing close and breathing hard.

'You'll keep,' Bianca tossed over her shoulder as she walked to the office. 'See you later alligator.'

'In a while crocodile,' Red tossed back, eyes locked with Ulla.

He winked at her then headed in the opposite direction towards the back door. Ulla watched him pull his boots on and walk towards the back gate, Mags trotting happily at his heels in hope he would whistle her into the back of the ute and take her to the yards.

With her heart in a flutter she cleared the bench. She loved this Australia so much. Hot, dusty and isolated, the complete opposite to the lush mountainous area of her home.

She couldn't find the words in her letters to her family to describe how she'd fallen deeply in love. She knew if she tried to tell Red he would understand. He would be able to help her find the words. He would know what she meant when she said she loved the red dust under her fingernails and the feeling of her shirt sticking to her back.

She felt real out here. It lived up to every romantic notion of her late teenage years when she came across a magazine filled with photos of outback Australia. She knew then she had to come and live it for herself.

Bianca smiled over her bookwork as Ulla sang in the kitchen. Although she'd been dreading Red coming here, it seemed his presence was exactly what the house needed.

'Fuck you Clive,' she muttered under her breath. 'Fuck you and your wicked ways. You can't knock us down the way you knocked Mum. We'll come out on top, we'll be the winners, you'll be the loser. Just you wait and see.'

# 4

'OUR JANE DOE'S name is Lucy Wallace. She's twenty-nine. Born in Warracknabeal, western Victoria. Just her and her Mum, no father listed on the birth certificate. No siblings.'

Rhiannon got out a notebook and started scribbling. Andy waited for her to catch up.

'Then she turned up again, five years later. As Lucy Smith. I know. Original. And her father, Harold Smith, who I'm still trying to track down. Do you know how many Harold Smith's there are in Australia? Hundreds!

'We found one of her old schoolteachers, Grade Three. She had a few photos in a box from the year Lucy was at school.

'She remembered her because of a family tree school project; she was the only child in the class who didn't have any family history. Said she felt sad at the time, that somebody could be so alone and not know anything about where they came from. She remembered seeing her with her Dad at the supermarket, but he was a bit of a recluse, and never went to any school functions. The teacher, when prompted, said it was a weird setup.'

Rhiannon interrupted.

'Jesus Andy, how did you dig all this up? And piece it all together?'

'Pure genius McVee. You should know that by now. Superior investigative skills, that's how.'

Rhiannon pursed her lips, not impressed she'd been left out of the loop while all this investigating had been going on. This was her case after all, she's the one who got up at four o'clock in the morning to sit in the middle of nowhere and wait for investigators to turn up to the crime scene.

'I know what you're thinking McVee, this is your case and I shouldn't have taken over, but I wanted to do a bit of digging around first, in case I was on the wrong track.'

To break the uncomfortable silence, he laid a series of photographs on the table of the most beautiful looking child Rhiannon had ever seen. Her hair was golden brown. She looked like she had stepped right out of a fairytale.

Andy continued. 'Fast forward a few years, she and her Dad, Mr Smith, moved regularly, we were able to track her through school records.

'Then they stop. From what we can gather she left school at fifteen.'

'Whoa, hold up a bit. She moves all around with her dad 'Mr Smith' then disappears aged 15?'

'No, she doesn't disappear as in goes missing. She just isn't on any more school records.'

'Right, okay, where was the last school record?'

'You do like to interrupt, McVee.'

Rhiannon had ants in her pants. Andy was so slow; it took all her willpower not to finish every single one of his sentences.

'Eden High School, on the South Coast.'

Rhiannon had never heard of Eden. She got out her map book so she could find it.

'Looks like we're going on a long road trip.'

Andy laughed dryly. 'Another one. You know how I love long drives.'

He kept on with the story. 'She hitched around New South Wales then back into Victoria, fruit picking along the Murray River. Under the name Lucy Wallace. Her real name.'

'Hang on a minute, isn't she Lucy Smith? Where does the Wallace come from again?'

'Born in Warracknabeal.'

'Where the fuck is Warracknabeal? I've never heard of it.' Rhiannon turned to the index of her map book.

'Victoria,' Andy explained. Head west from Melbourne towards Adelaide, it's somewhere in there.'

Rhiannon found it quickly.

'Okay, if she was born in Warracknabeal, where did she first turn up on the school records as Lucy Smith?'

'A long way away, northern Queensland would you believe.'

'Okay right, where were the other schools she went to? Before she got here that is.'

Andy glared at her. 'Can you just let me finish my broad brushstrokes story, then you can fill in the details in your own time?'

Rhiannon sighed loudly. 'Fine, resume from where you were, wherever the fuck that was.'

'Lucy Wallace, no longer at school. Floated here and there, living on hippie communes, one of those free spirits. No known address. She had a driver's licence but there's no other record of her.'

'How did you work out it was her?' Rhiannon skipped ahead.

'Hold your horses, I know I said I'm giving broad brushstrokes but you've got to let me set the scene, and you've got to stop, interrupting, me.'

Rhiannon sucked in a deep breath through her nostrils.

'We would never have known she existed if it wasn't for a dentist in a town at the arse end of nowhere she saw about five years ago. Actually, if you're born in Warracknabeal it's not really the arse end of nowhere, and if you're living in Bourke it's not really the arse end of nowhere either.'

Rhiannon glared.

'Oh, sorry, I got side-tracked by arse ends, given that I'm one right now. The dentist pulled out her wisdom teeth. A small country town named Wycheproof, in the Victorian Mallee. Almost as remote as here, but surely not as hot.'

Right on cue Andy retrieved his handkerchief from his pocket and wiped his brow.

'You're soft,' Rhiannon teased. 'It's only forty degrees today.'

She pulled out a small fan from her bottom drawer, the desktop one she kept for extreme days, about forty-five degrees Celsius, and for when Andy ventured out of the Sydney city limits for a taste of outback extremes.

With his face close to the whirring fan, Andy continued.

'She turned up with a fellow. The reason they stuck in his mind was because they were in such a state they drove their car onto the footpath and almost through the front door.

'She was only semi-conscious she was in that much pain. They had been fruit picking around Swan Hill and she'd complained of a toothache but by the time they drove through Wycheproof she'd developed an abscess so big she had to go straight into emergency surgery. They removed all four of her wisdom teeth.'

Rhiannon interrupted. 'I get it. You've set this part of the scene enough Andy. She had a toothache and got her wisdom teeth out. No more details on that please, just move on!'

Rhiannon had a phobia of the dentist. Fortunately, she had excellent teeth, straight, white and hole-free. Her visits to the dentist were rare, but the thought of an abscess in her mouth, having a needle in her mouth and teeth removed was enough to make her want to pass out.

Andy fanned himself, sweat running down into his eyes. 'Geez it's hot. Air conditioner isn't working all that well.'

Rhiannon had to go and make herself a cup of tea. Otherwise, she was going to strangle Andy and his convoluted, complicated story. She balanced her cup, a glass of cold water and a couple of Arnott's Scotch Finger Biscuits, Andy's favourite.

He snapped the biscuit in half, crumbs landing on his lap as he demolished it, swinging on the back two legs of his chair.

'Hasn't anyone ever told you it's dangerous to swing on your chair like that?' Rhiannon snapped.

'Come on, come on, take a chill pill.' Andy grinned.

'You're enjoying this aren't you? Giving me half the story then making me wait a full night and day, a sleepless night mind you, before you share the rest. When you finally do arrive and get yourself settled like the old Nanna that you are, you drag it out to the point I could wring your smug, sweaty neck.'

Andy put his chair back onto four legs and stood up. He was as wired as Rhiannon. This was big. Major. He'd been tossing it around for days, and the whole drive to Bourke he'd rehearsed the best way to tell the story.

He decided from start to finish was best, and was determined not to let Rhiannon make him jump forwards, backwards and sidewards so it got all mixed up and messed about.

The identity of Lucy Wallace was only one part of this story.
There were more.
Including Keely.

# 5

*1983*

'SHIT, SHIT, SHIT,' Lucy muttered under her breath as the sharp corner of something behind the boxes in Dad's shed sliced her finger. She watched the blood come to the surface and quickly put it in her mouth to soothe the pain.

It was her sixteenth birthday next week. She was searching for the box she kept as a young child with her favourite things, so she could add to the birthday cards she knew would come in the mail from the school friends in Eden she'd recently left behind.

The box also contained school sports ribbons, teacher's awards and trinkets from friends. She wondered how many more of these she'd add, she hadn't enrolled into high school yet, she'd do that once they were settled in.

She knew her box was in here somewhere, amongst Dad's tools, smelly oil rags and old bottle collection he'd been collecting from the faraway places he visited. This was their eleventh move in eleven years and each time the shed got messier, her special birthday box harder to find.

Dad's work at the local council called him away as soon as the removalist truck pulled into their new dirt driveway east of the isolated outback town everyone joked about, Back O' Bourke, so things were in even more disarray.

It had been left to Lucy to explore the falling down cottage, which showed few signs of its former glory, but had potential. He would be so excited when she took him down to the icy cellar she found underneath where she discovered several dusty bottles of red wine that looked like they'd been there for a hundred years, at least!

Eventually her finger stopped bleeding. She deftly flicked a hair tie off her wrist and pulled her long golden-brown hair back into a ponytail.

'Right, be more careful Lucy Lou, instead of going in like a Dalmatian in a china shop.

'I know, I know, it's meant to be a bull in a china shop, but I changed it when I met the crazy plum pudding dog at the house at the top of the hill in Eden.'

Lucy was always talking to herself and always changing sayings around, creating her own family vocabulary in the absence of any sayings handed down by relatives.

Her thoughts wandered to Eden, where whales leapt out of the bay, as she carefully removed the boxes the strapping, young removalists carelessly shoved against the shed wall.

Eventually she found the culprit of the cut. A padlocked, solid wooden box she hadn't seen before. A splinter on the edge was the finger-slicer; it looked like the box had caught on a nail protruding from the shed wall.

It was battered and looked like it needed some love. She went searching for sandpaper to sand the splinter, then decided to spruce up the whole thing. Every swipe of lacquer revealed a beautiful, rich timber and piqued her curiosity. She had to find out what was inside this beautiful, locked box.

She found a set of keys, at least 40 on a large solid ring, and methodically went through each one.

'Ta da!' She clapped her hands in delight with the familiar click of an opening lock.

Three hours later, after reading through his scrapbook of newspaper clippings and handwritten apology letters, Lucy's mind took a horrifying, twisted turn, sucking her into a dark, evil place from where she would never be free.


A WEEK LATER, the day before her sixteenth birthday, her pretend Dad, who she had always called Dad but would now be known as Harold, looked up from his plate of soggy Weetbix.

Lucy always ribbed him about drowning his Weetbix then procrastinating while eating so he always ended with white-grey slop for breakfast. Their in-house family joke clutched around her beating heart with sharp talons, leaving thin slice marks.

'Morning luv,' he said, scooping another mouthful of slop into a mouth she never found offensive, until now.

The faded newsprint of the first neatly cut out article, with dark marks in each corner where he left a splotch of glue, didn't make sense at first.

Police appeal for murdered Jane Doe.

Lucy only had snatched memories of a woman with a red umbrella who came to her in her dreams and read bedtime stories and sang soothing lullabies. In another dream this woman pushed her on a swing in the park, chanting encouragingly with each push, legs out, legs under, legs out, legs under.

The story from Dad was that her mother, his wife, abandoned them when Lucy was four. He wouldn't be drawn on what she was like, or why she left.

Lucy became more curious as she grew up, but he stuck with his simple, detail–free story. When she had to do her family tree for a Grade Three school project, she only had two people to put on it. Dad and herself. No Mum, or grandparents, aunts or uncles.

'Poor little Lucy,' her schoolteacher tut-tutted as she sipped her morning coffee in the staff room. 'Her whole family, gone. Just her and her poor father, on their own in this world. I do wish he'd find a girlfriend, or someone, so she can at least have a woman to help guide her through life.'

'What's her story?' another teacher asked.

'It's a mystery, I don't really know.'

The bell rang, interrupting their conversation, and in the busyness of that school day, and the days that followed, they never got back to it.

Soon after, Lucy left, and nobody gave the sweet little girl with the golden-brown hair and no family, apart from her reclusive father, another thought.

Lucy now knew the truth. Her mother was Jane Doe. Her mother was buried in a destitute cemetery somewhere in an unmarked grave. Nobody to claim her. Nobody to mourn her. Nobody to remember her.

'Morning,' she mumbled.

She couldn't get terrible images of what his mouth had done to her mother all those years ago out of her head. Goosebumps covered every inch of her body. She could even feel them on her scalp. How could she stand here and watch this man who had destroyed her life forever? How dare he pretend to be her father after what he had done to her only flesh and blood.

She clenched her fists and willed her mind to sit still and be quiet. She had to think this through, plan properly. A random act could never be covered up, she had to be calculated.

With her back hunched, she watched the coffee granules dissolve as the she poured steaming water from the kettle over them.

Dad, I mean Harold, always told her to add the milk first because otherwise she'd burn the coffee and end up with a bitter taste. It was a myth. Both ways tasted exactly the same, but this way was better because she never ended up with undissolved floaties around the edges.

Her mind went black again, a walker and his dog found what was left of her Mum on the edge of an isolated creek deep in the bush. She'd been there for more than a year before anyone found her and a broken red umbrella.

Reality left a dull ache and made her tall, graceful frame feel awkward and slow. Her Mum was never coming home, compliments of the brutal, horrifying act of the deranged taxi driver Lucy called Dad.

The man who decided to find the little girl whose picture he found in the blood-stained wallet of the woman he spent a whole week raping and beating, before strangling her in an overzealous attempt to get her to respond to his sexual fantasies.

When Harold found the hungry, dirty little girl named Lucy huddled under the blankets in her dark, damp bedroom she was beautiful, she was kind, she was strong.

When this murderer stepped into the role of her new pretend parent, Lucy remained beautiful and she remained strong. Now, she could no longer be kind.

She sipped on her hot coffee without attempting to blow on the edge like she usually did. It burned all the way down. Harold, you will pay for this. You will regret this for the rest of your soon to be shortened life.

AFTER LUCY LEFT Bourke, people still told her she was beautiful, she was strong, she was kind. But her kindness was nothing but a trap to satisfy the unhinged piece of her brain. After doing it once, she only wanted to kill, kill, kill.

# 6

'OKAY ANDY, I'M thoroughly confused now. Can you please just tell me a condensed version of how Lucy Smith/Wallace is linked to Keely?'

'Easy. It's the EH Holden.'

'How?'

'It was pretty random, but as I said earlier, I did manage to track down the dentist who removed Lucy's wisdom teeth in Wycheproof.'

'Where is that again?'

'West in Victoria, not quite as west as here, the Victorian version of the Australian outback. Turns out he's a bit of a car buff with a memory like a vault.'

*I'll never forget that day, there was a fair bit of excitement when this EH Holden roared into town. 1964, saltbush green. Ah, EH, the best Holden wagon ever made.*

'He said it just like that? Rattled off the make, colour and even the year?'

'Like I told you, he's a car buff. He went on to say his Dad had the same one, it was the fastest selling car of the time, and Holden made around 257,000 of them in about a year and a half.'

*Every time we went for a drive, Dad would recite the Holden slug line, 'Special Station Sedan, a new fun-filled family favourite!' For a minute there I thought it was my old Dad driving into town, except he'd been dead for a few years and the EH was long gone.*

'Okay, the EH Holden. Was this Lucy's car?'

'No, it wasn't. She never owned a car that we know of. There's nothing on the vehicle registry in her name, Smith or Wallace.

'What about the number plates from Mike, XEH 428?'

Rhiannon memorised the plates after Mike, a bikie gang leader from Sydney who confessed on his death bed last year he knew Keely and that she'd been seen getting into an EH Holden with this number plate.

Her investigation into the car had stalled, the neatly written dot point was unticked on her now almost full missing persons notebook she started straight out of the police academy. The first entry was her friend Leesa, who disappeared from her southwest Queensland property, found by Rhiannon in tragic circumstances. The notebook, entitled *Find Me Rhiannon McVee*, had become a collection of never-ending 'to do' lists on unsolved cases she couldn't let go of.

'Turns out they're plates belonging to one of the founding band members of The Pegs, Jock Beaufoy.'

'Never heard of him.' Rhiannon was still salty.

'Back before they were The Pegs, did you know they used to be called 'Purple'?' Andy was on a roll on one of his music-history jaunts. 'They formed in Melbourne in 1973. I saw them play in a pub once, Jock was the bass player, and left in 75.'

Rhiannon started tapping her foot. Andy raised an eyebrow, she stopped.

'I'm not sure exactly how, but at some stage his car ended up at some remote recording studio on the New South Wales far south coast, near Eden of all places, parked in an old shed under a tarp.'

'Let me guess, the car was a…'

'Yep, a green EH Holden wagon. 1964.'

'One and the same.'

Rhiannon's face glowed bright red, Andy thought he could even see tinges of purple. Her *angry with herself, disappointed with herself* face always came with colours.

'That doesn't matter, we've found a link between Lucy and the car now, and all you need to do is put your investigating hat on that fits you so well and dig around for the significance of that recording studio.'

Rhiannon recovered quickly, the thought of interviewing one of her favourite bands overshadowing her disgust at not discovering this link.

'Right. Aaaggh. I will not remotely consider the prospect of The Pegs being involved in something so sick and twisted as murder, I'm telling you that for nothing.'

Andy raised an eyebrow. 'Sounds to me like you're going in with your eyes wide shut McVee. They're not saints, you know.'

'Of course I know they're not saints, but they're harmless. It's all about the music for them. Good times, music, yes maybe a few drugs and definitely a lot of alcohol, plenty of women but not murder. No way.'

'All I'm saying is don't get star-struck or distracted. Your job is to find out how Lucy and her mystery boyfriend with the white-blonde hair got hold of this EH Holden. Simple, right?'

'Simple. Keely has made this so fucking simple.'

'Jeremy, your shearer mate you ran into at the pub, remembers Lucy and her boyfriend as Keely's 'cousins'. He has no recollection of their names but his description of Lucy matches. He has given a good description of the boyfriend too but look, he could be any surfer from Bondi to Noosa. Long white-blonde hair, tanned, fit, blue eyes. Who knows who he is, or where he is…'

'…or where Keely is,' Rhiannon said, despondent.

'Don't despair McVee.' Andy took a sip of his coffee. It was actually a slurp, Andy's sips were always slurps. Rhiannon didn't hide her cringe. Andy slurped again, with a wink.

'Here is what I think. We have found Lucy, dead, and we are safe to assume it was her boyfriend. All we need to figure out is who he is, and why he killed Lucy. When we do, it will lead us to Keely.'

'Simple.'

'Exactly. Simple. We know Keely was with Lucy and the mystery man in October 1993. You found Lucy a year later, almost exactly. Forensics put her time of death at about a year, which means she was killed not long after they left the station near Brewarrina they were shearing at.

'Things are starting to fall into place. See?'

Rhiannon did a ceiling sigh, head right back.

Andy was on a roll. 'We need to consider whether Keely killed her, which I think we both agree is unlikely but not impossible.'

Rhiannon rose to Keely's defence with a bolt of renewed energy.

'I refuse to believe Keely has turned into a killer. No way. Sounds like she got caught up in it, but it has to be the boyfriend. If we can find him, it's more likely than not we will find Keely.'

RHIANNON TOOK THE crime scene photos of Lucy to bed, unable to switch off after talking about the case with Andy for most of the day. She scrutinised every detail for so long her eyes struggled to focus.

Was Andy right not to close off the possibility Keely had something to do with her death? Could Keely have killed her?

Jeremy's story indicated Keely was trying to get away from her 'cousins'. His recollection was she was terrified as they dragged her into the car. Or was it the drama of the storm he was remembering rather than any drama between the trio?

Rhiannon didn't believe Keely could murder someone. She felt like she knew Keely almost as well as the family who missed her knew her, after so many years obsessing over her case. No matter how far off the wrong side of the tracks Keely landed, Rhiannon didn't believe she was capable of murder. It had to be the boyfriend, it just had to be.

Satisfied she had answered one question, she had another that was far more difficult to process. Long after turning out the light at three a.m. the question kept her awake. Did he also kill Keely, gouge her eyes out and bury her somewhere in the outback?

Was the discovery of Lucy's identity a nail in Keely's coffin? Was the boyfriend a serial killer?

Yes!

Rhiannon sat bolt upright and turned on the lamp.

'S.K.Y.' she said out loud. The paper on the stick at Lucy's burial site. She grabbed the pile of photos and flicked through to the close-up.

'S.K.Y. Serial. Killer. Yes.'

The wave built as it approached the shore. It crashed on her head and buried her face in the sand.

'Oh, Keely. Don't be dead. Please. Be alive. Please be alive.'

Serial. Killer. Yes.

This changed the landscape completely.

They weren't only looking for Keely.

There were more.

# 7

'HER NAME IS Harriet. She was nineteen the last time we saw her. A free spirit. Going her own path. Nothing sinister or terrible about it. She was carefree and not bound by rules. Said she was going to the Murray River to pick fruit. Said there was good money in it. She didn't know what she was going to do after that. She wanted adventure. We knew she would come home, eventually, but we also knew she needed to get away from here and see the world for herself.'

Andy and Rhiannon sat in the old–fashioned country kitchen of the Keith family, on a property thirty minutes' drive west of Coolah in New South Wales. They'd driven down from Bourke and stayed overnight at the Coolah pub, The Black Stump Inn.

Rhiannon felt right at home, Andy felt like he was at another end of the earth. Beyond the black stump, to be more precise. He hadn't slept a wink in the rickety bed in the back room where the floors creaked, and the windows rattled. Built in the late 1920s the pub was definitely looking tired. Andy was sure it had been the scene of murder between bushrangers and who still paced the corridors to this day.

Maybe it was the circumstances which had rattled him. They followed Rhiannon's theory the bloodied note near Lucy's body was a clue from a serial killer. A trophy, a stamp of pride that Lucy wasn't the only victim.

Rhiannon's go–to were old missing persons files, the ones nobody cared about, the ones meant to be loaded into the new electronic police database which went live last year but would probably never make it there.

If it wasn't for Rhiannon collecting dusty boxes from every station she visited, many of these cases would be lost forever.

Andy had become obsessed by Lucy Wallace, and his competitive streak made him try and impress his young prodigy. He could never outdo McVee though. She's the one who found Harriet. Missing eight years.

Linking her to Lucy's killer was a long shot, but still worth a shot.

'Did she keep in touch after she left?' Andy asked.

'Yes. Every Sunday night. She knew she'd always catch us. We have a Sunday roast at six, and spend the evenings watching television. Our only television for the week, creatures of habit. It used to be her on the couch with us, and her five brothers. Gradually they've all left, and it's just me and George now.'

Edna looked over at the elderly gentleman sitting in the corner. He refused to sit at the table, he didn't want to talk to anyone, he didn't want the police here, he didn't want to be reminded of his little girl who'd been gone since 1987. Eight years that felt like eighty.

'When she missed one of her Sunday night calls did you call the police straight away?' Andy had read the missing persons report but always liked to start from the beginning, to see how things matched up in people's memories.

'Yes, yes we did,' Edna said softly. 'They told us not to worry, that she was just being a typical nineteen-year-old, and that a teenager forgetting to phone her parents wasn't a police matter.'

Rhiannon was taking notes; she'd asked Edna when they first arrived if she would mind. Edna didn't. She might be getting on in years but was sharp as a tack.

George didn't think they'd live long enough to discover the whereabouts of their daughter, and was absolutely sure she was dead, but Edna remained hopeful. She prayed every night for their Harriet, their dear sweet Harriet. Their baby girl. Their gift.

By the time they'd had five boys they thought their family was complete. When Harriet came along, despite being in their mid-forties, Edna and George were smitten. As were her brothers.

She learnt to work as hard as they did on their cattle and cropping farm, and they all became gentler around her. Kind. Less crass in their language.

Edna was sixty-four when she said her last farewell to Harriet. George, sixty-six. Harriet would be twenty–seven by now. If she hadn't disappeared, maybe she would be married and starting to think about having children of her own.

They celebrated her last birthday with a quiet family dinner. All the boys came home, like they did every birthday. The seven of them sat around the table with photo albums and poured their memories into giant wine goblets, toasting to their little girl lost.

'Should we have a funeral for her?' One of the boys asked.

'What if she's still alive?' Edna said, sipping her red wine with tears in his eyes. 'What if she's still out there? How can we gather for a funeral if we don't know if she's dead or alive?'

'She's dead,' George said. 'I know it in my heart.'

'How can you say that?' It was Graham. He and Harriet were thick as thieves as kids. He was the closest to her in age, they played the same games when they were little and shared secrets in their teen years. 'How can you say she's dead when you don't know?'

Everyone stared into their glasses. Nobody knew what to say next. The thought of organising a funeral, the prospect of saying goodbye to someone who could be alive, or might be dead, too much to bear.

'Let's just celebrate her birthday,' Edna said brightly, the flush of red wine hot on her cheeks. 'This is a special occasion, a family occasion. Let's remember all the good times! We don't need to worry about funerals or any such thing. Tonight is about Harriet. Dear, sweet Harriet.'

'Hear hear!' The boys clinked their glasses in unison, deciding as a group the only way through this horrendous quasi celebration was to drink themselves stupid. The only way to deal with the pain lines etched on their elderly parents' faces was with the help of the well–stocked wine rack in the cellar.

ANDY AND RHIANNON waited patiently for Edna to return, sensing she was wandering down memory lane.

'I'm sorry,' she apologised. 'Off with the pixies for a moment there. What was the question again? Was there a question?'

'You were saying the police told you not to worry, the missed phone call was nothing to be concerned about,' Andy said patiently.

'That's right, the police.' George made a sound from the corner; Rhiannon had almost forgotten he was there. She looked over to see him wringing his hands, the guttural sound coming from deep within.

Edna shushed him tenderly. 'I know George, I know.'

She turned back to Andy. 'They were so mean to us. Thought it was one big joke. Our local coppers were of no use, so we all got in the car and headed to Coolah and marched into that police station, all of us.

'They thought we were a pack of hillbillies, but we weren't leaving until somebody took us seriously. We went to the local newspaper, they helped us make and print out posters, and people stopped us in the street, remembering they'd seen her.'

Rhiannon scribbled furiously, none of this was on the file.

'The paper did a story, printed a photo of her, and got many calls. We had a fantastic old editor, his name was Maurie, he did everything he could to drum up interest in her being missing. We recorded all the calls. But what could he do...' Edna said sadly, '...when the police were so disinterested?'

'Do you remember this newspaper editor's last name?' Rhiannon asked as she drew a circle around *Maurie* in her notes. She wondered if he was still alive and if she could track down clippings or any notes he had kept.

'Tonkin, it was Maurie Tonkin. I've saved all the clippings, and the notes of reports from people who called the paper,' Edna said.

Rhiannon felt like hugging her. This stoic, strong, rural woman. Tougher than steel on the inside. Shouldering more than her fair share of the load on this farm, and managing to hold everything together while George went to pieces in the corner.

Rhiannon felt sad for George and his *cracked face*, sunlight through the window highlighting his deep character lines.

Edna left to get the scrapbook while Andy gave Rhiannon his gesture–less thumbs up. After working with him all these years, Rhiannon understood exactly what he was saying with every look, nuance, nod and shoulder shrug.

HOURS LATER ANDY and Rhiannon said their goodbyes with Edna's bulging scrapbook and promises it would be put to good use.

Rhiannon resisted twirling down the path like a ballerina, they had struck gold. In her wildest imaginings, she would never have hoped for such a precious record of detail from the months following Harriet's disappearance.

George's final words as they left, his only words, were imprinted on her heart.

'We didn't think anyone cared anymore about our Harriet. We thought she was forgotten,' he said, his sharp blue eyes pleading with Rhiannon. 'She was a good girl. We love her very much.'

BACK AT THE pub, they talked over the top of each other while eating vigorously.

'I'm starving,' Rhiannon said, tucking into a giant T–bone that hung over the edge of her plate and covered a mountain of chips, steamed mixed vegetables and a generous hunk of cauliflower cheese.

'You're always starving,' Andy replied dryly, slicing into his slab of rump smothered in creamy mushroom sauce. 'You eat like a horse and still manage to fit into your strides without having to undo the top button.'

Rhiannon smiled. It was a familiar conversation. Next, she would tell Andy she worked out, went running or bike riding at least five times a week to keep in shape, then she'd politely suggest he join her for a jog around the block at sun-up before she hit the road back to Bourke and he for Sydney.

He'd grumble and groan and tell her he had forgotten his sneakers, damn shame, 'cause he really would love to join her on a run. Then he'd polish off his meal, order dessert, and undo the top button on his trousers that stretched over his round belly.

Once their plates were gone and the table clean, Rhiannon got out the scrapbook. They sat in a quiet corner away from prying eyes, their basic bedrooms having no table and being too small and dimly lit to spread things out properly and go through them together.

'She has dated absolutely everything,' Andy said with admiration. 'She should have been a copper, never seen anything so meticulous in all my life.'

Rhiannon arched one eyebrow. 'Apart from your files, of course, that goes without saying,' he covered quickly.

They read in silence.

'Look at this!' Rhiannon gasped, excitedly shifting the book around so Andy could read it.

'Someone called in to say they'd seen her get into a green EH Holden. Number plates XEH 428. Driver, female, long brown hair. Passenger, blonde. Most likely female.'

She took the scrap book back, not waiting for him to finish, and continued scanning the article, reading through to the end to see what the police had said about the report. Nothing.

'Edna has put an asterisk in red next to it; she must have thought it was important.' Andy commented.

'There's another report here that she was with a young couple, they all seemed to be good friends, travelling from orchard to orchard together.'

'And here's another,' Andy added, 'saying Harriet pretty much kept to herself, she didn't seem to be travelling with anyone, just arrived at this apple orchard under her own steam and asked for work. Frustrating, so what is it? Travelling with two others, or travelling alone?'

After another hour of reading, Rhiannon and Andy started yawning.

'Right, let's draw straws on who gets to take it to bed,' Andy said.

'You can take it,' Rhiannon said politely, even though she was itching to get into her PJs and keep reading. She was intrigued by Edna's red asterisk. If Lucy was one of the girls, who was the other? But what about the young couple? Who were they and why had they taken Harriet under their wing?

'Just messing with you,' Andy said. 'I know you'll be up until the wee hours but I'll be asleep in ten, so it's all yours, McVee.'

Rhiannon laughed and gave him her most grateful smile.

'I know, I know, I'm the best and all that.'

'Yes you are,' Rhiannon was grinning from ear to ear, re–energised and ready for a long night piecing together this mystery.

AS SHE WAS about to turn out her light at midnight Rhiannon ran her hands over a page where Edna pasted a large photo of Harriet. Freckles across her broad nose, big brown eyes, an old–fashioned hair cut with a straight fringe hanging low on her forehead and shoulder length brown hair.

Tanned, rugged looking. Like she could keep up with the strongest and fittest farmhand or fruit picker in the crew. Which she could, having spent her life keeping up with her older brothers so they wouldn't call her a sissy, or say she was slacking off. She had a broad, open, friendly smile and her front teeth were slightly crooked.

'Speak to me, Harriet,' Rhiannon whispered in the dark. 'Tell me where to look.'

At that moment her window rattled. The wind? Or perhaps Harriet saying, *Find Me, Find Me, Rhiannon McVee.*

# 8

MAC LOOKED DOWN at the speedo, he was up to one hundred and twenty–five. He eased off the accelerator, the road would narrow up ahead and he didn't want to have to get out in the rough dirt edges if he happened upon a truck at that speed.

He looked at the seat next to him, admiring the stack of newspapers and brochures he collected in his search for the perfect property for him and Rhiannon. And as many brochures he could find on chook farming. He couldn't wait to pore over them with her, looking forward to her enthusiasm feeding off his.

He hadn't seen her for what felt like forever. She'd been gallivanting all over the countryside with her big city detective Andy, working on some big case Mac knew he couldn't ask about.

It was late by the time he pulled into Bourke. He rumbled past small groups of loiterers getting geared up for their Friday night shenanigans, pleased Rhiannon had the night off and didn't have to deal with them tonight.

Honey heralded Mac's arrival long before he pulled into the street, her sharp ears tuned into the familiar sound of his WB.

'Wonder dog, that's what you are,' Rhiannon grinned as she congratulated her brilliance with Honey's favourite pat, firstly a gentle touch on the top of the head then left to fondle one ear, right to the other ear, finishing with a scratch under the chin.

Honey was torn, she wanted to stay and enjoy Rhiannon's love and affection, but Mac's ute was getting closer and she couldn't wait to see him.

'You're just as excited as I am, aren't you girl?' Rhiannon laughed, enjoying the ritual that happened every time Mac arrived. 'Come on then, out you go.'

Honey raced out the back door, around the side of the house and to the front gate, her front paws on the top, whole body wagging.

'Well hello Honey dog. My special welcoming party,' Mac called, casually leaning out of his window. 'Gunna get the gate for me?'

'She's pretty clever,' Rhiannon said, coming up behind, 'but not that clever.'

Mac pulled in behind Rhiannon's Mazda and before he could take his seat belt off, Honey had jumped through the window and onto his lap, licking his face and snuggling in close.

'You should have brushed your teeth before I arrived. Your breath is pretty average!'

He opened the door and she obediently got down after a sharp 'out' from Rhiannon.

Mac unstretched from the driver's seat and was barely out himself before Rhiannon grabbed him in an excited hug, jumping up and wrapping her legs around his waist.

Honey stood patiently watching them kiss deeply and passionately.

'I missed you,' Rhiannon whispered in between kisses.

'Not as much as I missed you,' Mac replied, out of breath due to the pace at which his heart was pumping blood around his body.

She ran her hands over his arms, his back, through his hair.

'Perhaps we'd better take this inside,' Mac suggested, conscious they were standing under the garage light for the neighbours to see.

'I'm going to take you right here, right now,' Rhiannon giggled.

'Oh, no you're not. You have a reputation to uphold.' Mac started walking to the side door, knowing exactly which direction he was taking her.

'Hang on, you'd better shut your door and lock up, never know who's around on a Friday night.'

Rhiannon ran back to the ute before running back to Mac who was waiting at the door for her, opening it wide with one hand, leaving the other free to pull her into him.

Honey, knowing she was forgotten for now, jumped into the back of the ute and settled into a small gap between his swag and esky, waiting patiently for someone to let her back inside. It could be a while.

THE NEXT MORNING over breakfast Mac spread out the papers, brochures and leaflets across the table, talking animatedly about a property he'd seen advertised in The Land.

'It was once a profitable and thriving chook farm at Manilla, until divorce cleaned out the husband's bank account and now he has to reluctantly walk away,' he explained.

'You know the whole life story then,' Rhiannon marvelled at Mac's investigative techniques, not for the first time.

'Yeah, could've been a reporter…'

Rhiannon cut in and they spoke in unison, '…or a detective!'

'Jinx on the 'or a detective',' they said in unison again.

'Jinx on the jinx on the jinx!'

After they'd finished their first coffee, Rhiannon got out an A4 lined notebook and started a list.

'How are we going to do this? Step one, step two?' she asked.

'Sounds good. Step one is pretty easy…let's do this!'

'Whoa back there, Mister Jump in Feet First. I think you've forgotten one small, teensy tiny detail. As in, where are we going to get the money?'

Mac grinned like a schoolboy. 'Don't worry about stuff like that Rhee, we'll get the money.'

'Where from?' Rhiannon was getting annoyed, Mac knew as well as anyone not to be reckless about finances after the trouble his parent's property got in during the eighties when they couldn't afford to pay him to work full time after he left school. He had to work off–farm to earn an income to help them get back on their feet.

'Be sensible, come on, this is serious,' she said with exasperation.

They went around in circles about ways to get the money. After an hour and still nothing written on the list, Rhiannon was feeling like their plans were over before they started.

A random thought entered her mind. They could sell *Hillview*. It was like a physical king hit to the back of her neck and the pain shot through her entire body. No, how could they? Dad loved the property so much.

Another thought quickly chased it down. He's gone. And it's too much for Mum, she might welcome a fresh start. Another thought. But where will Jane go?

She can come with us. She looked at Mac, knowing he wouldn't mind. Or would he? This was their life now, their new start.

'Penny for your thoughts,' Mac reached over to wipe the deep frown line that had formed between Rhiannon's eyebrows. She wasn't sure if she could say them out loud. When she tried, they came out like a stutter.

'I was just thinking, you know, maybe we could, um, ask Mum if she wants to sell up, and maybe she will lend us some money from the sale to get us started, and we can pay her back...'

Mac grabbed Rhiannon's hand and squeezed hard.

'We can't do that Rhee, she won't want to leave. There's too much of Bill there, she can't leave him.'

'But he's not there! He's gone. Dead and buried!'

Tears appeared from nowhere. The way Jane spoke about Bill as though he was still alive was a constant worry. She hadn't cleared out his wardrobe, or any of his things around the house. His glasses and the paper he'd been reading the day before he died still sat together next to his armchair. She set a place for him at dinner. She always said *we* instead of *I*.

'I don't think we can ask her.' Mac stuck to the topic, knowing how tangled Rhiannon got when she started talking about Jane's refusal to let go of her memories of Bill. 'Where would she go?'

Rhiannon blurted out the words before she lost her nerve. 'She could come with us?'

Mac wasn't sure.

'Forget it, forget I said that,' Rhiannon swept away her words by neatening the stack of brochures in front of her. 'It's a silly idea. We need to strike out on our own, do it ourselves without asking our parents for help.'

She had another thought. 'Oh, but what about your Mum and Dad? Richard will be heartbroken if you don't stay and take over *Leander Park*.'

'I know. But it doesn't feel like it's going to happen anytime soon. Maybe we just leave it open ended? He's got plenty of years left in him, he's never going to retire. He'll still be belting around those paddocks when he's eighty. I reckon I'll start with Mum, she'll help pave the way.'

Rhiannon grimaced. 'It's not easy being a grown up.'

Mac nodded thoughtfully. 'Not really, but it's fun to pretend we're grown up.'

He had no idea how they were going to convince the bank to lend them the money to buy, but this felt so right. It was the solution to so many things. It was the path to their future together.

'Everyone needs a dream Rhee, and if you'll share this dream with me, it's going to happen, I know it will.'

# 9

'MCVEE, IT'S FOR you!' Annoyance fluttered in the pit of Rhiannon's stomach at the slap–dash phone manner of the new young female constable, Zoe Chesney, who didn't know how to use the hold or transfer button.

She probably didn't even bother covering the mouthpiece of the phone so the person on the other end didn't hear her trailer park screech from the front desk all the way to the tiny room at the very back of the poky Bourke Police Station which served as Rhiannon's office.

Rhiannon waited patiently for the next words she knew would come.

'Hey fellas, anyone know how to transfer a call to McVee's phone?'

Zoe was trying so hard to fit in she'd adopted an ocker, tough girl image. What nobody knew was this was nothing like her; she was quite meek and mild and found this whole experience in a real working station terrifying.

Rhiannon rearranged her pens, sitting neatly in rows on her immaculately clean desk, and re–stacked the files to her right while opening her top draw to retrieve a notepad from the bottom left corner where a small plastic container kept her stack of clean white notepads exactly where she wanted them.

It also stopped them from sliding around and interfering with other sections in the drawer which contained sticky tape, scissors, staplers and yellow sticky note pads.

'One, two, three, four...oh, a record,' she muttered to herself as she noticed the red button flashing, indicating the person on the other end of the phone was on hold.

Last time she counted to twelve and almost got out of her chair to walk to the front desk to do it herself.

'Rhiannon McVee,' she answered in her best professional police voice.

'McVee, what's doing?'

'Not much,' she scrambled as she tried to place the voice. It only took a second or two. 'Richards, I wondered how long it would be before I heard from you again.'

Pat Richards from Sydney, a nosy parker, who preferred Rhiannon to describe him as an 'investigative journalist'.

'You know me, persistent at best.'

'I've got nothing for you,' she replied. 'Things have gone quiet.'

'Oh, c'mon McVee, surely you've got something to revive this story. I notice the bastard is living it up on the North Shore, *shorely* that's not right, pardon the pun.'

'Ha ha Richards, very funny.'

ABC reporter Pat Richards was on the up and up in his career, starting to make a name for himself in breaking the big stories. Working behind the scenes on Four Corners under the guidance of Andrew Olle, Pat soaked in everything he could learn from his mentor who he aspired to emulate.

Pat also worked on radio news and was part of the ABC's shift into a digital launch planned for August this year.

Breaking the Clive Philips story was one notch in his belt but he knew there was much more to tell. All other media were still focussed on Clive's possible involvement in Ayala's disappearance but after a gift from Rhiannon, Pat knew police were more focussed on Clive's paedophile activities.

Their case was unravelling, thanks to Clive's contacts and substantial financial wealth affording the best lawyers in the country.

What Rhiannon and Bianca knew, but nobody else, not even Pat, was Clive had admitted to crimes against one of his own children. He then withdrew his admission, saying he had a moment of temporary insanity, that his grief of missing Ayala had made him say things that weren't true.

'Clive Philips is an innocent man…' her voice tapered off.

'…until proven guilty, right?' Pat finished for her.

'Come on, I know you. I was there that night in the Coaches and Arms when you spilled everything. You wouldn't have told me all those things if you didn't believe he was guilty, so what's happened? I saw him the other day, partying on a yacht with all the beautiful people.'

'Really?' Rhiannon's voice suddenly went squeaky.

Bam. He had her. Pat knew this would get right under her skin.

'Yes, really. Mostly young men mind you.' Pat was enjoying this, drip–feeding Rhiannon to lure her into his trap of getting her to tell him more.

Rhiannon felt an overwhelming urge to pour out her frustrations over Clive's ability to weasel his way out of the charges she was trying to prove, but Andy's voice I gnawed in her ear. He'd given her a major *chewing* for speaking to Pat in the first place at the time of Clive's arrest, and had risked his own arse to cover hers.

'Sorry Pat, no can do. Gotta go, see you later.'

She hung up before he could use his nosy–journalist investigative techniques on her. She thought she knew every trick in the book, but he was good. He'd make a good policeman, maybe she could recruit.

PAT INSPIRED RHIANNON to put in a call to Bianca, as much to see how she was going as to settle her own unease at visions of Clive sleazing all over young men on his yacht, doing goodness knows what behind closed doors.

The audacity of that man made her skin crawl. She straightened her desk, again, in an attempt to order her thoughts but the neatly stacked pile of paper and perfectly placed pen holder with three red, three blue and three black pens were of no comfort.

While the phone rang and rang, she closed her eyes, but that was worse, because all she could see was the glittering, glistening water of Rushcutters Bay and Clive, at the helm of his yacht, his head thrown back in ecstasy, laughing at the sky (and her).

'Allo?' A foreign voice answered just as Rhiannon was about to give up. 'I can help you?'

'Hello Ulla, it's Rhiannon McVee, from Bourke Police Station.'

'Oh, allo Miss Detective,' Ulla said in her singsong voice. She adored Rhiannon, with her smooth skin and big warm eyes. She brought hope to this sad family Ulla was trying to hold together with recipes handed down from her Swedish grandmother who firmly believed good food fixed people in the worst of times, the saddest of times, the hardest of times.

'You have news for them?'

Ulla was always direct, she was not nosy or asking to satisfy her own curiosity, it was just her way.

Rhiannon delicately avoided answering.

'How are you enjoying the outback Ulla, are you longing for home yet?'

'No, not at all, this is like home now. I love this place you call the outback.'

Rhiannon smiled, she loved when the stillness and wide, open Australian outback wrapped its remoteness around overseas visitors, climbing under their skin and settling quietly into their hearts.

'I thought it might be too hot, not many people want to face our endless hot summers.'

Ulla laughed. 'Yes, it is hot. I am okay with that, this is a good home to be looking after, good people to care for. But I wish they weren't so sad,' she confided, her tone changing.

Her voice changed again when Bianca walked into the room, quickly handing her the phone. 'Miss Detective Rhiannon for you Bianca, I am sorry if you overheard my words, it is not my business.'

Rhiannon listened to Bianca reassuring Ulla it was okay, that she wasn't offended by her caring about their wellbeing.

'Hi Rhiannon, to what do I owe the pleasure of your call?' A slight edge to her voice gave away Bianca's nervousness.

'Nothing really, just checking in. Things are a bit quiet today in Bourke, so I thought I'd take the opportunity to see how you were going.'

Bianca relaxed. 'Okay, thanks. Yeah, all going well. Um, well, considering...'

'Have you heard from him?'

'No, well I have, but I have refused to speak to him. Ulla is screening all the calls now.'

Rhiannon laughed. 'You've got yourself a keeper there! I bet she gives Clive the short shrift.'

Bianca joined her mirth. 'Oh yes, she's pretty direct. It's funny hearing her tell him to 'go jump off his boat' and 'stop calling this house you bad man'.'

Bianca dropped her voice to almost a whisper. 'Letters still arrive every week but I've stopped reading them. And now Red is here.'

'I see.' Rhiannon waited for Bianca to elaborate.

'He refuses to say anything. I don't know how to broach the topic, and not sure if I can. It's much easier to pretend things are okay, as okay as they can be.'

Rhiannon didn't comment, what could she say? This would require patience and understanding, there was no point trying to force Red to lay charges against Clive. It would be very public. Red needed to have more strength of character than the average person to be able to withstand the screaming headlines, the photos journalists would dig out from his old school albums and anywhere they could find one, and the continual hailing blows of insensitive questions.

'Do you think maybe Clive lied that day?' Bianca asked softly, hopefully.

'No, I'm sorry Bianca, I think he was telling the truth,' Rhiannon replied gently.

'Sometimes I catch myself thinking a good memory with Clive in it,' Bianca admitted. 'A family holiday, or him teaching me to drive, or laughing at one of the boys' stupid jokes. We weren't an unhappy family, despite how things ended up. I always thought we were a really close, happy, loving family.'

Rhiannon listened with care, knowing Bianca needed someone to talk to and unburden herself with.

'Then I feel so hateful towards him, all in the same minute! How can that be? How can I love and hate someone at the same time?'

'He's your father Bianca, every little girl adores and looks up to their father.' Rhiannon's voice trailed off as she remembered her Dad.

The most wonderful man in the world in her eyes. Losing him so suddenly such a shock, she didn't think she'd ever get over it. Time did dull the pain somewhat, but it was always there. That longing for one more conversation, one more opportunity to thank him for all the things he had taught her. If she was faced with the prospect he wasn't perfect, she'd find it impossible to bear.

'How can I still love him, when I know what he's done? Oh, my blood boils whenever I think about how he treated Mum and when I think about what he might have done to her, maybe killed her! I don't know what's worse, the possibility he killed Mum or what he did to Red and all those faceless boys from his overseas trips.

'We are just normal, everyday people, how can all of this happen to us?'

Small sobs interspersed Bianca's sentences, adding to the rawness of her words.

'I'm not sure how to answer that Bianca. I am so sorry all this has happened to you. You have been amazing in holding everything together, don't forget that. You were so brave to come forward with Ayala's diary, and to face up to Clive the way you did.

'And look at what you're doing now, looking after a property, managing staff, keeping a busy life in order. I know when the chips are down it's tempting to huddle in a corner and hide away from the world. Unfortunately, life never stops, and the best thing we can all do when dealing with tragedy is to get up in the morning and face the day. Day after day.'

Bianca pressed the phone hard against her ear, willing Rhiannon's words to absorb and balance her addled brain.

'You're right,' she said eventually. 'You're absolutely right, as always. Thanks Rhiannon.'

'Anytime. Remember, you can call me whenever you need to, you've got my home number as well if you can't catch me at work. And you can drop into the station anytime, even if there's nothing new to talk about. Just pop in and I'll make you a cuppa.'

'Thanks again, I will, I definitely will. And if anything new crops up this end, I'll be straight on the blower.'

'Vicky Verka,' Rhiannon replied, enjoying Bianca's laughter at one of her favourite sayings.

Bianca sat quietly, unaware Red was outside the office door wringing his shaking hands in a state of such distress, that, not for the first time, he thought he would be better off dead.

# 10

*1983*

'COME ON RED!' Clive called. 'You're right mate, best thing you can do is get back on that horse!'

Red wiped the dust smear on the back of his size ten RM Williams moleskins and used the back of his dusty hands to wipe the tears from his eyes. Clive jumped down from the timber railing encircling the horse yard and strode over.

He was wearing matching moleskins, boots and shirt. Ayala loved to dress them the same. Like father, like sons. The rest of the family, Ayala, Bianca, Jack and Lachie, still on the rail, yelled words of encouragement.

It was the first school holidays for the year, and everyone was together. Ayala loved these precious moments. She hated that Bianca and Jack were away at school and knew it wouldn't be too long before she had to say goodbye to Red, now ten, and Lachlan, almost nine, who were still home doing School of the Air.

Ayala resisted the temptation to jump down and mollycoddle Red. He was her softest on the inside, not as tough as the others. Her third child, her sensitive soul, who worried and felt *the little things* the most.

She worried how he would cope in the boarding house. Red wasn't as robust as Jack, and she'd confided in Clive on several occasions. She knew he'd be a target for bullies, they would know they could get to him.

His big brother Jackson would look out for him but couldn't be there the whole time.

She watched Red intently, looking for signs of serious injury, but knew Clive would check him carefully before he let him back on the horse.

Clive leaned down and went to put his arm around Red.

'Get away from me,' Red said angrily, shrugging Clive off, his eyes flashing the same colour as his hair. Clive recoiled and stepped back, the only one who knew the real reason for Red's anger.

*Oh, what have I done?*

Clive laid awake all night, tossing and turning, disgusted with himself. He was an intelligent man, he knew that, but the weakness in his brain for what was totally unacceptable, completely wrong, the worst sin against another person – a child, his own child – had overtaken.

What he did when he went in to say goodnight to Red wasn't pre-planned, it just happened.

'I'm sorry Red,' Clive whispered, so low that only Red could hear. 'I'm really sorry.'

Red was confused. Standing before him was the man he idolised, who he had followed around the paddock since he could walk. The man who made them laugh, who lavished them with love and affection.

The confident, capable father at the helm of the yacht, who showed them how to steer through both calm and stormy seas. The man who sat at the head of the table and tested their general knowledge over chops with three veg. The man in charge at shearing time, giving orders left right and centre to make sure things ran smoothly.

Red's Dad could do anything, fix anything. He knew so much about the world, and brought the world into their happy home.

Red crumpled and moved into Clive's hug. He loved his father with all his heart. Clive crouched down so they were at eye level.

'Hey, how about we get back on that horse young fellow.'

Red grinned. 'Righto Dad, good idea.'

LATER THAT NIGHT, in bed with Ayala, Clive unveiled his plan. 'I've been thinking about what you said, about Red at boarding school. Maybe it would be better if he went now, when he's younger.'

Ayala's heart fell, but she knew she should hear him out. 'Really? What makes you think that?'

'He'll get a bit more care and attention from the boarding house, I'll make sure of that. But I'm thinking the younger he is, the better chance he has of finding a good friendship group before he gets into high school. Then he'll have more support when he needs it. It's only a year earlier than we sent Bianca and Jack, but that extra year will do him the world of good.'

Ayala wasn't convinced.

'It will do him good to see Jack every day, I know he misses him.'

'Yes, you're right. He does look up to Jack. And Jack misses him too.'

'Family sticks together, that's how we've raised them,' Clive said vehemently. 'You and I didn't have siblings to look out for us, we had to do it all on our own, but they've got each other.'

Clive could be very persuasive when he wanted to be. He leaned over and put his arms around her, snuggling into the softness between her neck and shoulder, kissing her lightly and tenderly.

He concentrated hard on wanting her, needing her, being attracted to her. She was more than everything a normal man could wish for. It was taking more and more effort, his heart wasn't in it. He was grateful they had the light off; in the darkness she couldn't see the lies in his eyes.

'Okay Clive, you're probably right. I'll contact the school tomorrow and get him started for the new term.' Ayala's voice wobbled as she snuggled close.

Her babies – her beautiful, happy, lovely, bundles of love and joy – were growing up so fast. She yearned for time to stand still, and felt an overwhelming urge to get down on her knees in the middle of their most desolate, bare paddock, where if you stood on your tippy toes you could touch the stars, and conjure a magical spell to keep her children young and innocent. Away from the harshness real life would no doubt deliver.

Little did she know that for Red it was too late, real life and the sickness that lived within it, had already crept under his skin and into his fragile, sensitive heart.

# 11

AFTER A SLEEPLESS night trying to steer his mind away from his thoughts Red crept out of the deathly silent house before the morning birds greeted the new day with their bush concert.

He was at his lowest point, where he could see no reason to continue in this living hell. His favourite childhood horse stood patiently and quietly, sensing his distress but instinctively knowing it was her job to be calm.

She knew exactly what to do, she'd done this many times before when he snuck out before daylight to take her for a long ride and escape the horrors of his bedroom during school holiday visits.

Sending him to boarding school young hadn't fixed Clive's problem, it just made school holidays the worst possible time for Red until he got old enough to find ways to not come home and spend his holidays with mates instead.

She walked quietly and slowly, her only pace these days. The sun was also quiet and slow, gradually erasing the dark shadows Red rode through. By the time they reached his final destination the sun was ready to announce its arrival in its usual blaze of outback sunrise glory.

The horse stood perfectly still, not moving a muscle, knowing somehow this ride was different. Sensing it might be their last she couldn't stop the tremble that started at her head, travelled along her back and all the way to a final twitch of her tail.

BIANCA WOKE WITH purpose. Unburdening herself to Rhiannon had cleared out the muck. The only way to move forward was to move forward, and sitting around feeling sorry for herself wasn't going to change a damned thing.

Still in her pyjamas she raced into Red's bedroom, just like when they were kids. Their favourite thing was to beat the sunrise, jump on their horses or motorbikes and ride to the top of their sandy hill where they could see to the sun and back, then to the moon and back.

'Red,' she whispered into the dark room. 'Red! Get up, let's go for a ride!'

No answer. She flicked on the light to discover the perfectly made bed in his immaculately tidy room.

'He beat me to it,' she mumbled, closing the door quietly.

In the kitchen Ulla was preparing breakfast, a deep worry line denting her forehead like an inside out trouser crease.

'Good morning Ulla, you're up bright and early,' Bianca greeted her enthusiastically. 'I think I'll take an early morning ride to watch the sunset.'

'I have bad feeling Miss Bianca,' Ulla muttered as she moved gracefully around the kitchen. 'Bad, bad feeling. Where is Mr Red? He sneak out early. He too quiet. Too sneaky. You need to find him.'

Ulla handed Bianca a picnic pack with two warm bacon and egg rolls wrapped in aluminium tin foil, a coffee–filled thermos, two apples and a shortbread assortments biscuit tin filled with home–made raspberry coconut slice.

As they crunched across the gravel to the shed, Bianca could also hear ice clinking together in a second thermos of water Ulla gripped tightly, one step behind.

'You take motorbike, and dog. It will be faster.'

'You're very bossy this morning Ulla,' Bianca joked, trying not to go into the same panicked state.

She noticed Red's favourite old horse was gone, as was Red's saddle. A fleeting thought crossed her mind to check the gun cabinet but Ulla was hustling her to get going.

'I worried for Mr Red. He has sadness, how you say it when too sad?'

'Depressed?'

'Yes, that is the word I look for. Depressed.' Ulla rolled it around for practice, adding it to her growing English vocabulary.

Bianca strapped the picnic pack and water to the back of the bike and whistled for Mags to jump on her lap.

Leaving Ulla in a cloud of red dust she took off at speed. She knew exactly where to go, she just hoped she wasn't too late.

# 12

AFTER A RUN of night shifts Rhiannon was facing four glorious days off in a row and knew exactly what she wanted to do, to go home to *Hillview*.

Jane was waiting at the gate, arms outstretched, her face alight with joy.

'Rhiannon!'

Tears welled as they hugged, Rhiannon wishing Bill was there like he always used to be, welcoming her home with shining eyes that required a hanky wipe when nobody was looking.

It had been a long time since her last visit, and she did the usual scan of the garden, house, sheds, chooks, dogs, cats and yards to make sure things were in order. Then she went further afield, checking bore drains, fences, sheep and troughs.

Mac and Duncan were doing their best to help Jane with upkeep, but they had been busy on their own places, so Rhiannon spent the first couple of days home fixing gate latches, repairing fences and unblocking the main trough in second paddock.

Day three was when the flies getting in behind her sunglasses did more damage than usual. 'Bloody things,' she cursed. The barbed wire she was trying to strain let go and nearly took her head off.

With twittering, hopping red robins as her audience she cursed and stomped, threw her gloves onto the ground and kicked powdery red dust at them until they disappeared.

She yelled and screamed and put on a performance like no other until finally collapsing on the dirt, defeated and forlorn.

How on earth was she going to broach the topic with Jane that *Hillview* was too much for one woman to manage on her own; that she needed to consider her longer–term future? That she needed to sell up and start a new life, one without Bill in it?

'I NEED TO talk to you Mum, a serious talk.' Rhiannon spoke in between hungry mouthfuls. She was ravenous after her day on the fenceline and couldn't get the loin chops, cooked the way she loved them with the perfect crispness on the thin fat strip, into her mouth quickly enough.

She scooped the mashed potato onto her fork until it enveloped her meat, and put the whole delicious ball onto her tongue.

'But first, eat,' Jane laughed, enjoying watching her daughter eat her chops, mashed potato and peas the same way Bill used to.

They ate dinner at record speed until both plates were clean. Jane didn't often cook this family favourite, it wasn't worth the effort when she was on her own, but knew she could serve it up every night for Rhiannon and she'd never complain.

'Thanks Mum, delicious.' Silence crept slowly, filled the room, squeezed into all the corners. Jane sensed what was coming and decided to get in first.

'I'm thinking of selling up,' she said quietly.

It was like being a front-rower, so intent on charging headlong into the pack ahead that you didn't see the winger coming in for support from the side. Rhiannon's rehearsed speech, which included responses to what she was expecting Jane to say, hit the deck and the whole team piled on top.

'It's not the hard work that worries me,' Jane continued.

'Things mightn't be as ship shape as when Bill was around but generally I'm managing fine with that side of it all. Finances are good, there are no major disasters to worry about and although a bit more rain wouldn't go astray, the place is holding up.'

Rhiannon watched intently as Jane fought to compose herself. 'It's me that worries me. I'm so lonely out here. I'm so lonely without him.'

That was it for both of them. Rhiannon moved to Bill's empty chair beside Jane and wrapped her arms around her. The tighter she squeezed, the more tears came out. Thick sponges that could never dry.

'AND THAT WAS how it came about.' Rhiannon's breath couldn't keep up with the pace she was trying to get the words out, her hands flailing wildly in her excitement.

She and Jane sat up until two in the morning making plans for the future, and after the initial shock and sadness of accepting her childhood home would not always be hers, Rhiannon was a bubble about to burst.

She radioed Mac first thing and they met in the boundary paddock – MacVee's Corner – for morning smoko. Rhiannon had made one of Mac's favourites, tea cake. It was still warm.

'I didn't even have to say anything I didn't want to say. All the words that had been scrambled like last week's eggs weren't needed. Mum had it all worked out.'

Mac took a soft buttery mouthful of cake and the cinnamon sugar danced on his tongue.

'Oh, this is good. Did you say anything about our plans...?'

Mac didn't like to sound pushy but was desperate to know.

'No, not yet. But I will. I didn't want to put too much on her plate when she's obviously been through a lot of soul searching to get to this. But it feels like someone is smiling over us. With what Mum makes on the sale, I will be able to borrow a portion, enough for a deposit, and we're off and away!'

Mac pulled Rhiannon close, lost for words. He couldn't help indulging the vision of the small homestead behind a white picket fence, roses lining the path to the front verandah where children played with their Tonka trucks and dolls in prams. Call him old-fashioned, he didn't mind.

The thought of a proper proposal and setting a wedding date darted in, but before he could catch it, the thought was gone.

Rhiannon's thoughts were similar to Mac's, but without the wedding, children and white picket fence. Her visions were more career-focussed, especially since some of the more recent developments in the S.K.Y. case.

If this all worked out, and they did end up at Manilla on Mac's dream chicken farm, she would be closer to Andy, which would help her career progress more quickly. Closer to the action with better opportunities to advance her detective dreams.

It wasn't that she didn't want the same things as Mac, but she was content to coast along in their relationship as it was for a while yet. Best friends, business partners, lovers and eventually husband and wife. Kids? Maybe, one day. The husband, wife, family part was a tiny speck on the horizon; she had so many other places to get to before she reached where Mac was ready to go yesterday.

'Gotta go,' she said, giving Mac a quick kiss and a squeeze on his firm right cheek that she'd been admiring encased perfectly in his Wrangler jeans. 'Mum and I have a few things to sort before I hit the road.'

Mac groaned and wrapped himself tightly around her. 'Can't you stay a bit longer?'

'As tempting as you are, I really can't.' Rhiannon pulled away reluctantly, keen to stay but more eager to get back to Jane. 'We'll have more time next weekend, when I come back for a couple of days. Maybe you could stay over if you can fit it around sheep work?'

Mac only had his mind on one thing.

'You're not listening,' Rhiannon scolded. 'I. Have. To. Go.'

He frowned as she went from zero to sixty on her motorbike. Always in a hurry, she was. Squeezing every last drop out of every single minute. He often felt there weren't enough drops for him.

Would it always be this way?

### TEA CAKE

1 cup plain flour
1 teaspoon baking powder
½ cup sugar
1 egg
½ cup milk

*Method*: Combine all ingredients until well mixed. Bake in sandwich loaf tin or round tin for 20 minutes on 180 degrees Celsius. Melt butter and pour over the top while cake is still warm, sprinkle with cinnamon sugar.

# 13

ROUTINE, ROUTINE, ROUTINE. Get up, open the window to breathe in today's air, then let the air decide what next.

Today's 'what next' was a bike ride down the steep hill at full speed, the wind in her ears so loud it drowned out the morning birds who had started with a twitter but as the sun got higher in the sky, they struck a more feverish pitch.

Lucy had been drifting east for a year, if Mum was still alive they would have just celebrated her seventeenth birthday. One year since she killed her 'pretend Dad' Harold, and hidden his body in the cool cellar of the rambling homestead east of the hot, dusty outback town of Bourke.

She'd drifted back to Eden, perched on a hill with a glittering ocean stretching further than the horizon. She had fond memories of their time here, and after the vast open skies of the outback she needed to feel more closed in. She was living in a densely forested area, her tiny seaside cottage invisible amongst the trees.

She rode her bike everywhere, getting stronger and fitter every day thanks to the steep hills and mountain tracks she bashed through.

She reached the bottom of the hill and passed the grid with the faded timber sign *Pri a e P op ty N T ess ass rs*. Feeling curious she jammed on the brakes, leaving a large skid mark in the gravel, and turned her bike around, bumping over the grid to enter a pristine, peaceful place. Morning sunlight streaming through the trees created a gold wash.

To her left, morning mist rose from a small dam bordered by wild rushes. She caught a glimpse of a small dark face as a wallaby leant through the rushes to take a cold sip.

As she rounded a corner the gravel changed to bitumen, and she wondered who could afford to bitumen a private driveway as long as this. The gravel wasn't maintained, and obviously laid a long time ago. She swerved left and right around potholes, misjudging occasionally when the sun hit her right between the eyes.

Ten minutes later she reached the top of a hill and was surprised to see the ocean, so close she felt she could touch it. Hundreds of kangaroos munched quietly on the lush green pasture paddock that continued all the way to the ocean's edge.

A small, fenced yard with a rusty iron tank and leaking trough housed an old grey pony who gazed at her through its long dark lashes.

She leaned her bike against a post and slowly approached.

'Hello boy, aren't you beautiful.'

He limped towards her.

'Oh, careful. Don't forget you're not a spring chicken anymore,' Lucy laughed as he nuzzled her hand, looking for treats she would remember to bring tomorrow.

LUCY RETURNED EVERY day, with carrots and apples. She named the pony Prince. Some days she'd find him munching on a bale of fresh hay and wondered who was looking after him.

She couldn't see any houses, although if she rode a little further she'd discover a gate with another sign KEEP OUT attached with rusty wire, then beyond that a mud brick two-storey mansion with six-foot ceilings and floor to ceiling windows on both levels curving around to take in the ocean views.

Lucy had her head resting on Prince's neck so didn't hear the car approaching from the mansion. It wasn't until Prince whinnied and pulled away, she realised she wasn't alone.

'Hey there.' She turned to the deep voice and took an intake of breath. Leaning against an EH Holden wagon, green, was a male version of herself. Tall, lean, long hair, blue eyes, tanned skin. The only difference was his hair was white-blonde, a stark contrast to her golden brown.

'Hey there yourself,' she said cautiously.

'I wondered who was feeding him carrots and apples,' he said, as he casually walked closer. Lucy stayed where she was, wondering whether it was a friendly approach.

'I hope you don't mind. He asked me the first time we met, and now he just expects it.' Lucy's luxurious laugh broke the awkwardness and stopped the young man in his tracks.

He had come here to tell her to get off the property, that as caretaker it was his job to make sure nobody came any further, that the owner didn't want anyone here. Ever. Her laugh, a magical, tinkling stream in the woods, distracted him from his purpose.

'I'm Lief,' he said as he put out his hand to her.

'I'm Lucy,' she responded warmly, clasping his slightly calloused hand in her smooth, long fingers.

'You do realise you are on private property, don't you?' he said in a much softer tone than initially intended. Lucy took a step closer, still gripping his hand.

'You do realise the sign at the grid is illegible, don't you? So no, I had no idea.'

Lief smiled at the sparkle in her eye. He let go of her hand but didn't step back.

'You look very familiar,' Lucy continued, 'if I didn't know any better, I'd think maybe we were related.'

'No chance of that I wouldn't think, although I must admit, we do look alike! You from around here?'

'No, a blow in. I did live here briefly when I was little, but only briefly.'

'What brought you back?'

Lucy turned her head towards the ocean. 'That. The big blue. Water everywhere I look. Can't get enough of it.'

'Yeah, it's pretty nice.'

'You don't sound like you're from here? What's your accent?'

'International accent. No, not from around here. I just look after Henry.'

'Henry? I've named him Prince. He looks like he was a Prince in days gone by, not a plain old Henry.'

Lief laughed.

'I have no idea if he was. I've only known him in his Henry life, he was well past his 'Prince days' when I arrived at this joint.'

'What joint? All of this, private property?'

'Yep, there's a big old house with a recording studio in it just around the bend. If you kept coming you'd realise you aren't supposed to be here. The owner doesn't like anyone here.'

'Why's that? Secret business going on?'

'No, nothing like that. Just famous people. They come here to get away from it all. They come here to write, create, sing, record. It's the most sophisticated recording studio on the east coast. Worth millions.'

Lief stopped, he'd said too much. He wasn't usually like this; he was a closed book. Lucy had enchanted him and put him under a spell. He stepped back, awkward.

'I'm in strife,' he joked. 'Now I've revealed all these secrets, I'll have to kill you.'

Lucy squinted, the sun came out from behind a cloud and she temporarily lost sight of Lief. It was a strange feeling, out here in the remote wilderness, just her and a stranger. He could be anyone; he could be a serial killer. She could be anyone, she was a serial killer.

She walked to her bike, calling out over her shoulder.

'See you tomorrow, Prince, I'll be back.'

A MONTH LATER, with daily visits to Prince Henry, the new name they'd given him, turning into daily visits to Lief's caretaker's cottage in the bottom corner of the expansive gardens that enclosed the creative coastal getaway for up-and-coming rock bands like Cold Chisel, ACDC, The Angels, The Diviynls and INXS, Prince Henry died.

Lucy didn't return the next day, or the next.

Lief stopped waiting and after a few months left his coastal home behind the wheel of the EH Holden everyone had forgotten was stored in the bottom shed. He told himself he was seeking adventure, but if he was truly honest, he was searching for the magical tinkling laugh that had buried itself under his skin.

# 14

BIANCA TORE THROUGH the brigalow and gidgee, weaving around logs and large sticks. Noisy yellow-tailed black cockatoos screeched from the nearby watercourse that ran through the property and a lonely crow *caw, caw, cawed* in the distance.

She noticed none of this, her concentration purely focussed on finding Red. Her precious brother, who, unlike her other brothers, when growing up rarely pushed or shoved or told her she was an annoying brat.

He was always the one to move in for a kind hug when she fell off her bike or horse. The one who fetched bandages when she came a cropper and needed something to stop the blood gushing from a leg, arm or head wound.

They were allies against the others in childhood games of hide and seek, and automatically paired up during shearing and mustering – a silent language between them ensuring they knew exactly who was doing what.

She slowed down as she drew closer to one of their favourite spots on the top of a sandy rise.

She and Red would come here often at the end of a long, hot, dusty day. The remoteness, the stillness, the feeling you were at the top of an ancient landscape which lay relatively untouched by European settlement.

For hundreds of thousands of years Aboriginal communities sat on this rise, and here Bianca felt a connection to the bush she could not explain.

Their favourite tree was where she knew she would find Red. It was a leopardwood, *Flindersia maculosa.*

They would run their hands over its smooth, spotty trunk, fascinated by the way its spots changed with the light. After rain the spots turned a brilliant white; the leopard was washed clean and you could see it from miles away, glittering amongst the brown, grey, black and rust coloured trunks of eucalypts and acacias which paled in comparison.

'Please don't be dead, please don't be dead,' she pleaded over the roar of her motorbike.

As she got closer she slowed down, both because she didn't want to scare Red's horse but also because she wanted to delay this moment where life as she knew it could change dramatically. From a life where Red was okay, alive and well, to a life with added shock and trauma to the heavy, heartbreaking load she was already carrying.

She putted towards the leopardwood with glazed, unseeing eyes. As she got closer she could no longer unsee what was in front of her. She slowed the bike to a stop. In slow motion she kicked its stand and dropped to her knees.

# 15

*1985*

'TELL ME WHO you are Lucy Lou,' Lief joked as they headed down the Hume Highway, away from the bright lights of Sydney towards Melbourne.

'I'm whoever you want me to be,' she teased, tucking her hair behind her ear in a way that made Lief melt into the cracked leather passenger seat of the EH Holden wagon.

He'd been trying to get her out of his mind for the past year, moving from orchard to orchard along the Murray River following fruit picking season, until eventually they locked eyes across a campfire while he had his arm around the cute curly-haired backpacker whose name he couldn't remember.

She smiled casually at him through the flames, unphased that he'd moved on from her. This mythical creature who appeared out of the spooky forest and into his life, then just as suddenly, disappeared, then appeared again.

He could have any girl he wanted with his combination of exotic Dutch accent and devastating good looks, but Lucy was the only one for him.

They went to Sydney for a change of pace but Lucy quickly grew tired of the noise and bright lights, which is how they ended up on the Hume Highway.

'I want you to be mine,' he said softly, reaching over to touch her golden hair.

Lucy's laugh sprinkled around the inside of the car like soft rain.

'That will never happen,' is what she wanted to say. Instead, she moved his hand from her hair to her lap. Deftly, like she'd done this many times before, she used his hand to pull back the hem of the light cotton dress she found in an op shop in a cute little town called Cobargo.

Lief moved closer so he could cover her perfect neck with soft buttery kisses while she shifted in her seat to make it easier for him to get his hand into her pants and gently put one, then two fingers inside.

It had been like this from the first time Lucy laid him on a patch of fresh herbed grasses underneath one of the giant eucalypts she called the Magic Faraway Tree.

She always took charge and put him under a spell he had no hope of breaking. Each time was more exciting than the last and it got that way where he couldn't breathe if she wasn't within touching distance.

He could only touch with permission. It came in a variety of ways. He was an obedient kelpie, continually watching and waiting for a signal, a nod, a gesture.

Lucy spotted a gravel driveway leading to a rusted gate hanging from its hinges beside the highway, willows lining a bubbling creek in the paddock beyond.

While Lief continued to stroke, kiss her neck, pull her spaghetti straps off her shoulder so he could get her perfect breast and nipple into his mouth she calmly put her blinker on and guided the car past a patch of yellow flowers fighting for attention amongst stinking nettles and purple thistles.

The flash of an empty coke can catching the sunlight dazzled her briefly, or maybe it was the way Lief's fingers went even deeper when they hit the grid. By the time she stopped under the shade of the willow tree he was almost fully on her lap, his boardies stretched tight as he fought to break free.

They tumbled out of the driver's door and onto more of the yellow weed flowers beside the creek. Lief used his shirt to cushion Lucy and she guided him around her body, showing him how to explore places he'd never tasted before. It wasn't until he had satisfied her in every possible way that she allowed him to remove his shorts and join the party.

She guided him slowly into her and moved his hips where she felt him the most. With more control than he'd ever needed before he moved in and out until she whispered, now.

He closed his eyes and the billions of stars in the sky joined together to shine so brightly they blinded him, before exploding and eventually returning to where they belonged.

# 16

*1987*

HARRIET HAD FIFTY dollars in her back pocket and carried everything she needed in her backpack.

Her plan was to follow the Murray River, shift from orchard to orchard to earn some money to put away for a rainy day. Meet new friends, get experience and party. No set plans, take things one day at a time. She knew this would be her only chance – once she went back to the farm, she'd be into the daily grind that never ended.

She heard a car approaching in the distance and automatically put her hand out without looking. If they stopped they stopped, if they didn't, no matter. It wasn't until she heard the slowing down of the engine she threw a glance over her shoulder.

With her slightly crooked front teeth on full display she clapped her hands together and skipped, hopped and jumped towards the green EH Holden. Two beautiful people grinned at her from the front seat, the passenger reaching into the back to open the door.

'Hey, I'm Harriet,' she said breezily through the open window, slightly taken aback when she realised the passenger wasn't female as she thought from a distance. Instead, she locked eyes with the most beautiful man she'd ever laid eyes on.

'Hi Harriet, I'm Lief. This is Lucy. Where you headed?'

'Hoping to get to the Murray, looking for fruit picking work.'

'Perfect!' Lucy smiled and Harriet felt faint. Never in her entire nineteen years had she seen anyone as beautiful as Lucy. She should be on the cover of Vogue. Completely dazzled Harriet threw her bag into the back seat and slid over to sit in the centre.

'We're heading to the exact same place. Meant to be.' Lucy tucked her glorious long hair around her ear and Harriet admired how perfectly it stayed in place. Lief turned up the music and Harriet leaned back into her seat. With the wind on her face, she missed the exchange in the front seat. In fact, she missed all the exchanges between Lucy and Lief over the next few weeks. When she happened to catch one, it was too late.

THE SUN BEAT down, burning the top of Harriet's head through the holes in her straw hat.

'Bit tropical today,' she said to Lief, who was at the same ladder height as her on the adjoining peach tree.

'Pushing thirty-five I'd say,' Lief said, handing her his drink bottle.

'Thanks,' she said shyly, flattered by the attention of this beautiful man, the man of her dreams. She pushed her feelings aside; he wasn't hers to dream about. He belonged to Lucy.

They were the perfect power couple. They were so in love with each other, nobody could penetrate. But he was paying Harriet a lot of attention the past few days, and Lucy didn't seem to mind.

'Want to join Lucy and I for a swim later? We've found the perfect waterhole. Nice and deep, surrounded by big, old red gums.'

'Sounds great. I think I'll sleep in the river. I've been hot before but not this hot.'

Harriet felt Lief's eyes on her muscled and now, very tanned body. She had never been conscious of how she looked; it didn't matter much if anyone noticed her. She'd always been plain, and years of working on the farm with her big brothers protecting her and scaring off any potential suitors, meant she wasn't wise in the ways of the world.

Lief was the first male to really notice her. The way he looked at her with an intensity she'd never known. The way his eyes scanned down her face, neck, chest, torso, legs. He would scan down then back up, catching her catching him and smiling in a way that said *nice*.

It made her stomach flutter and her fanny tingle. She wondered if he knew she'd never been touched before. Her strict upbringing had prepared her for marriage so far into the future that she hadn't even considered it. As far as sex before marriage, that wasn't even an option. As soon as anyone even thought about looking at her, her brothers would swoop in and sweep her away.

Later, cooled down from a long swim in the brown waters of the Murray River, Harriet dozed on her towel. It was just her, Lucy and Lief. Everyone else in the picking group headed to the pub straight from the orchard, nobody even noticed they were missing three.

She opened her eyes when she felt a fuzzy peach being placed gently on her bare stomach.

'Hey, you,' Lief said as he rolled it back and forth over her firm abs.

'Hey, you,' she replied, looking around to see where Lucy was. She was nowhere.

Harriet sat up and started peeling the skin off with a small knife, offering Lief a slice as she bit into one herself, the juice dribbling down her chin. He reached over and gently caught the drips with his bare fingers. Harriet couldn't help herself from looking at his bronze-coloured torso, also bare, and resisted the temptation to squeeze a slice of juicy peach over it and lick it off.

She stood up, embarrassed by her runaway mind.

He grabbed her hand and pulled her back down onto the towel.

'Don't go,' he whispered.

'What about Lucy? I'm not that kind of girl.'

'Lucy doesn't mind sharing me, we are cool that way.'

'I don't understand. It's not the way I was brought up.'

'Tell me about home, tell me about your upbringing.' Lief seemed to understand when to back away. It was part of his undeniable charm.

Harriet told him about her parents, how hard they worked. Her brothers. How protective they were. A hard-working, old-fashioned, country family. Church on Sundays, taking it in turns as to who would do the Sunday chores, milking being the main one with the herd her Mum bred.

Her life revolved around the farm, around her family. She had little time for socialising and loved the freedom of being on the road like this. No alarms, no ties, no chores.

Work when she wanted, stop working when she wanted. Meet new people, see new places she'd only read about in the papers or seen in a magazine.

'How about you?' Harriet asked, worried she was hogging the conversation.

'I'm pretty boring, I'm far more interested in hearing more about you.'

Harriet lay back on the towel, relaxed, charmed.

'Hey, you two,' Lucy reappeared, and Harriet quickly sat up.

'Hi Lucy, sorry,' Harriet mumbled, and stood, ready to leave. Lucy stopped her with a hug.

'Don't leave on my account,' she said kindly. 'Stay.'

Harriet's stomach churned in confusion, like the butter churner in the small steel bench in their dairy Mum topped up continually during milking to make butter for them and to sell in the grocery store in town for $1.50 a stick.

Harriet wasn't sure when her body took over her thinking brain and melted into the moment. It might have been when Lief kissed her behind the ear from behind while Lucy kissed her gently on the lips. Or maybe it was when Lucy removed Harriet's bikini top and cupped her small breasts in her two hands, leaning down to kiss and suck each nipple.

Or when Lief laid her on her back and gently removed her bikini bottoms before placing his mouth over her. It was definitely when he put his tongue deep inside a place she'd only ever explored with her fingers. Also definitely when he removed his shorts and brought her hands to hold his erection before Lucy put her mouth over it.

So much pleasure, followed by so much pain. Tears rolled out of the corners of her eyes as the pain of seeing Lief sob overtook the pain of the rock Lucy hit into the side of her head, over and over again, until Harriet couldn't see anything anymore.

'STOP YOUR CRYING. It's done now. Time to clean it all up, quick, in case someone decides to leave the pub early and come looking for a spot for a dip.'

'I thought you said nobody knew about this place,' Lief wiped his dripping nose with the back of his hand.

'Who knows, but you need to hurry.'

Lief didn't move, he couldn't drag his eyes away from Harriet's, wide open and looking straight through him.

'Lief. Move.' Lucy was getting angrier by the second, now was not the time for Lief to have a conscience attack.

He shook as the adrenalin kicked in. Lucy had gone over this with him before. How to clean up the mess, how to dig the hole, how to bury the body so it would never be found, or if it was, it would be so badly decomposed it couldn't be identified. He wasn't supposed to leave any clothing, jewellery or other items that could leave a clue with the body.

He was efficient. His years cleaning up after the wild rock and roll parties at the mud brick recording studio, disposing of drug paraphernalia and cleaning up vomit, blood and women who weren't meant to be there made him perfect for the clean-ups. Lucy worked that out early on when she came up with the idea of bringing him in as her co-pilot.

She never stayed for this part – it was time for her to make an appearance at the pub and create a story about Lief dropping Harriet at a bus stop for an emergency dash back to her family. They were an itinerant bunch and didn't form close friendships. Here one day, gone the next.

She was long gone when Lief placed Harriet's brown string bikini top in his secret pouch before carefully folding the bottom and placing it next to her body. If someone ever found this spot, the bikini would contain traces of her which may eventually lead her back home. It was a small act of rebellion against the power Lucy held over him, a thin thread of hope he might one day find his way out of this mess he'd gotten himself into and make things right.

SIX YEARS LATER, a group of fishing mates on a drunken riverside camping trip, where they caught more hangovers than Murray Cod, got the shock of their lives when they dug a pit a reasonable smelling distance away from the waterhole where they could empty their bowels in peace and solitude.

A human skull and a neatly folded brown bikini bottom lay undisturbed while a hard-working farming family from Coolah in New South Wales grieved for their much-adored daughter and sister who still hadn't come home.

The police retrieved the bones and bagged them with the bikini, which would lay unclaimed in a box for many more agonising years to come. The unmatched, unidentified remains added to the ever-growing pile of unsolved cold cases that just needed a dedicated, stubborn, determined detective by the name of Rhiannon McVee to find them.

# 17

ULLA TAPPED QUIETLY on the door before coming in.

'Here is tea for you Mr Red.' She gently placed the fresh brew on his bedside table, taking in the masculine room that didn't suit him one bit. She ached to fill it with fresh flowers to soften the hard edges of the chocolate timber bed setting, black floor rug, black curtains and black bedspread. She didn't understand why Ayala made the room so dark, did she not know her son?

She tut, tutted her way around the room. 'You need colour in here, yes? These black curtains, blah. They is, how I say it?'

'Black?' Red replied in a deadpan voice.

Ulla glanced at him, noticing the corner of his mouth twitch. She smiled her beautiful smile and for Red the black in the room turned golden.

'Ah, you having a joke with me? That is good. Very good. I am happy to see your mouth move up, not down.'

She went to leave.

'Don't go Ulla,' Red said quietly. 'Sit with me.' He reached his hand out to her and she laced her fingers through his as she sat on the bed.

His face slowly relaxed and she kept hold of his hand while his eyes closed. It didn't take long for him to drift off, his chest rising and falling. Ulla's eyes wandered to the red welt on his neck where the rope dug in before the branch of his childhood leopardwood tree saved his life, unable to bear the weight of the tragedy he tied around it.

'Mr Red, you must stay until your heart grows strong. I will stay with you,' she whispered.

Red could hear her but his body was like jelly; jelly limbs, jelly bones, jelly eyelids. He was not strong enough to will his eyes open or command his arms to pull her into him. He lay there, helpless but hopeful, letting her soak into him and fill the dark corners of his mind with light.

BIANCA WAS ON a plane to Sydney, fired up and ready to confront Clive. Enough of sitting back and feeling helpless and hopeless because of the shitty life he'd dealt them.

She channelled the sadness of what he'd done to Red into anger, along with what she knew he'd done to Ayala and what she imagined he'd done to Ayala which put them all in this mind-blowing state of constant ambiguity.

She grasped for a phrase to describe what it was like when someone close to you disappeared so mysteriously. Sometimes she entertained the thought her Mum had run away and escaped this life, starting fresh somewhere new, safe from the man-turned-monster who she'd promised to have and to hold, for richer or poorer, for better or worse.

Before her thoughts could fully form and create visions in her mind of a happy, content Ayala sitting in a cosy cottage by the sea, darkness descended like a drenched oilskin riding coat.

Darkness visited often. It brought with it the horror of their dog Maggie covered in blood from the death blows someone rained on her, clumps of dirt stuck to the blood from being buried in one of Ayala's garden beds.

Maggie became Ayala, Maggie's blood became Ayala's blood, Ayala was buried deep beneath the earth while she was still alive. Suffocating, trying to spit the dirt out of her mouth and wipe it from her eyes. The dirt pinned her arms to her body as its weight pushed her down, down, down.

'M'am, M'am...are you okay?'

Bianca startled from her restless, dark dream as the air hostess gently touched her shoulder. She stared into pale green, worried eyes. Blink, blink, blink. Gradually she became aware of dribble running from the left corner of her mouth, her clenched jaw, tears weeping from her eyes and the book she'd been reading in the hostess's other hand. She'd rescued it from the middle of the aisle after Bianca swept it with one of her flailing arms during her fitful dream.

'Can I get you anything M'am?'

All Bianca could manage was a shake of her head. She attempted a smile through her tears and tried to rearrange her face from something resembling Edvard Munch's *The Scream* into something more like Leonardo da Vinci's *Mona Lisa*.

She opened her book and went to a blank page at the back. After scrabbling around in her bag for a pen, she gripped it tightly as she wrote.

'This is the beginning of the rest of your life. Start living it now.'

CLIVE SQUIRMED UNCOMFORTABLY under the fierce scrutiny of her gaze.

'Well?' Bianca insisted. 'Happy now? Happy another death could have been on your hands? It's only by some stupid twist of fate Red isn't dead. If that branch hadn't snapped when it did, he would be dead. And it would be your fault. Yours. All yours. More blood on your hands.'

He looked away, feeling sweat trickle down between his shoulder blades and resisting the urge to blubber like the big, pathetic, weak baby of a man he knew he was. Facing his only daughter, who had always been Daddy's Girl, stripped him bare of his bravado and the influence his masses of wealth brought to him.

Clive was nothing but an ageing, balding, sick and despicable man who'd abused his own son and the sons of too many others to count. A man who'd also abused his wife, mentally and physically, to the point of no return.

Now, he was bare and exposed in front of his independent, bright, intelligent and beautiful daughter who had cherished and adored him so generously from the moment she was born. Guilt tiptoed across his conscience but didn't have a hope of penetrating the layer of selfishness and arrogance that shrouded his heart.

'How many more lives do you plan to ruin before you man up and face the consequences of your actions?' Bianca knew she only had one chance to be this brave, and if she didn't take it, she'd never be able to walk this path again.

Clive stuttered and stammered. After a while he gave up, shoulders slumped, head hung low, face slack, arms hanging by his side.

'Don't put on any acts with me, Dad. CLIVE.' It was like someone had taken over. Someone far stronger, tougher and braver than she ever thought she was. 'I've come here to stop all the lies, stop all the splashing yourself around the place like you haven't got a care in the world.'

He looked at her again. She didn't break his gaze. 'Tell me. Where. The fuck. Is Ayala?'

There was no way Clive was going to be a man. He knew that, and although she was crossing her fingers behind her back in a childhood, and childish, gesture, she knew that. He stood silently, wishing and hoping she would just walk away.

Clive couldn't change a damned thing. But most of all, he couldn't survive in prison. Every action, every word, every move was purely for his own self-preservation. He was incapable of considering anyone else.

He turned away. She clawed at him, trying to twist his shoulders back towards her to force him to look in her eyes. He was a slippery slug, and shrugged off her grasping hands.

In that one split second he knew he could give in and confess everything to Bianca, and the thought of being able to reduce her pain, his precious little girl, almost won over.

A picture of him in prison, with tough tattooed and intolerant inmates crowded around him, their furious faces unable to hide the contempt or the desire to hurt him, took over.

Clive slowly, calmly, walked away.

Devastated in the knowledge she hadn't achieved anything on this crazy mission where she had envisaged her father making heartfelt confessions to his sins, Bianca's insides shattered. Then, just like The Terminator, the pieces joined together and became solid again. She muttered under her breath, and her words gained strength as they escaped from her lips.

'Fuck you Clive. Fuck you to the end of the moon and back. Your time will come, and you will pay for what you've done. You won't get away with this. That much I promise.'

PAT WATCHED THE exchange through binoculars he'd invested in since becoming one of those journalists who stalked people. His obsession with

Clive was growing with every day the man, who Pat believed was guilty as all sin, walked free and flaunted his freedom like a cocky male peacock strutting its iridescent feathers.

It was Ayala who drove him. Such a beautiful, poised woman with so much to contribute to this world. So vibrant and alive. With passing time people would move on with their lives, Ayala a faded memory until eventually she was forgotten. Meanwhile Clive was out and about, boastful in his aliveness, seemingly unfazed by what Pat believed he had done.

Without the advantage of sound, he tried to interpret their hand gestures and facial expressions, turning them into stories of an imagined conversation between father and daughter.

He didn't even look at the notepad on his lap while his hand transcribed what as unfolding before him into shorthand to digest and pick to pieces later.

Ring marks formed around his eyes from pressing the binoculars so tight. His shoulder blades clenched together, forming a tight knot he'd have to release during his gym workout later.

He finally understood. Bianca was the key to this story, not Clive. It was Bianca who would unravel this mystery. He needed to shift his stalking from the glittering water views of Sydney to the rust-coloured outback. His hand continued its frenetic notetaking.

'Bianca shouts obscenities as Clive exits the scene, tail between his legs, knowing she's won this round and it won't be long before it's all over red rover for him.'

By the weekend Pat had checked into the backpackers in Bourke's Old London Bank Building, built over one hundred years ago on the corner of Oxley and Sturt streets, his window providing a perfect vantage point of the comings and goings in this notorious wild west town of barred shop windows and unsolved mysteries.

# 18

'Bloody hell,' Andy ranted on the phone. 'What is going on McVee? We are so close to this, and then his daughter swoops in and nearly stuffs the whole thing. I thought you had her in check. The last thing we need is her here trying to solve this herself.'

'I know, I know,' Rhiannon tried to placate Andy, who was walking around barefoot on a hot tinned roof.

Rhiannon also wasn't impressed. But what could she do? If Bianca wanted to confront Clive, and put their undercover surveillance at risk, along with every other tactic they were using to solve this case, it was out of Rhiannon's control.

'She's just gone through finding her brother with a rope around his neck, it's bound to create some sort of knee jerk reaction none of us could anticipate.'

Andy simmered down. 'Geezus,' he muttered. 'That was a gift from above for sure.'

Silence, as they digested how lucky everyone was not to have to attend a funeral in amongst all this.

'Are you any closer to working out what he's done with Ayala?' Rhiannon diverted the subject to the left.

'No. Not one bloody inch. I don't know what he's done with her. How could someone vanish like that? I feel like vital clues are staring me right in the face.'

'Me too. Me too,' Rhiannon admitted. 'I'm getting a fair bit of stick about it. Everyone telling me it's unsolvable and I should just file it away in the cabinet and forget about it.'

'Since when have you listened to what anyone else said?'

Rhiannon was swift in her reply. 'Vicky Verka, Andy.'

Andy swerved left. 'I haven't spotted that pesky journalist for a while. He's turned himself into some sort of private sleuth, pretty good at it too if I'm completely honest, but he must be taking a sabbatical.'

Rhiannon groaned. 'No, he isn't. He's here. Turned up just after Bianca got back. Sticks out like dog's balls in Bourke too.'

Andy laughed. 'I'll give him points for trying, that's for sure. Not many of these city journos would go to those lengths; they go to Newcastle and think they're in the outback!'

'Exactly! He's pretty thorough I've got to admit. I'm not putting any reigns on him, you never know, he might uncover something we can't.'

'You reckon?'

'I do reckon. People get stars in their eyes at the prospect of being on radio, television or in the paper. Their five seconds of fame and all that. He offers far more than us coppers do for someone to spill their guts. Clive must have confided in someone; he couldn't have kept this all a complete secret. Maybe he got drunk one night at a race meeting or farmer function, let down his guard, 'fessed all his sins.'

Rhiannon sat with the thought for a moment. 'Plus, Pat's a pretty genuine bloke.'

'Be careful,' Andy warned. 'Don't want you going all soft on me with the media, they're the enemy you know. I also don't want you to dump yourself into the sheep dip, you've been there before.'

'I'm impressed Andy, dumping myself into the sheep dip, you're learning a thing or two from the bush!'

Andy humphed, not wanting to admit one of Rhiannon's sayings had become one of his favourites. He had gotten a few impressive reactions when he ripped it out around the office.

'Anyway,' Rhiannon continued, talking over the top of Andy's reference to her leaking information to Pat in a desperate attempt to create some movement in the case. 'I've learnt from past mistakes; I know what I'm doing.'

'Okay then but keep him on a short leash.'

Rhiannon mulled things over long after Andy was gone.

'Where the fuck are you, Ayala? Where the fuck?'

# 19

PAT WATCHED FROM his window in the old bank building, recognising Bianca as soon as she got out of her dusty, new Toyota Landcruiser 80 Series, white, beside a phone box. He was working on a story scheduled to run in this Friday's news bulletins, which he also expected to get picked up by the major dailies.

The story had minimal 'new' news but Pat had managed to convince his program manager it was worth running to keep the Ayala Philips' case on people's minds.

He stopped typing on his new laptop the paper had issued to watch her hunched in the phone box, hair falling over her face, feeding coins into the slot.

'I'm not sure if my phones are tapped,' she whispered to the gravelly, familiar voice who picked up on the third ring. 'I'm ringing from a phone box in Bourke.'

'How are you holding up?' Kenneth asked, squashing down the guilt at not sharing what he knew.

'Terrible. Red tried to hang himself.'

Shocked silence reverberated through the stiff, squeaky cord which had been replaced more times than any other public telephone box in Australia. Every time they tried a thicker, stiffer, more vandal-proof cord, the problem youths who lurked the dark streets fuelled by alcohol their genetics couldn't handle always found a way.

'He's okay?'

'As okay as one could be after deciding he was a failure and his life was so unbearable he didn't want to be part of it anymore, then failing in that. It's all Clive's fault. Everything is Clive's fault. I hate him so much, and it's eating me from the inside.'

'Red has always been the sensitive one,' he said gravely. 'Your mother's disappearance would have had a major impact on him.'

'It's not only that.' Bianca's voice cracked. He knew what was coming. He knew everything Clive had done. Everything. He waited patiently for her to go on.

'Clive abused him, since he was a little boy.'

Pat watched Bianca's legs give way and she slid to the floor of the cubicle, the cord now at full stretch. She pushed her hair away from her face and her pain reached out across the street.

Who was she talking to? A girlfriend? A boyfriend? And why a phone box? He figured it was because she couldn't talk on the phone at home, in case her brother overheard her. Knowing about his recent suicide attempt from Rhiannon, strictly off the record, this was most likely the topic of the conversation. That had to be it.

But one should never assume, he reminded himself. It could be something completely different. She could be talking to Ayala. The thought was so wild and off the wall it was laughable. Or was it?

RHIANNON WAS CAREFULLY selecting from the pile of apples which has just arrived from the Sydney fruit markets, when she felt hot breath on the back of her neck. Slowly and with control she turned around and found herself nose to nose with Pat Richards.

'What the fuck are you doing here!' she laughed, taking a small step backwards while trying hard not to topple the apples from the wooden shelf behind her.

Pat grinned like the Cheshire cat who had eaten the cream.

'That's for me to know and you to find out, Detective.'

Rhiannon turned back to the apples, taking her time to select while she got hold of herself at the sight of Pat on her home turf.

'This one looks good.' She held it up to show him. 'Want one?'

'Sure.'

They munched in companionable silence as they walked up the street towards the police station. Rhiannon finished first and pegged her core into the vacant block where dry grass created a haven for all creatures great and small from rats to snakes to the local tomcats and town chooks that roamed free before heading back to their respective backyard pens at night.

'Spill,' she said.

'I was going to ask the same of you.' Pat took another crunchy bite.

'It's pretty obvious what you're doing here but what I don't understand is what inspired you to leave your yuppie streets of Sydney for this heat and dust and flies. Surely you could have just picked up the phone and ask me a few questions?'

'I guess I could have, if you had the answers to the questions I have.'

'Smartarse.'

'Smarter than you, I'm guessing. Nah, just joking. I got pretty sick of watching old Clive living it up on his yacht with all the rich and famous who don't seem to be concerned about hanging out with a paedophile.'

'I think you're wasting your time out here, I really do.'

'You're not trying to just get me off the scent of something big?'

'Come on Pat, you should know me better than that, if I had something, I'd tell you.'

'Well, what would you make of Bianca in a phone box in the main street of Bourke, having a conversation so difficult her legs collapse from beneath her?'

Rhiannon raised one eyebrow. If Pat hadn't been watching her face so intently, which he often found himself doing, he would have missed her small expression of surprise before she quickly hid it away.

'She's had a pretty tough run, you'd have to admit.'

'Agree. But that doesn't really explain who she's calling from a phone box when she's got a perfectly good phone at home.'

They reached the back door of the police station and Rhiannon nodded to check if Pat wanted to come in.

'No thanks, not gonna find out much in there I wouldn't expect. I think I've got more chance of solving this mystery on the street.'

Rhiannon watched him walk away. Pat was right. Nobody was going to solve this mystery from the confines of a police station. The street was where it was at. Not this street though.

# 20

LIEF WATCHED THE bus pull away; the empty space it left on the kerb yawned as large as a hippopotamus's open jaws.

He ambled casually, and an ordinary observer wouldn't notice a thing out of place. Their only reason for stealing a second glance would be his perfectly symmetrical features – chiselled good looks was a phrase inspired by men like him.

He'd parked the car, registered under his real name, Lief Janssen, in a secluded street. Once inside, windows shut tight, he lost it. The steering wheel bore the brunt of his rage. His right elbow bounced off the side window. He didn't feel a thing even though he carried the bruise for weeks.

HIS MUM AND Dad would be turning in their graves. They were so proud when Lief, their golden child, their only son, set out on a world adventure which eventually landed him in Australia. He had an ordinary, happy childhood, he was loved, albeit from a distance.

He wrote home to Rotterdam, where he grew up in a privileged, wealthy household, every week for the first year he was away. His letters gradually became less frequent, eventually they stopped. His parents were kind, hard-working upper class who loved their son, but loved each other more. A string of nannies and boarding school from a young age established his independence early. He knew when he left the Netherlands he'd never return.

It wasn't until he called home one night, three girls into Lucy's killing spree (not his, hers, he told himself), he found out they both died in a car accident. They left a large sum of money in a bank account in the

Netherlands, and he could return home at any time to pick up his life. However, Lucy had him by the short and curlies, an expression he heard around a campfire one night. He presented the idea of them both going but she had no intention of moving to the other side of the world. Who would avenge her mother then?

What had he become? He hardly believed it himself. How could he fix this? How could he make this right?

Spent, he rested his forehead on the steering wheel that hadn't changed shape despite the pounding.

It came to him. He needed to go back to the beginning, back to when he met Lucy at the horse yard on the isolated seaside retreat on the NSW Far South Coast. Retrace their steps. He'd kept something from each victim, knew where they all were. He would leave a clue at each location to link them together and make it easy for police to figure it out.

He'd already left one to help them identify who Lucy really was.

S.K.Y. Serial. Killer. Yes.

*March 1988*

'WHAT DO WE have here?' Lucy mused, spotting two people in the distance, thumbs out, on an isolated road west of Dubbo. Lucy and Lief were headed to Trangie for the cotton-picking season. The hours were long, but the money was good.

'Looks like they've got the same idea as us.' Lief tried to be casual and upbeat while his dread built as Lucy lifted her foot off the accelerator.

He was still reeling from what they'd done to Harriet. Lucy spent months reassuring him, counselling him, telling him she forgave him for what he'd done. He was confused, he hadn't done anything. He'd been there, he'd known what was coming, but it wasn't him. It was all on her.

Then she begged and pleaded with him to forgive her; told him it would never happen again. She didn't understand why she did it, something took over when she thought about what 'he' did to her mother, she went into a rage and didn't know where she was or what she was doing. *Please forgive me, it won't happen again.*

Of course he forgave her; she was his life, his obsession, his everything. She was his twisted world.

The girls came to the passenger window first. Lief rolled it down and flashed his perfect smile.

'Hey there, need a lift?'

'That would be grand,' the stocky looking one replied in a strong Cockney accent. The second girl hung back, less confident, the follower.

Lucy flashed her beautiful smile as they slid into the back seat, backpacks wedged into the boot amongst mattresses, doonas and camp gear.

'What brings you girls all this way out in the middle of nowhere?' she asked, her voice like honey on hot toast.

'We heard there was good money to be made on the cotton farms. Trying to get a bit of money together so we can get to the beach in Queensland and put a shrimp or two on the barbie! I'm Helen.'

'Hey Helen, love your accent, where are you from?' Lucy dazzled both girls, they'd never seen anyone so beautiful.

'Let me guess,' Lief cut in. 'East London?'

Speaking of beautiful, Lief had the girls equally dazzled.

The quieter girl, Sheila, nudged her friend who'd been doing all the talking. 'He got you first go,' she said, her lilting Irish accent like a song. 'Now guess where I'm from?'

'Wexford?'

'Enniscorthy. How did you know?'

'Ah, Enniscorthy, I spent time there after I left on my big world adventure. Prettiest town in Ireland between the mountains and River Slaney.'

'He's a Lonely Planet Tour Guide in the making,' Lucy laughed. 'He plays this game every time we meet new people. Never seen anything like it in my life, missed his calling he has. This is Lief. I'm Lucy.'

Lucy eased her foot onto the accelerator as everyone got comfortable and settled into the long drive ahead.

Helen from East London and Sheila from Enniscorthy never made it to Trangie. Neither did their backpacks. They lay buried well off the beaten track by a tiny waterway that only flowed in a one in one-hundred-year flood.

The families of Helen from East London and Sheila from Enniscorthy didn't know if their girls were dead or alive. The last calls to home were from Sydney a week before they disappeared, and there was no mention of Trangie, or each other.

They met at an Irish bar a few days after they called home and made a last-minute plan to go to Trangie together. Footloose and fancy free, with no commitments or plans apart from seeing as much of the country they'd dreamt of visiting since they'd seen the good-looking Paul Hogan say *G'day* on the Australian Tourism ads.

Letters they posted from Dubbo Post Office the day Lucy and Lief picked them up arrived home a month later, giving a vital clue that narrowed down the search area to somewhere between there and Trangie.

Police response was more casual than a Sunday afternoon backyard barbecue.

'Bloody backpackers, they come out here and expect they can walk to the next town in a few hours with a small water bottle in their backpack,' the Dubbo police sergeant mumbled after the tenth call from Sheila's parents who had been hounding him since they got the letters post-stamped Dubbo.

'Probably perished beside some dry creek bed, thinking they would find a bubbling stream. We're nothing like the green, lush farmland of Europe where everything is in spitting distance.'

The simple fact was, after basic enquiries and an appeal in the newspaper, the police had no information. No clues. All they knew was the girls were heading out to Trangie. If they walked the whole way without a lift, it would take fourteen and a half hours to get there. It was November and the day they posted the letter had been a scorcher.

How could these two young girls who had a lifetime of adventures in front of them vanish from the face of the earth?

Easily.

Just like that.

*1995*

HE HADN'T PASSED a car since he turned off the highway onto the shortcut road he traversed with Lucy seven years earlier. He pulled off the bitumen onto a bush track, and soon he wasn't visible from the road, he wasn't visible from anywhere.

It was approaching dusk when he reached the cleared area which would lead his car down to the dry creek bed. A glorious bright orange sunset with pink streaks filtered through the trees as the sun gracefully moved towards the horizon.

Lief wound down the window and soaked in its glory, momentarily forgetting the horror of this place. It wasn't until he stepped out of the car in bare feet, straight onto a giant patch of goat heads, that he remembered.

'Yeeeoooowwwwwww!'

The sunset birds relaxing into their evening startled, disturbing the crispy crackling leaves of the trees waiting for a rain revival which was taking a long time to come.

'Noooooooo!! How could you Lucy??!!!!! I hhhaatttteeee what you've doooonnneee!!!'

Lief yelled louder and the birds flew faster but the sun ignored them as it went about its daily routine, eventually disappearing completely and plunging everything into darkness.

*March 1988*

THE GIRLS HAD no idea Lucy was driving them in circles; neither had any concept of geography, distance or direction. They could easily find their way around a city, and were adept at reading bus and train timetables, but as soon as they left the built-up areas of Sydney they didn't know their left from their right or their east from their west.

It was stinking hot by nine in the morning, on a day with an expected top of thirty-six degrees Celsius, and they wondered if they'd made the right decision to hitchhike out to Trangie or if they should have spent the money on a bus ticket.

'It's all part of the adventure!' Helen was upbeat and ready for anything, Sheila less so.

'But it's so hot, and it's just past breakfast,' Sheila couldn't keep the whine out of her voice. She couldn't believe how hot this wide brown land got, especially this far from the beach. She looked around at the trees, more of a brownish green than the lush green she imagined. Shrivelled up grass the colour of straw, or no grass at all and just dirt. Dust. Ugly. Brown.

Helen saw it through completely different eyes. She loved the space and vastness. Every shade of brown from gold to red to everywhere in between. She loved the warmth, the feel of sweat on her skin. She never wanted to leave.

Their progress was slow. They stopped every hour to rest under the shadiest tree they could find. It was penetratingly hot when Lucy pulled over and Sheila had been pleading with Helen to turn back.

'You saved us!' Helen gushed after they settled into the car.

LIEF WASN'T EXPECTING the day to turn out the way it did. Lucy caught him by as much surprise as the two innocent backpackers who had no idea their lives were about to be cut short.

Even now, Lief didn't know what triggered Lucy's rage as they sat around a small campfire he lit to heat up tinned baked beans and boil a billy on.

All he knew was one minute they were laughing and joking and the next he was plunged into hell with a flash of a knife in Lucy's hand. Sheila had no idea what was coming, but Helen saw the whole thing. She acted quickly and ran for her life but had no hope of outrunning Lucy in this unfamiliar bush.

It was a moonless night and once she was away from the fire she couldn't see a thing including the branch that tripped her and landed her face-first in a patch of goat head burrs.

She didn't even feel them as she crawled in a panicked attempt to get back on her feet, but Lucy was right there, grabbing her ankles, her legs, her waist. Then Lucy was on top of her, pushing her face into the unforgiving goat heads that left small holes in her cheeks, chin, lips, nose and forehead.

With a mouthful of dirt and Lucy's sour breath in her ear, Helen only had time to ask once.

'Why?'

Lucy didn't answer. She didn't really know. She could say it was to avenge the death of her Mum. But she'd done that when she killed the man she thought was her father who'd taken her whole world from her then tried to present her with a new world filled with lies.

Now it wasn't as clear cut. She just did it. Because she couldn't stop.

LUCY WAS NOWHERE to be found while Lief cleaned up the mess she'd left. The dirt was rock hard but became softer and more malleable the closer he moved towards the dry creek.

He dug for hours. Four holes, an hour each. One for each girl, one for each backpack. Helen was wearing a gold necklace with a small cross attached to the end. Sheila was wearing a large silver ring with a square top and an S stamped on it. On the underside were engraved words. Love Dad & Mum.

Lief gently, tenderly removed them and placed them into the small leather pouch he hid from Lucy. It was getting full; Harriet's brown bikini top took up a lot of room.

Every time he thought he would cry he called on his mind to take him to when he was a small boy, still wide awake long after his final kiss goodnight. To try and get to sleep he would visualise an ice skater on a frozen pond slowly skating around the edge, left leg, right leg, arms opposite. Everything was white and there was no sound apart from the knife-sharp edge of the ice skate. Skate, skate, skate, skate. Some nights took longer than others but he always reached that other place, not here, not anywhere.

IT TOOK HIM thirty minutes to find the spot. In the seven years that had passed it didn't look like floods of any consequence had washed through. Maybe the creek had a trickle of water during a heavy shower since he was here last but the trees and landscape still looked much the same.

He recognised the large rocks he'd arranged in a pattern to look haphazard to a casual observer. Had he known he'd be back? Maybe. Had he known he'd one day need a clue from each girl Lucy killed? Maybe.

He bought a shovel and sturdy gardening gloves in the hardware store in Dubbo, essential tools for any backyard gardener. To add to the guise he bought two proteas, parsley and chives. The plants were sitting on the nature strip of an unsuspecting homeowner who would wonder for a moment who had bought new plants for them, before planting them without a fuss after concluding they were from a friendly neighbour.

He was heartened to see wheel tracks and the remnants of campouts not far away. The spot was not as isolated as he thought. People used it and judging by the labels on the VB stubby bottles that looked brand new; someone had been here not too long ago.

He thought it best to dig up the backpacks to trigger a closer look around. Once the backpacks were easy to see he found a stick for the piece of paper he'd calmly written on earlier, and pushed it deep into the ground beside them.

He pierced the piece of paper and pushed it down halfway so it wouldn't blow off. The words weren't written in blood, but he'd used a red pen for effect.

S.K.Y.

He pushed the silver ring over the end of the stick to hold the paper in place, before weaving Helen's gold necklace around and around. Still on his knees, he drew his hands together in prayer and as a lonely crow cawed in the distance, begged for forgiveness.

# 21

RHIANNON WAS BURIED in files in the only private room she could find at the Bourke Police Station – the storeroom – where she'd set up a table and chair behind the bulk toilet paper and meagre stationery supplies.

She had boxes underneath the table; these were the ones she wanted to keep close, and others stacked against the wall – the ones she'd been through which didn't fit the profile.

She was looking for girls in their late teens and early twenties. Backpackers, runaways, hitchhikers who had possibly worked as fruit pickers, corn tasslers, or any other farm work where it was cash in hand, no experience necessary, no questions asked, all welcome.

She had a several pieces of butcher's paper taped together pinned to the only bare wall space in the storeroom not covered by shelves or other useless crap. On a map were marked out Lucy's known addresses, making an assumption these were places of interest she may have been drawn back to after she left school.

The paper also had an image of the mystery man a police sketch artist drew based on the eyewitnesses who'd seen him, mostly Jeremy's account. The only real distinguishing features they felt sure of were the white-blond long hair and a tall, lean build. This man kept Rhiannon awake at night, and when she finally did get to sleep, he came to her in her dreams, chasing her down and gouging her eyes out so she couldn't see him.

She'd also started a timeline. When did Lucy first meet this mystery man? Was it just before they picked up Harriet? Or had they been together longer than that?

This raised the question of how far back to go with missing teenagers who might have jumped into the EH Holden with Lucy and her male companion.

Then more questions. Did Lucy know her companion was a serial killer? Could they really make the assumption he was a serial killer? Just because they picked up Harriet didn't mean they killed her.

They still couldn't discount Keely's involvement in Lucy's death. Had she seen so much when she was living with Mike that she lost who she was, and become involved in serious crimes that scared her enough to run away from him, keep running and never come home? Aagghh, Rhiannon's mind raced like a rabbit startled in the bushes.

By the end of the day she had set aside four possible missing girls who could be connected with the serial killer who'd killed Lucy, mostly based on where they'd gone missing. They were all long shots, wild guesses, but you had to start somewhere, right?

That night, she relaxed in front of the six o'clock news in her Dad's armchair, Honey at her feet, TV dinner on her lap. Tonight, she was having frozen fish fingers with mashed potato and fresh vegetables from her elderly neighbour's garden – carrots, corn and broccoli. Plus a glass of milk to keep her bones strong.

Within seconds of the lead story about discovering two backpacks owned by young girls from overseas, last seen in Dubbo before disappearing without a trace, Rhiannon was dialing Andy's direct line at Kings Cross Police Station. When she couldn't get him at work she called his home number.

Nobody called him at home apart from Rhiannon, because nobody had his home number, apart from Rhiannon. She prised it out of him early in their working relationship, convincing him he needed to be reachable in case she had an urgent lead.

He wanted her to use his pager like everyone else did but she had a more personal motive – he needed someone to check in on him now and then even though the crusty old bachelor he had become after his wife left him decades ago, taking their only daughter with her, would never admit it.

'Andy, I've got a feeling about these girls. I think they're definitely connected to S.K.Y. They've got to be.'

'Whoa up a bit,' Andy reasoned, eating his dinner with one hand while trying not to upend the new cushioned TV dinner tray he'd bought from

Danoz Direct at two o'clock in the morning.

'Don't go jumping to conclusions just yet. You said they haven't found any bodies?'

'No, not yet, but I reckon I could be there in less than three hours and get fully up to speed.' She looked at the clock. 'It's 6.15 now; I can be there by 9.30, give or take.'

Andy sighed. You just didn't turn up to a suspected crime scene without going through a few hoops.

'I guess that means I need to spend the next couple of hours jumping through hoops for you so you get a decent sort of welcome when you turn up.'

'You're the best Andy, I owe you one.'

'Another one, you mean.'

But she was already gone, a whirly gig packing a bag, bolting down the rest of her dinner, spilling her milk down her front after not fully connecting with her mouth, and filling Honey's bowl with dry biscuits.

She was in the car by 6.23pm, at the station by 6.26pm and on the road in a police vehicle by 6.31pm. Sirens on for effect, she hurtled down the highway at breakneck speed, knowing in her heart. Serial. Killer. Yes.


RHIANNON FOUND THE crime scene easily thanks to it being lit up like a Christmas tree in the middle of nowhere.

She pulled in slowly and parked just off the road with a few other police vehicles, not wanting to roar in like she owned the place. Her police issue torch helped her avoid tree stumps, rocks and other bush obstacles.

Despite Andy's best work, Rhiannon was not welcomed with open arms. She greeted a couple of officers milling about, getting nothing in return apart from blank stares. She was used to it though. It wasn't until she found the Dubbo sergeant who'd dismissed the girls' parents and put so little effort into searching for them when they first disappeared, that she made headway.

'Good evening,' she looked down at his badge which she could read under the scene lights, 'Sergeant Wagner. I'm Detective Senior Constable Rhiannon McVee from Bourke.'

She put out her hand and they exchanged a firm shake.

'I heard you were coming. Talk to me.'

Rhiannon knew she had thirty seconds, at best, to hook him in.

'I'm looking into missing girls in Victoria and New South that might be linked to what I suspect is a serial killer. I have been going through old files and have a few possibles. I haven't come across this one, but from what I read between the lines on tonight's ABC News, they fit into my theory.'

She had plenty of practice with the next part of her elevator pitch, knowing if she went into too much detail she'd lose him at the three-minute mark. If she failed to include the right detail, she'd still lose him at the three-minute mark.

'You're probably confused by what Kings Cross and Bourke have to do with this, but Detective Sergeant Andy Cassettari and I are working on an old missing Sydney teenager's case which is linked to a body we found out near Bourke.

'We've since found one other backpacker, a young girl from Coolah, who we've linked to the Bourke body, also linked to the missing Sydney teenager.'

She was losing him.

'But before I go into too much more detail, are you able to tell me a bit about what's going on here?'

The Sergeant, despite eating remorse for lunch when he arrived on scene, parted with only the basics.

'A couple of young fellas came out with their motorbikes to hoon around and came across two backpacks. They come here regularly but it's the first time they've ever noticed them.'

'So, just the backpacks then?'

The Sergeant didn't know how much he wanted to share.

'Look, I know I've just rocked up here out of nowhere and you don't know me from a bar of soap, but I wouldn't have dropped everything, including my dinner down my front, if I didn't think there was something in this. I'm not here to take over or anything, I'm just here to help connect some dots I've been trying to connect for some time.'

The Sergeant warmed to her. She was straight down the line, and he could tell she was a country girl. Plus, she'd know more details soon enough when they were on the news.

'No, not just the backpacks.'

He paused for effect. 'We've since found two bodies.'

Rhiannon's legs trembled as the adrenalin of the last few hours kicked in.

'What else can you tell me?'

Sergeant Wagner took a step closer.

'There was something strange, which doesn't make any sense. A stick with a piece of paper stuck to it.'

Rhiannon grounded her feet as best she could, willing herself to exude calm despite being about to burst like a balloon with one breath too many.

'Let me guess. Three letters?'

'Yeeesss. How did you know?'

It was Rhiannon's turn to step closer and pause for effect.

'If you tell me those letters are S.K.Y. then I'll tell you we definitely have the same serial killer on our hands.

'And I have no idea just how many more are out there.'


RHIANNON BOOKED MOTEL rooms side by side in a basic motel next to the railway line in Narromine. With its cracked sign, out-of-control weeds along the side fence and algae floating on the swimming pool, she decided to be grateful for the small things. Like a fridge that kept the beer cold, a working air conditioner and a dining room serving steaks which covered the entire plate.

The dining room was gigantic, and could easily fit 200 diners. Rhiannon wondered if the people who'd built it were being a tad over ambitious, she didn't imagine the sleepy, run-down motel got numbers like that very often.

It was perfect for her and Andy though, they could pull a couple of tables together in the corner and spread out maps, papers and photos and not get disturbed.

Rhiannon was doing all the talking. 'Now we know they spent time at Trangie in 1988 and so I reckon they went from Coolah after Harriet and eventually to here. There's a time gap between the two, so I wonder if he killed anyone between them?'

Andy didn't respond, things weren't sitting right, it didn't fit.

'Okay. We're assuming it's the male travelling companion we're pinning all these murders on. Where was Lucy while they were going on? Was she part of it? How did she then become a victim if she was his accomplice? It makes no sense.'

'I agree, it's a head fuck. It would make more sense if Lucy was still alive because it would then feel like she was retracing their steps and leaving clues to hopefully lead us to him.'

'We need to work out who 'him' really is. I can't believe we haven't worked that out yet.'

Rhiannon groaned. 'It's doing my head in. Is he Australian, or did he slip into the country unnoticed? The bureaucrats tell me they're doing the best they can…'

'Everyone has a different 'best we can' to you, McVee,' Andy's dry delivery inserted humour. 'We have to be patient and shift away from that and solve the other pieces.'

'You're right Andy, save me from going into the secret inner sanctums of Australian bureaucracy and sorting through boxes of paperwork, I'm going to have to wait. What we need to figure out is who is leaving these clues?'

'We are pretty confident Keely was with Lucy and this mystery man, well, we have to assume she was because we have no other information suggesting otherwise. Is she leaving the clues?'

'How would she know about these girls though? That was long before she even ran away. If it is him, why is he leaving clues leading us to him?' Andy pondered.

Rhiannon's mouth couldn't keep up with her brain. 'We have two scenarios. Keely is dead, Keely is alive. Ironic, that's the two scenarios we've had since that girl went missing. She sure has created a tangle for us to untangle.'

'You're not wrong. Far out! I could kick her arse for the trouble she's caused,' Andy said.

'Hear, hear, if I wasn't so endeared to her. I just hope she's alive. I hope we find her before it's too late.'

'It might already be too late, you know that. I know that.'

'Don't crush all my hope, Andy. Some days hope is all I've got.'

Rhiannon needed a break. She headed to the bar. Diet Coke for Andy, soda water for herself. As much as she would have preferred a brandy, they had a lot of work to get through and she needed to keep a clear head.

Andy needed to cut back on his sugar intake, she was tempted to get him a soda water with a lemon slice in it, but that would be pushing things too far.

Once she'd settled back in and the soda bubbles fizzed her brain back to life, Rhiannon picked up from where they left off.

'Someone very deliberately exposed those backpacks and led police to the bodies. The clue they left clearly links them with Lucy's body.

'Then there's Harriet. She was with Lucy and her travelling companion, so did they kill Harriet? Do we assume she's dead even though we have no evidence?'

Andy was doodling on a piece of paper and had almost filled half a page with S.K.Y. before he realised what he was doing.

'I think we rule out Keely as leaving these notes,' he said. 'She's no way connected with the backpacker girls; it's also unlikely the killer would have shared that information with her.'

Rhiannon picked up the thread. 'It comes back to our mystery guy being the killer. Was the intention all along to kill Keely?'

Andy continued. 'Maybe it was just pure luck, the opportunity didn't arise? She obviously wanted to break free from them at the shearing shed with Jeremy. Maybe she was scared and knew what was coming?'

Andy sat back in his chair and folded his arms over the top of his protruding belly.

'We keep coming back to it, don't we? It's looking more and more likely Keely is dead and we're looking for her body along with goodness knows how many more.'

# 22

THE EFFORT OF revisiting the burial site of the English backpackers left Lief feeling like the small piece of lemon that came with the salt and tequila shot, after he'd sucked it dry.

Rational thinking floated out of reach, leaving him only one choice. He had to go to where he and Lucy always disappeared when they needed to recalibrate.

He pushed in the radio knob, tuned into outback radio 2WEB, turned up the volume, and let Slim Dusty take him home.

White fluffy clouds turned grey, then black, and as the sun got lower in its stormy sky he drove into an orange, yellow and pink painting, a tiny speck in a giant universe.

It was dark by the time he got to the small creek, dry and cracked, that would lead him to the homestead.

Howling winds on the edge of the thunderstorms surrounding him tossed his car from side to side. He pelted along straight dirt roads, avoiding the bulldust which Lucy had taught him grabbed at the wheels and took the car off the road and into the pungent trees.

As he got closer the wind dropped, pushing his dust trail straight behind. He wound down the window to breathe in clean air where nobody had lived for over a decade, since Lucy and her 'Dad' moved here, avoiding clumps of saltbush and bogan burr bushes growing over the unused track.

A hundred years earlier, original settlers picked their way through this rugged bush on horseback and in carriages carrying women dressed in their long, white party dresses edged with the finest lace from the merchant ships into Sydney Harbour.

Wearing matching gloves and pretty lace-up boots, they sat expressionless as they bounced uncomfortably over rough tracks cut by poorly paid, often unpaid, Aboriginal labour.

On their laps were perched elaborate broad-brimmed hats tied with velvet ribbons. Leaning against their neatly crossed legs were parasols from Paris, bought in bulk to protect their alabaster complexions from the harsh Australian sun.

Tiny dust particles made their way through the open window and onto Lief's teeth, coating them with an invisible powder that made his mouth dry.

He turned off the radio and had to look twice in the passenger seat as he felt Lucy sitting beside him, along for the ride to their favourite place. The only home they knew together, their secret place, their sanctuary.

The longer he lived without her, the easier it became for him to pretend it was all her. He could push the truth further than his homeland now it was just him in his own head.

He didn't have to admit to anyone, including himself, he had been complicit in seven of eleven murders Lucy admitted to. Or that he had been part of the lure and he didn't stop her even when he could. Or that he had killed her as easily as he'd watched her kill the others.

Keely didn't know about any of the others, only about Lucy. He convinced Keely he loved her, that Lucy was jealous and planning to kill her. He said he wanted to start afresh, he wanted to leave this life behind and start a new one with Keely.

Lief recreated himself from murderer to hero; he cajoled the distressed Keely with the lies he spun, telling her he had no choice, he was defending her honour. His magically bright blue eyes, leg-weakening good looks and sex appeal that went for days brought her out of shock and the more he caressed her, delighted every inch of her and made her feel like the most beautiful girl in the world, the less she thought about what he had done.

She was used to pretending, she'd been pretending since long before she ran away from her real life. Together they pretended their way through the days, weeks and months after Lucy died.

The sunset painting turned black as he rounded the final curve. He hoped to arrive before darkness laid its heavy blanket over the giant homestead with its expansive corrugated iron roof, gable design and double chimneys.

Here in the heat of the day the ladies removed their hats and folded their parasols down so they could take tea on the gauzed-in front verandah which curved around the west side to catch the afternoon breeze.

The men remained on the front lawn, standing between immaculately tended rows of white rose bushes, white on white against the fresh white timber. They started blooming in October and continued right through until January when scorching forty-five-degree winds blowing from the inland Australian desert burnt their deceivingly delicate petals.

The evening bush birds were almost silent by the time Lief pulled up at the back entrance guarded by a rusting single gate twitched to solid timber posts with tie wire. In its more modern heyday, a perfectly graded airstrip was the main entry point for politicians and wealthy graziers and this entry gate was perfectly swung and perfectly oiled.

He arrived at what Lucy referred to as the 'quiet time' between the end of the day and start of the evening, when all the day creatures tucked themselves into bed before the night creatures came alive.

The silence reached its icy fingers out as he alighted from the car and walked towards the creaking timber homestead.

Too many years had passed for it to be restored to its former glory and although it stood through a mini tornado which ripped the roof off the much newer shed built many years later, it was weighed down by the ravages of time and the secrets hiding behind the peeling wallpaper.

People came and went with big dreams of a fresh lick of white paint, stripping back the original timber to reveal its historical beauty, retiling the bathroom and bringing in a claw foot bath discovered in the timber cottage near the tank which used to be a garden shed. Spiders built their homes in the fingers of the steel rakes, underneath stacks of garden stakes and trellis made from wire for the square kitchen garden where hired cooks long ago picked fresh vegetables and herbs watered from the nearby creek.

After the settling generations died out, new owners never stayed long. Just as they were starting to get comfortable, they would notice little things that didn't make sense. Plates and cups stored in high kitchen cupboards would be laid out for breakfast; it would sometimes take weeks for a conversation between husbands and wives revealed it hadn't been either of them.

One couple with a child six months shy of her third birthday left after she asked them who the lady in her bedroom was who sang her to sleep each night. An older couple whose retirement project was for him to restore the house while she restored the garden left after someone pressed a hand over his mouth while he was sleeping.

'Lucy Lou, Lucy Lou,' whispered the wind as it passed through the crispy eucalypts patiently waiting for rain.

Lief felt the hairs at the base of his hairline prickle as he searched his pockets for his torch at the gate, only visible because the bright white paints of years before still held strong to the fancy circles curved together to form a centre dot in each one.

Damn, he must have left it in the car. The power hadn't been connected for years; he had come prepared with extra torches and candles.

He turned away from the homestead and the wind grew blustery. At the same time a light went on in the long sash window facing the gate to reveal the ghostly pale face of the grieving woman who walked the long hallways where a little girl used to hop and skip in her frilled party dress with tiny pink roses embroidered across the smocked bodice while nobody was watching.

Lief wasn't the only one who had paced the rotting timber floorboards in this sagging outback homestead. Although he had secrets keeping him up in the night, this house he came to for peace and forgiveness held even more.

# 23

'BRIGALOW MOBILE TO base, Brigalow mobile to base, are you on channel Alice?'

Alice raced to the two-way. Number one rule. When mobile called base, base must drop everything, no matter how important, to answer.

'Gotcha Duncan.'

'Have you heard from Hank?'

'You mean Hunky Hank?' Alice teased. She blushed, realising she had shared her private nickname for their young strapping backpacker from Canada with every single property, truckie and roadhouse on Channel 16 within a forty-kilometre radius.

Duncan was in no mood for jokes.

'He hasn't turned up for work, the last I saw him was Friday night. He was heading to St George. He's done a runner,' Duncan said brusquely.

'You think so?'

'Yes, I do. Bloody backpackers. I'm sitting out here like a frog on a log, and he's pissed off on me.'

Alice blushed. Duncan was under immense pressure to get a twenty-kilometre section of fence built. They couldn't find a contractor and he needed a helping hand, but none of the local lads were available. Then Alice hit on the idea of getting a backpacker in.

Alice's thoughts turned dark. Something terrible had happened. Her imagination ran wilder than most, after experiencing the trauma of her ex husband Toby going missing. She pictured Hank laying bruised and bleeding in the gutter in some back street in St George.

'Maybe he is hurt or something? Perhaps we should contact the police?'

Duncan didn't answer. He was too busy fuming. He was out on the fenceline ripping outposts he and Hank had spent ages sighting in on a hot, dusty Friday. Duncan couldn't figure out why they couldn't get the dog leg out of it, but they'd preserved and pushed on.

In the light of a new week, after a rare couple of days off, Duncan could see exactly where the mistake had originated. Hank had put the sighter post on the wrong side of the line. A simple, stupid mistake by a simple, stupid backpacker who'd built himself up as being skilled in this, an expert in that and a master of the other.

'He's done a runner. Over and out.'

'Roger Roger.'

Duncan couldn't help but roll his eyes and a tiny smile tugged at his downturned mouth and danced its way to his forehead to smooth out the deep frown line between his eyebrows. Alice watched far too many American movies and as a result, she was the most uncool Base radio operator in southwest Queensland. Oh, but he loved her so.

As she was about to call St George she had a change of heart. She'd call Rhiannon instead. It would be a good excuse to catch up and she knew Rhiannon would take her seriously.

She didn't know Hank well, but thought she knew enough to know he wouldn't take off like this. Also, they owed him money, which he'd earned. If he was going to do a runner, logic said he'd wait until he was paid first.

LATER THAT NIGHT, cuddled side by side, Alice updated Duncan on the conversation with Rhiannon.

'She got onto St George police and they're doing some basic enquiries. If Hunky Hank hit the Cobb & Co he would've stuck out like a sore thumb, and if he picked up one of the locals I'm sure another one of the locals would be more than happy to talk about it.'

'Did she tell you not to worry?'

'Of course she did, you know how she is. Cool, calm and collected. Unflappable. Organised. Efficient. Onto it.'

Duncan laughed. 'Onto it. She's certainly got a handle on this police business. Don't know how she does it to be honest. The things she must see.'

Alice wasn't really listening. She had other big news to share.

'She also told me Jane is selling *Hillview*.'

'What?' Duncan sat up straight in bed, all thoughts of Hunky Hank obliterated. He'd always dreamt of expansion and there was no better way to expand out here, with such vast distances, than to go next door to his family property *Charlotte Downs*.

*Hillview* was ideal goat country too, and he saw the future looking brighter with goats, who could handle the tough years, than with sheep.

Last time he spoke to Mac, he told him he came across a mob of at least one thousand in Bill's Paddock, where Rhiannon and Jane sprinkled some of his ashes and built a seat under a giant Coolabah tree beside the creek that filled in the wet.

They were planning to muster and truck them off for export as soon as they had a free weekend, splitting the proceeds between them and Jane. If Jane was selling, they might need to get in sooner rather than later. Unless…

Duncan lay back down on his pillow, deflated. He couldn't afford to buy, not the way sheep and wool prices were. He couldn't even afford to employ a decent worker and instead had to put up with a useless backpacker who decided to go and get himself 'missing'.

Alice watched his mood swing the full pendulum before she spoke. She turned on her side so she could get closer.

'We could do it you know.'

Duncan rolled to face her, grabbing her by one bare butt cheek so he could shift her whole body closer.

'Not that,' Alice giggled, distracted for a moment.

'*Hillview*. We could put in an offer.'

'No way, where would we get that kind of money?'

'From the bank. Between this property and your property, we've got plenty of security.'

'It's not a good time to borrow I don't reckon. Interest rates are going to chain us to the fence.'

'Yes, I know they're high, but they're never going to go back to what they were in eighty-nine and ninety, we were all in debt to the hilt, but we didn't die. Plus, land prices are pretty low right now.'

'I wouldn't want Jane and Rhiannon to lose out though,' Duncan stressed. 'Bill worked so hard to improve the place and get it into the good condition it is now.'

'I understand, I wouldn't either. But we would offer a fair price.'

Duncan rubbed his hands over his face and through his untamed hair which could do with a cut.

Alice's enthusiasm didn't waver. She was on a mission.

'You were talking to Mac recently about getting onto some goats, that'd be a good way to make a few dollars while we wait for sheep and wool prices to improve, and every day is closer to rain.'

'What about Toby? I'm not sure he'd be all that happy with you using his half to help you set up a new life with your new hubby?'

'That's just it. It's not his half; he didn't contest anything done in his absence. It's all settled. He doesn't want a penny from us.'

Alice beamed proudly. She received the news earlier in the day from her best friend from school Steph, who had moved in with Alice when Rose was born, only a day or two after Alice's first husband Toby disappeared.

Steph helped sort out the legal nightmare that ensues when a husband vanishes from the face of the earth – a task Alice was incapable of at the time. Fortunately, Toby's parents still owned the property, and were happy to put it all into Alice's name when Toby didn't return. Everyone accepted he had died. They even had a funeral.

Life got complicated when Toby turned up a few years later, well and truly alive. He'd learnt from his mistakes and his goal was to rebuild the relationships he'd ruined, one step at a time. His main focus, after realising he'd never win Alice back, was Rose. It was the least he could do to not dispute the arrangements his parents had made for the two girls he'd abandoned so thoughtlessly.

Toby was now pursuing a promising football career and earning more money than he'd ever dreamed of. Returning to southwest Queensland was not part of his long-term plan. He'd just about ruined his life, and the lives of everyone around him, but was learning it was possible to start from below the very bottom rung.

He'd proved to himself that despite the despicable things he'd done, he still deserved to be happy. He didn't have to carry his mistakes like a chastity belt, he could leave them in the past and live a better future. Part of that was making sure Rose, and Alice, lived a better future too.

Duncan's green-eyed monster reared its ugly head.

'Why would he do that?' he snapped.

'Because it's the right thing to do,' Alice patiently explained. 'Nothing more, nothing less. He told Steph he needed to set things right for Rose and me. He doesn't want to come back out here, he's going well with his football, and he has new plans and new dreams that don't involve any of us.'

'Bloody arsehole, I don't believe he's doing this out of the goodness of his heart.'

'You'd better believe it Dunc. It's a done deal, it's in the bag. This place is ours – yours, mine and Rose's. We can move there together, make a fresh start for us all. Now, you'd better get up and get on the phone to Jane and make an offer.'

# 24

THE SUN WAS so bright it bounced shards of light off every surface, drenching everything around her in a colour somewhere between yellow and orange. The ocean glittered and twinkled, and she could hear the waves crashing below.

She closed her eyes and saw memories of family holidays by the sea. Short, frantic visions clamoured for her attention. Bustling and rushing around her head until she felt her brain could explode.

She sensed him rather than heard him, as he put a pot of tea on the white wicker table between their two comfy white cane armchairs. She opened her eyes and smiled.

'Thank you Lucas, what a perfect day.'

He poured into the blue and white china teacups he found at the second-hand shop in town, followed by a dash of milk from the matching blue jug with a tiny chip on its rim.

He had gradually collected all the things they needed, unobtrusively, quietly, carefully. Nothing matched but everything went together.

It was important to have lots of white, then lots of colour.

'Yes Ayala, it sure is. Another perfect day in paradise.'

'ARE YOU SURE you will be okay on your own?' The pot of tea now empty, Lucas broached the subject of their plans thoughtfully.

'Yes Lucas, yes I will be fine.'

'It's just if something happens, if you need something, there's nobody around to help. If you refuse to connect the telephone, what line to the outside world do you have?'

'I don't want a line to the outside world,' Ayala said softly.

Lucas didn't reply. He knew it was painful for her to think any further ahead than the next hour, let alone the next day or next week.

He was booked onto a boat as Paul Evans. A one-way passage to Europe. He wasn't fussed where he landed.

'There is no turning back,' Ayala said quietly, pouring another cup. 'You can never go back. Go and chase those fashion dreams, make your mark on the world. You have the talent, and the world is waiting for you to reveal it.'

Lucas blushed. He dreamed big yet felt small. As a teenager he'd sit up late into the night cutting out catwalk models from glossy magazines then trace the outline and recreate Coco Chanel, Versace, Lagerfield, Valentino – gradually moving towards his favourites. Givenchy, most recognised for designing for Audrey Hepburn and his creations of casual chic, aristocratic elegance and femininity. Armani, who gave women the power suit using elements found in men's suits. And his most treasured obsession, Christian Dior, who revived haute couture in Paris post the Second World War with collections shifting from the nipped waist, full skirted ensembles that redefined post-war fashion in the 1940s to *The New Look* which emphasised an hourglass shape.

He'd become embroiled in Ayala's elaborate plan, sparked by her enthusiasm for his dreams and charged with reckless abandon that came with his youth. He was living in a Jeffrey Archer thriller novel, but after the adrenalin required to get to their hideaway in the west wore off, he struggled to take the next step.

He quite liked it here, hidden away from the world in this peaceful place. Endless days, no interruptions, no hustling, no bustling.

Lucas sank into the wicker armchair which had moulded perfectly around someone else's body for many years before he found it at the same second-hand store as the tea set, and stretched his gaze beyond the horizon.

He had to move forward. It would be easy to blend into European life and thanks to Ayala's generosity, he didn't have to worry about money for a while.

As tragic as the circumstances were that threw them together, it also gave them a chance to start afresh and change their lives in directions they'd never dreamed of.

Their half-empty glasses were now filling, steering their ships towards new futures. Still, neither of them could stop the dark invading thoughts about whether they were doing the right thing. Whether they had taken things too far, or if they would ever be forgiven for their sins.

AYALA HADN'T STEPPED foot off the isolated seaside property since they'd arrived. Nobody even knew she existed. Everyone thought Lucas, the quiet young man who lived in the white cottage on the point, lived alone.

The locals made up their own stories about his life, guessing amongst themselves about his occupation. Was he an artist? A painter maybe? A writer? Yes, he had to be a writer. The next Bryce Courtenay, sitting in the quiet of the Australian bush writing a bestselling novel with nobody to interrupt him.

He'd shopped in every store in town. The nursery-come-hardware store, where he bought all he needed to make his own backyard vegetable garden beds and bags of seeds so he could fill it with herbs, onions, lettuce, broccoli, beetroot, spinach, tomatoes, potatoes, beans and snow peas. He even took a couple of chickens home after seeing the handwritten note covered in dirty thumb prints tacked to the noticeboard, *Isa Brown laying hens for sale, $5 each*.

They loved pecking about in the wild yard which Ayala was gradually restoring to its former glory after the cottage sat empty for the past year or so, since Kenneth bought it for her. At night they slept in the hand-made chicken coop in the back corner which a previous owner with enviable handyman skills had made from used bits of wire and old steel posts.

Then there was the friendly butcher, where Lucas ordered a half beast, after picking up an old chest freezer he saw on the side of the road driving into town for twenty-five dollars. He bought in bulk quantities flour, sugar, long life milk, rice, a small amount of pasta even though Ayala mostly made her own, tinned foods including tomatoes, spaghetti and peaches, plus bread and butter blocks at the grocery store. He quietly explained to the elderly woman behind the counter with wispy grey hairs escaping from her loose bun, that he liked to keep a full pantry so when he got involved in his work, he didn't need to worry about running out of supplies.

At the pub, he ordered four dozen mixed wines, mostly cabernet sauvignons which thrived in the Margaret River region with its constant sea breeze protecting it from extreme winter and summer temperatures. Plus, several bottles of brandy 'to have with a dry' and gin, 'to have with a tonic' he said with a quiet smile as he handed cash notes to the sea dog barman who made no judgements on how many boxes of alcohol walked out his door.

At the newsagency, owned by the elderly couple who prided themselves on knowing every single person by their first name along with knowing their children, their children's children and any family friends who came to visit, he arranged for delivery of all the major newspapers. Also, a selection of magazines, from Home Beautiful to Cleo to Vogue, Better Homes and Gardens, Rolling Stone plus Australian Smocking and Embroidery to keep them guessing.

He was the only one reading the newspapers; he hadn't been able to turn the world off completely. He hid them underneath his bed so Ayala wouldn't catch a glimpse of today's headlines, which she featured in regularly.

They had no television, although Lucas had bought one and suggested they watch for light entertainment, the Sunday night movie.

'I don't want to see the news,' Ayala explained. 'I don't want to see anything about my life splashed over a television screen.'

'I understand. But maybe you could just switch it off when the news comes on?'

'No.'

The subject was closed, and Lucas wasn't about to add to Alaya's trauma that seeped slowly from a frost crack in a garden hose. He bit his tongue many times, wondering if she might be better off knowing what was happening in the lives of her family.

To be honest, there was very little 'new' news on Clive and Ayala Philips once the initial story faded away. Lucas was most interested in Pat Richards, the only reporter who seemed to cover the story with any attention to detail. He worked for ABC and his name popped up regularly in print, as a reliable source of factual details.

Every other report was hell bent on sensationalism, just a rehash of what had been written before.

Lucas was also looking for any mention of one female detective who Pat mentioned in his reports. At first, he wasn't sure why Rhiannon McVee's name grabbed his attention but then it clicked. She'd been involved in another Sydney case he'd been following – the young teenager Annabelle Brown who disappeared in the late eighties and was still missing.

When he was younger, partying most nights in Kings Cross underground bars and night clubs, did he brush shoulders with Annabelle? Had he stood beside her at a bar while they ordered drinks? Had he bumped into her while cracking out his best dance moves under flashing lights at three o'clock in the morning when the party was just getting started? Had he passed her on the street, given her a subtle smile but not a second thought?

Lucas knew Ayala's story was far from over. His firm opinion was Clive Philips was not a man true to his word, and that Ayala was living in denial. Lucas knew he would resurface, reinvent himself. It was highly unlikely he would learn from his mistakes.

It was also highly unlikely Rhiannon McVee would let go of this case until she answered the question on everyone's minds, 'where the fuck is Ayala?'.

# 25

*October 1993*

'I KNOW WHAT you've done,' Ayala whispered as Clive's hands tightened around her neck. A flash of surprise in his eyes was the only sign he heard her.

He was choking her, on their bed, and she found herself wondering how he was planning to dispose of her body so nobody would see signs of their struggle.

'I had to stop you once and for all. I know about the boys in Phuket. I know the whole story. I know about the affairs. I know about your obsession with boys. I know it all.'

His hands tightened. Ten minutes ago, he'd confronted her with the arsenic he found. He was livid, teetering on a dangerous precipice which could easily tip him to commit murder.

He didn't recognise the woman he convinced himself as a young man he loved. The woman who gifted him four beautiful children. The woman duty bound him to. The woman he grew dismissive of, took for granted, wanted to control, needed for show. She belonged to him, she was his trophy wife. Her presence was necessary to do the things he did.

His hate started when she stood up to him. She made him into the violent man he had become, she drove him to this moment. Discovering the arsenic and realising she was trying to poison him, was the final straw. He had to put a stop to her behaviour, her rebellion against the life he wanted to present to the world.

Killing her was the only way. Especially now she knew the secrets he worked so hard to hide. His hands tightened, her eyes widened.

Yes, he could do it, he would do it. He would make it look like she'd disappeared, gone missing. People went missing every day. Hers would just become another unsolved mystery.

Maybe she'd wandered into the bush, depressed, and ended her life. Maybe she'd gone on a trip somewhere and met up with someone unsavoury who'd disposed of her body in a place nobody would ever find.

Nobody would ever suspect him, he would make sure of it. He had plenty of contacts in high places who would make sure his story was solid. If anyone did find out, he would pay them off.

Ayala was gasping, trying to speak, desperate to know the truth before she breathed her last breath.

'What I really need to know, have you touched any of our children?'

Clive loosened his grip and Ayala watched in horror as the surprise in his eyes turned to shame.

Coughing and gasping for breath, she rolled away and onto the floor, desperate to get away but with no strength to do so. Tears appeared and Ayala's inability to breathe had more to do with what she now knew than with the bright red marks around her throat.

'Who?' she asked hoarsely.

Clive hung his head. Of all the sinful, despicable acts, this was the one thing he couldn't live with. He had pushed it so far back, pretending it never happened, some days he convinced himself it hadn't.

He paced the room, his face getting redder with every step, muttering 'no no no'.

Ayala slowly stood up and moved backwards to the bedroom door, banshee wails reverberating off the walls, waiting for him to turn and look at her. Her mind went back like a movie reel, grasping for memories and moments that would give her clues to what Clive had done to their children.

'Who?' Her voice was louder now, and she felt stronger.

She looked around for a weapon in case he came at her again. A ceramic blue blossom umbrella stand by the door caught her eye. She stepped sideways and closed her hand around the smooth, timber handle of her father's golf umbrella which she could never throw away even though she didn't play golf.

'Tell me you sick bastard. Tell me the truth for once in your life. You sick, pathetic excuse for a man. What have you done?'

Clive started to cry, large gulping sobs. He sank onto the bed and collapsed into himself like a high-rise apartment block with weak foundations. How had his life come to this? What was it that drove him to do such hateful, inexcusable things?

'CLIVEY, CLIVEY, WHERE are you?'

Clive huddled in his cupboard with his hands over his ears, trying the block out the voice that reached around his throat to strangle him. Her one and only spoilt, molly-coddled son was all she had to fill her empty days and lonely nights.

'Come on Clive, I know you're here somewhere. I'm not in the mood for hide and seek, so just come out.' The word 'out' had a shrillness to it that started at the top of his head and crept like silent pin pricks to the back of his neck.

Long absences by his father since Clive was a baby twisted this needy, insecure woman into folds and crevices she had no business in visiting. Clive loved her deeply, but he knew their relationship was wrong. Fifteen years old, still hiding behind the thick coats he collected to protect himself from a life he didn't understand.

He had to escape, as soon as he could. He decided, then and there with dust sticking in the back of his throat, he could not, would not, let her control him anymore. It was time for him to take control, be a real man. He stepped out from behind the coats, shoulders back, chest out, and pushed straight past her out the door.

It was the last time he ever cowered from the sound of his mother's voice. She never got over her heartbreak, but he didn't care.

CLIVE RELAYED THE story of his mother to Ayala, hoping it would go some way towards explaining the man he was, the man he had become.

'I always disliked your mother as much as she disliked me, but I never really understood her hatred. She hated me because she had to finally accept she could no longer have you. I always knew she didn't like sharing her only son, but I didn't know it was jealousy of a woman scorned.

'You chose me over her. It must have felt like a husband cheating on his wife, but it was scrunched into this sick revolting ... I can't even find the words for it.'

'You were so good and pure, and I did love you,' Clive tried to explain.

'You did not! I was just an escape. I was your way out of your pathetic love affair with your own mother. My God, I can't even bear to think about it. That woman. That horrible, horrible woman. Who does that to their child?

'Still, it's no excuse for what you've become. It should have made you understand how much damage that can do to a child. Your own child, or children.'

Ayala paused, wondering if she could face her own truth.

'Who, who, for fucks sake?'

It took him a long time to answer.

'Red.'

Ayala lost all empathy and compassion for what Clive's mother had done. Nothing, absolutely nothing, could excuse what he had done to her precious boy Red. Something exploded. She gripped the umbrella more tightly to ground herself in the here and now. Her hatred dug into Clive's skin so deeply he was surprised not to see blood when he looked down at his hands and arms.

The power had shifted. Clive was now a simpering, weak shell huddled on the floor at the end of the bed. Ayala, mother bear, transformed into an Amazonian woman with an iron rod spine.

She moved her face close, no longer scared of the man who less than an hour ago she thought was going to kill her.

'I should have added more arsenic, you are a pathetic excuse for a human being and don't deserve to breathe another breath...'

Ayala turned on her heel, unable to continue the conversation. She longed for a normal life with normal problems. Not this unbelievable, twisted tale. It wasn't real, it couldn't be.

Next thing she remembered she was in the kitchen. She laid her hot cheek onto the cool, smooth bench top and ran her hands over it. She held onto the solid surface to stop herself from floating out the window, across the lawn, over the red dirt roads and into Goat Paddock a hundred kilometres away.

She opened her eyes and they settled on the butcher's knife block in the far corner. Knives of every shape and size, sharp and shiny. She dropped the umbrella with a clatter on the kitchen tiles.

Could she do it? Flashes of Red's childhood blurred her vision then came back into focus.

Yes, she could. Clive did not deserve to live after all he had done. He had driven her to this, she had no choice.

# 26

THE DAY LUCAS left the ocean was moody. The sky as well.

'Looks like you might be in for some rough seas,' Ayala said from his bedroom door as he packed the last of his things into a black leather backpack. He also had a black suitcase, and his clothes were tones of black, denim, grey and beige. He was leaving all his flashy things with Ayala. Maybe one day he would be reunited with his selection of brightly coloured shirts and shiny glitzy shoes.

'That'd be right,' he said with dry wit teetering on the precipice of sarcasm. 'Looking forward to spending the next month with my head hanging over the side of the ship, emptying my guts into the clear blue waters beneath. Oooh goody, it's what I've dreamt of my whole life.'

Ayala laughed. 'I bet you have. Not to worry, makes good fish food you know. They'll be reeling in the biggest fish you've ever seen and serving them up to you for dinner each night. Then you can eat your own vomit-filled fish then start the cycle all over again the next day.'

Lucas zipped up his backpack and swung it over his thin shoulders.

'Right, that's about it for me,' he grinned, unable to contain his excitement.

Ayala had so much she wanted to say to this young man who had rescued her. Not only that, but he'd also been there through the worst of times. Like a cracked teacup and saucer that had fallen to the floor, he gently swept her into a dustpan and instead of putting her broken pieces into the bin, he patiently sat with invisible glue and put her shattered heart and soul back together. He was so careful while doing so, only the faintest of crack lines were now visible.

'Thankyou Lucas. I couldn't have survived without you.'

He came in close, putting his gentle hands on her shoulders.

'Yes, you could have. All the things you've been through, you can survive anything.'

'I'm not so sure,' she faltered. 'With you going, I'm not sure how I'm going to survive completely on my own. I haven't been completely on my own, without someone closeby, Clive, the children, for as long as I can remember.'

'Try and remember the Ayala you were before things went south with Clive. Channel that version of yourself into this version of yourself. That's your way back.'

'How can I keep going without my children? I am not complete without them, I can't go on without them.' Ayala choked on the words on the spinning wheel in her mind.

Lucas didn't have the answer. He kissed her on the cheek and enveloped her into a hug.

'You're like hugging an ironing board,' she laughed.

'And you're like hugging a very small bird! Not as small as the bird you were when we first arrived, but you need to make sure you keep tending to the vegetables and chooks, and don't forget to eat the fresh wholesome goodness they will provide.'

'Yes, Mum.'

'I have also arranged a grocery order every few months to leave on the verandah if I'm not home, the delivery dates are pinned to the fridge so you know when to make yourself scarce. I also told the post office if any mail comes for me to deliver it out here.'

'You've covered all bases by the sound of it.'

'Well, I had to make sure your cover wasn't blown, so I told them I had a major project which meant a lot of travel and although they might not see me in town, I will still be here for periods of time.'

Lucas looked at his watch.

'Oh, time to go! My ride is probably waiting out the front.' On cue, a horn honk cut through the seaside bush sounds.

'Travel safe young man.'

'Stay safe young woman.'

And just like that he was gone. Ayala stood on the verandah that opened to the ocean in its full, glittering glory, waiting for a glint of the ship Lucas was departing on. Hours later, the sun caught the flash off the railing or a window and she raised her hand and waved.

She wondered if she should have gone on the ship with him, disappeared into Europe somewhere, never to be seen or heard of again.

No, she couldn't. The pull of her children was too strong. Even if they didn't know where she was, or that she was still alive, she could never leave.

AFTER LUCAS LEFT Ayala settled into a comfortable routine. She yearned and longed for her children, but she couldn't face the terrible mess her life had become. She wondered if Bianca had found the diary. Or if Clive had done what he promised and sold the holiday apartment in Phuket and never returned again.

'Probably not,' a little voice niggled at her, 'it's highly unlikely he has done what he promised now that you're out of the way.'

Ayala had to believe Clive was upholding his part of the bargain they made on that terrible, terrible day where he came close to squeezing every living breath from her. Where she came close to sticking the knife from the kitchen block into his heart to break it as much as he'd broken hers.

After he confessed to what he'd done to her beautiful, lovely, sensitive soul Red she wanted to wound him, kill him, punish him. When it came to those final moments when she pushed all her anger into her right arm down to her hand which had a steel grip on the knife, she couldn't do it. Even though she wanted to, there was no way she could.

He was so much larger than her. Stronger.

Once he recovered from his confession the evil returned to his eyes. They spoke volumes. 'I will win if you go hand to hand with me in a fight to the death.'

He had the evil in him she didn't. He could follow it through, he could kill her then live with himself after the act. She couldn't.

His sins were worse, but her conscience ran deeper. That night was a sick, twisted horror movie on continual replay, when she made a deal with the devil.

He wouldn't tell their children she tried to poison him, but he put a high price on his silence. She must disappear from his life, and the lives of their children, and he would stop his sick, perverted, shameful and disgusting wrongful acts.

The plan made perfect sense back then but made no sense now.

There had been no time to retrieve her diary, hidden safely under the floorboards under the colourful rug in Bianca's bedroom. Even if Bianca decided to take the rug outside to bash the dust out with a broom, she'd never discover the tiny fault in the timber floor that hinted to a secret place, or would she?

Regret pinned her to her bed at the thought of Bianca reading her deepest, sickest and most desperate thoughts. What would she think of her? Would she feel sympathy or rage? Bianca was Daddy's girl, would she take his side? Or would she understand the torment and torture which pushed Ayala to the brink?

What did it matter? She'd never see her children again, so regardless of whether someone found the diary or not, it was too late. She was already dead to them.

# 27

LARRY WAITED ANXIOUSLY outside the bedroom door while Ayala and her Mum Barbara fussed and primped. Kenneth came around the corner, startling Larry out of his trance.

'How's the bride to be going?' Kenneth asked, putting his hand out for a firm friendly shake which turned into a man hug between these long-time friends who used to tussle on the rugby union field at Kings.

'Better than the father-in-law to be, that's for sure,' Larry said wryly.

'Come on, she's a smart girl, she knows what she's doing.'

Larry raised his eyebrows. 'I don't know Ken. She's naive, gullible. Easy to manipulate. We've shielded her too much, maybe spoilt her a bit too. Being our only child, it's hard not to.'

'She's definitely not spoilt. She's a clever, sweet, kind, clever young woman who will go far.'

Larry smiled. 'You're right, I've just got the jitters.'

'Clive is a good man,' Kenneth said. 'He's got all the qualities you want in a man. Ambition, brains and bit of spunk.'

'Spunk?'

'Yes, you know, he has an air of confidence that will take him places. He is good looking, and that will hold him in good stead in certain situations...' Kenneth's voice trailed off when he noticed the expression on Larry's face.

'What is it, my friend? This looks like more than just jitters from the father of the bride.'

'I don't know. I really don't know. But I have a strange feeling, Ken.'

Larry stepped in closer, lowering his voice to a hoarse whisper. 'I worry he's only marrying her for the money, for status. And I also worry he seems controlling. There's something in his eyes when he looks at her. She adores him so much and it's written all over her face, but his eyes are colder. It's like they don't connect.

'I really wanted her to insist he sign a pre-nup, but she refused. Said I was being controlling. Overprotective. That I had to let her go. I haven't slept a wink in the lead-up to this day.'

Kenneth put his arm around Larry's shoulder.

'You seem genuinely concerned; do you need my help? You know, to set things up for her so she's not left completely dependent on her new husband?'

'Yes, yes, that's exactly what I need.' Larry's face relaxed into a smile. 'You've been a good friend for a long time, I knew you'd understand. We'll get working on it once the fuss dies down.'

'Sounds like a plan. Now, old man, time for you to be the best father of the bride there is, and walk your little girl up the aisle!'

Larry managed to wipe all concern from his face when he heard Ayala and Barbara's voices as they got closer to the door.

He gasped when it opened, as the past twenty years flashed before his eyes in fast-forward, starting from when she was a tiny tot of a thing twirling around the lounge room in a ballerina's outfit.

'Hello Dad,' she beamed, kissing him on the cheek. 'Hello Kenneth, lovely to see you.' She kissed Kenneth as well.

'You look so...' Dad's eyes twinkled with tears, and he looked over the top of Ayala's head into Barbara's shining eyes.

'Yes, she does. She is the most beautiful girl in the world.'

Kenneth hit rewind, play. Rewind, play. The four of them in a luxury art deco hotel hallway with white walls offsetting rich timber features and gold patterned carpet. On a precipice of something they could never have predicted, heading down a path none could ever imagine, not in their wildest dreams.

# 28

AS HE GOT closer to Manilla, Mac felt a sense of home. Although there was no red dirt, the mix of plains and mountain country looked prosperous.

Rainfall was more reliable than in the southwest and if he wanted to dabble in sheep on the side, he could. Or maybe he could go into grain to save buying it off-site and have one hundred percent control over what went into his chickens.

He could look into something he'd been reading about in a US magazine Dad subscribed to about farming with less chemicals and more nature-based methods like mixed species crops and switching the focus from what was happening above the ground to what was going on below, in the soil.

Mac's head buzzed. He wanted this. He really did.

He hadn't told Rhiannon he had organised an inspection. It had been impossible to pin her down. When he called to tell her, he couldn't reach her. Not wanting to leave a message about his planned trip, he made a snap decision one night, called the property agent, and was on the road before dawn the next morning.

Rhiannon's initial enthusiasm in making plans for their future had waned, she used work pressure and Jane needing her full attention to help get ready to hand over *Hillview* to new owners Alice and Duncan as excuses. She was petrified of the changes ahead. Every time she thought about packing up her life and moving to a new place with Mac, it was like wearing an itchy woollen skivvy on a warm winter's day.

She would be furious to know he was pursuing the idea without her, but he was sick of waiting. He was restless for this new challenge, and the more he pored over the brochures, the more he felt he needed a change. If she ended up deciding it wasn't what she wanted to do, he'd find his own way.

It was a six-hour drive from Bourke to Manilla, and a six-hour drive from Manilla to Kings Cross. Mac figured being halfway between the two places Rhiannon spent the majority of her time was a good way to hedge his bets.

With his new Brooks and Dunn cassette turned up loud and his foot to the floor, he couldn't have felt happier.

The family who were selling had been running the chicken farm for over ten years. In that time they expanded from two thousand to ten thousand birds and had secured contracts with major supermarkets. Along with their farm gate sales, supplying cafes and restaurants in Manilla, Tamworth, Gunnedah and everywhere in between, it wasn't a life for the faint-hearted.

While family and work life were in balance, they pursued opportunities to expand by purchasing land surrounding the original block, dreaming one day of one hundred thousand birds and supplying restaurants from Sydney to Melbourne to Brisbane to Adelaide. They even drew up plans for developing a broiler farm.

A bitter marriage split set their dreams on fire, and although they'd hoped their two sons would take on the business and continue the dreams they made when they believed they'd live happily ever after – after the boys finished high school, they never wanted to see a chook's bum again.

He recognised the impressive entrance from the brochures. He got out for a stretch and a leak behind the stand of eucalypts a few metres off to the side, admiring the handiwork that had gone into the timber rails which looked like they'd been cut off the place.

The sales pitch had promoted fences being in good order, and he was pleased to see they were. Someone who knew what they were doing had them in perfect alignment, and the railway line end assemblies would withstand any challenges nature threw their way.

It had been a wet month, and the paddocks were green, fresh and inviting.

A timber deck wrapped itself around the old homestead which looked like it had been recently restored. The suited-up real estate agent with the limp handshake met him at the homestead gate, leading him through a rambling lush garden with plants Ronnie dreamt of but would never grow on harsh bore water.

'A swimming pool for the kids,' he rattled off, 'and plenty of room for the family to grow with four bedrooms, two bathrooms...'

Mac cut him off, feeling guilty about doing the house tour without Rhiannon. She'd love it, who wouldn't when not a single cent had been spared, but was it a bit much?

'Thanks mate, it's great, but my main interest is in the sheds so if you don't mind, maybe we could head down there.'

Walking into the large chicken shed where the birds were caged filled Mac with a sense of deep longing.

He knew this was the most efficient way to egg farm, and it was easier to control disease, they weren't at risk from predators, and this would give him the highest rate of return. But his dreams lay in the paddocks. His vision was to take them out of the sheds under a controlled pasture system and move them around so they didn't graze down to bare earth. They would lay and seek shelter in a mobile hen house prototype he'd been tinkering with at home for his own chooks.

Several hours later Mac knew he was ready to sign on the dotted line.

'Thanks for your time,' he said to the agent. 'I'm really interested, I've just got a few things to sort out though.'

'Well, you'd better be quick, this won't be on the market long, I've got several very interested buyers lined up.'

Mac smiled, not fazed by the standard sales pressure spiel. Okay, maybe a little bit fazed. He was living in a dreamland, he had no idea how to fund the purchase on his own and truthfully and honestly, he didn't want to do it without Rhiannon.

He drove out the gates with his tail between his legs, not even looking in the rear vision mirror. What was he thinking? This dream was over before it had even begun.

# 29

'HEY JANE, ARE you sure you want to put this in?' Mac lifted his hat to wipe the sweat with the back of his forearm. He was standing at a vintage tractor Bill always intended to restore but never got around to.

Jane, carrying a red clipboard, wrote the tractor details on her items list to pass onto the auctioneer who was running next month's clearing sale.

'I'm sure. I'm certainly not going to restore that old thing and I doubt you'll have time, so it's better off going to a good home.'

'Okay, as long as you're sure.'

Jane didn't hesitate. She couldn't. If she did, she'd never go through with it.

Next thing was the Ford Pilot car from the 1950s, a V8 Bill also planned to restore. He had all the restoration gear, and had made a good start.

'You could get up to five grand for this I reckon,' Mac said, admiring the car.

'Or you could have it,' she said. 'Finish off what he started.'

'No way, that's too much, you'll get a really good price for this, you should put it in.'

'Now Mac, Bill would want you to have it. I can just see you putting around the countryside in this one day. It's a classic. It should stay in the family.'

Mac's dry laugh gave his true feelings away.

'I'm not doing so well on that score, can't seem to get her to settle down so I'm not exactly family.'

Jane knew Mac had gone to look at the chicken farm at Manilla. Ronnie confided in her last week when they ran into each other in the Cunnamulla Post Office. They continued the conversation in The Club a few hours later

132

where they met for toasted ham, cheese and pineapple sandwiches and a sneaky Pimms and lemonade.

'You're always family to us Mac and you should know that, regardless of what happens with you and Rhiannon. You're both still young and have plenty of time to settle down. You know as well as I do, she'll only commit to something when she's good and ready.'

The homestead at Manilla flashed into Mac's mind, before he quickly pushed it away.

'Don't I know it? Let me think about the car then, it feels like too much but I'll consider it.'

Jane put a question mark next to the car. She'd have to get Rhiannon to convince him. She knew he'd already spent hours with Bill working on it and that it meant more to Mac than he was letting on.

Rhiannon had promised to help that week but used her work as an excuse for not being able to get away. The simple truth was she couldn't bring herself to go anywhere near *Hillview* to prepare for the clearing sale. She supported Jane's decision, and was beyond happy Alice, Duncan and Rose and any children they had in the future would live here, meaning she could visit whenever she wanted. But every time she faced the reality of leaving, she became a blubbering mess.

Mac was staying the week to help Jane sort through things. Although Bill kept a pretty tidy ship, Jane had hardly touched his things since he died so the red back spiders, brown snakes and mice had well and truly moved in. Some of it would end up in the big hole in Plains Paddock they used as their rubbish tip, but there were many treasures that would fetch a good price.

The phone rang while Jane and Mac were having dinner, steak, potato bake and Surprise dried minted peas, forever known as *Surprise Peas*. Potato bake was of Mac's favourites – Jane's was renowned as the best in the district. She had baked her home-made apple pie for sweets, also a favourite at every camp draft and polocross weekend. Many tried and failed to get their pastry as flaky as hers.

'I'm pretty sure that will be Rhiannon, how about you get it?' Jane said.

'Hello sexy,' Mac took a punt it was her.

'Hello sexier, how's it going?'

'Pretty good, we're just having dinner.'

'Of course, sorry, didn't check the time. Just got home from work and needed to hear your voice.'

'How about you get your cute butt up here and you can hear it all day, every day.'

The hot flush came quickly at the mention of joining him, literally. It had been too long between visits. The flush that followed at the thought of packing her Dad's things up for someone else to buy and take away was of a different kind.

'I can't. I'm on this really hot case, I have to be here, I just can't.'

'I know it's not your work,' Mac said quietly, hoping Jane couldn't hear. 'I know it's more than that.'

Rhiannon crumbled. He'd found the soft place he always found.

'Does Mum know?'

'She hasn't said. I think she'd understand, if you wanted to talk to her.'

'No way, I can't. I'm supposed to be the strong one, I'm a tough copper remember?'

'Not as tough as you think you are,' Mac joked. 'Seriously though, just tell her how hard it is for you. Maybe it will feel better once you get it off your chest.' He paused, his mind wandering. 'Speaking of chest.'

'Very funny, you and your one-track mind!'

'I can't help it, I need to see you. I need to hold you. I need you, need you.'

That was the end of the serious talk, the rest of the conversation was well below the waist. As she fell asleep with thoughts of Mac on her mind Rhiannon made a decision.

She had to say goodbye to Dad properly, it's what he would want. He would want her and Jane to support each other and go through this together. She would regret it for the rest of her life if she didn't go.

# 30

SHE LOOKED AT the large rust coloured clock on the wall of the back verandah at the sound of vehicle. It sounded close, but she wasn't sure. Sound was an illusion on these perfectly still mornings when she could taste rain on the horizon. Vehicles which were miles away sounded like they were driving up her driveway.

With her cup of tea frozen halfway to her next sip, she listened intently. Ah, the mailman. She took a sip and relaxed. She couldn't see her mailbox from her favourite morning chair on the verandah. It was a five-minute walk from her back step, and bushy low trees shielded her house from the road, and the road from the house.

He never stopped at her gate anyway. Who would write to her? Nobody knew she was here, absolutely nobody.

She waited for the familiar gear change as he slowed down respectfully, something country people did when passing a house so they didn't cover it in dust, then gear up again to continue along the isolated laneway.

Instead, she heard the clunk of several downwards gearshifts as the vehicle slowed to a halt.

Her breath caught in her throat, and she felt like she might faint on the spot from the thought of someone stopping here. When they couldn't open the gate because of the large padlock Lucas attached, what if they decided to climb over and take the long walk to the house?

The humid stillness carried the sound straight into her ears. *Crunch, crunch, crunch,* on the gravel drive. *Swoosh, swish, crackle,* as they caught themselves on the eucalyptus branch hanging over the mailbox.

Ordinary bush sounds became the sounds of evil people sent by Clive to finish the job he wished he had the courage to go through with on the day she disappeared. Little did she know how truly capable he was of murder, and she'd be even more terrified if she knew what he did to her beautiful dog Maggie as soon as she left.

A loud bang shook her from her wild imagination.

It was the sound of her mailbox lid slamming shut. Mail?

*Crunch, crunch, crunch,* back to the vehicle. Her heart galloped as she listened for revs as it continued its run. After it drove away she counted to one hundred, slowly, tiptoed down the front steps onto the path, through the gate and along the driveway with its scribbly trees and happy, chirpy birds.

She almost laughed out loud. Why was she tiptoeing? Crazy woman.

With a deep breath she realigned her body and walked like a normal, everyday person on their way to the mailbox to see what the day would deliver.

She tasted the faintest layer of dust on her tongue as she breathed in and out through her mouth, and the air around her was hazy. They really needed rain. She hoped it would come today. This weather reminded her of home, the endless wait for moisture to arrive and drench the roasted earth.

She paused in the last stand of trees before stepping into the open for the final few steps, her ears alert to any strange sounds, such as the mail van coming back the way it had come.

With shaking hands she pulled up the heavy white lid covered in rust. Spiders scurried into dark corners as she reached in for a lonely, thin envelope.

She read the address on the front. No name, just her road, nearest town, state and postcode. It was a miracle it found her. The postmark looked foreign. Italy?

Her gasp was loud in the eerie silence that descended at that moment.

Lucas.

Why was he risking everything to send mail? Her mind reeled and her fingers stuck together like glue as she prised it open. A single sheet of newspaper fluttered onto the ground, settling into the dry dust at her feet. Clive's face peered up at her and she resisted the urge to yell out loud.

Slowly, ever so slowly, she crouched down and picked it up.

The headline screamed at her. THE LIFE OF A MURDER SUSPECT. Then the opening paragraph: *Prominent Australian businessman Clive Philips lives a life of luxury despite being a key suspect in the disappearance of his wife Ayala.* She scanned through the remaining words which ran into each other and became back to front, mixed up sentences.

The report was brief. But it did reveal he'd wined and dined with the businessmen she knew he travelled to Phuket with, and although he was on bail, the police case appeared shaky and ready to topple. Which would leave him a free man. Tears caught in the back of her throat.

She understood why Lucas took the risk. He had to let her know Clive hadn't held up his end of the bargain.

He had to warn her Clive had punched a giant hole in their plan.

She needed a new one.

# 31

'MAC!' RHIANNON TRIED to keep the panic from her voice as the king brown snake as thick as her arm slowly uncoiled itself from behind the old washer Bill hadn't gotten around to throwing out.

Moments earlier her and Jane were laughing at Jane's memories of turning the large handle around and around to wring the water out of the bed sheets, which always seemed to tangle despite her best efforts to become friends with this 'modern' machine.

'Modern my arse,' Rhiannon laughed. 'Oh my, how did you even manage? Far out, I couldn't even imagine having to face up to this contraption every time I wanted clean clothes. I think I'd just swish them around in a bucket and hang them dripping wet on the line and leave it to the spring wind to do the rest.'

'Exactly! I hated that machine so much, and I'll never forget the day your Dad turned up from town with a brand-new automatic machine in a box. It was right after he'd banked the wool cheque, which had been a good one that year.

'He marched straight into the electrical goods store come hardware store and bought me a washing machine and himself a new workshop gadget, not sure exactly what. I suspect he hadn't actually gone in there with the intention of buying me anything but I didn't comment on that.'

Rhiannon roared with laughter.

'Good old Dad, even if it wasn't his original intention, he always seemed to come home with the latest gadgets for you as soon as they came out – old Benny from the hardware store always knew he could get a sale, you were probably the first one in the district to get every latest fan-dangled thing to come on the market.'

'I think so! Bill was a soft touch and Benny knew it.'

'Do you think anyone will want this old thing now?' Rhiannon grabbed one corner while Jane grabbed the other, and they pulled it out from the wall in awkward jerking movements.

'Shit it's heavy, I might need to get Mac to help us.'

'No way! We can do it Mum, we'll just edge it out slowly and get it onto the trolley, then I'll be able to wheel it out. Which pile? Sale pile or tip pile?'

Jane rolled her eyes. Little Miss Independent.

'Definitely tip pile. Surely nobody wants to relive this moment from the past.'

'Oh, you never know. Maybe it could go into the historical museum or something.'

They had it well away from the wall now.

'Hold on, I need a blow.' Jane retrieved a handkerchief to wipe the sweat from her forehead. Rhiannon looked behind the machine to see if she could get better leverage.

Oh fuck,' she said quietly. 'Don't move Mum.'

Rhiannon slowly backed away, not taking her gaze off the two beady eyes assessing the threat on two legs that had disturbed it from its comfortable, safe place. The snake, threatened, had nowhere to go and Rhiannon was within perfect striking distance.

Jane froze. She'd killed a few brown snakes in her day, mostly with the shotgun by the back door, occasionally with a shovel when she didn't have time to get the gun. She didn't like to kill them and mostly left them alone, but the house, garden and sheds were out of bounds. As were the chook and dog yards; Bill had lost several good dogs to snake bite.

The light changed, and Rhiannon knew Mac was at the door. He looked around for a weapon, grabbing a steel rake. It wasn't ideal, he'd have to be exact, but there was no time for anything else.

Rhiannon took another backward step; the snake took another slide towards her. Step, slide. Mac slowly approached from behind until he was between her and the snake, bringing the rake down over his shoulder, aiming the round end of the handle at the top of the snake's head.

As he struck the snake, the steel rake end caught him behind his head, knocking him out cold.

The blow stunned the snake but only momentarily. Rhiannon grabbed the rake and stepped over Mac, rake end down, and sliced the head off, swiftly dragging Mac backwards out of the way with her other hand.

Jane raced over to Mac, laying his head in her lap and smacking his cheeks. Blood from the rake wound leaked onto her jeans and she used her handkerchief to stem the flow.

'Mac, Mac, Mac.'

Rhiannon passed a pannikin of water and Jane tipped the full cup over his face. He opened his eyes and mumbled incoherently.

By now Jane had ascertained his head wound was only minor. Rhiannon kicked the dead snake well away and knelt down next to Mac, joining in on the cheek smacking. She looked from him, to Jane, back to him, over to the wriggling snake in its final death throes. If she had to guess, she'd say it was two metres long.

'Well, if that wasn't the funniest fucking thing I've ever seen, I don't know what is,' she said, deadpan.

They rolled around the dusty shed floor in hysterics for the next ten minutes. 'I'm dying' Rhiannon kept saying. 'I thought I was dead,' Mac replied. 'I thought you were both going to be dead,' Jane squealed, sending them into a fresh bout of laughter.

Years later, Mac would retell the story to his children and grandchildren, the snake getting longer and more menacing with every telling.

TWO DAYS LATER, each with a cold XXXX, they sat on Bill's work bench finally cleared of all its clutter, admiring the organised workshop with items neatly arranged for sale,

'That's the last of it then,' Jane said quietly. It wasn't necessarily planned that way, but it was fitting for them to finish sale preparations in Bill's workshop, where Jane found him on the floor, way too late to save him from the heart attack he had suffered hours earlier.

Rhiannon, in the middle of the two people she loved the most, put her arms around their shoulders and hugged them closer.

'Dad's never seen his workshop in such good order, you could eat off the floor it's that clean.'

Her timing and tone were spot on, and they erupted into laughter.

Since Rhiannon arrived, she stepped quickly into the role of keeping the mood fun and light. It made the days fly by and helped them all push through the physical and emotional exhaustion of the mammoth task of sorting through a lifetime of memories.

None of them wanted to say this final goodbye to Bill, and all of them worried about how they'd remember him when they were no longer following his footsteps around *Hillview*.

Jane finished her beer and jumped down. 'I'm going to wash up and get dinner organised, I hope you don't mind but it's plain old lamb fritters tonight.'

'I love fritters,' Rhiannon and Mac said in unison. 'Jinx on the *I love fritters*! Jinx on the jinx.'

Rhiannon rested her head on Mac's shoulder, allowing a few tears to fall once Jane was gone.

'I'm glad I'm here, even though it hurts all over.'

'I'm glad you're here too, it's made it easier for your Mum too.'

'I don't know what we're going to do once this is all finished. To not be able to come home to this home, belt around our paddocks…'

'I'm sure Dunc will let you belt around the paddocks as much as you like. He won't mind putting you to work here one bit!'

'True,' Rhiannon said wryly. 'So true.'

'Your Mum will find a new home, and she'll make it feel like home. This place is too much for her, and Duncan and Alice will continue the great legacy your Mum and Dad have left.

'They've looked after everything so well, but it's starting to fray around the edges without your Dad here. It's a good time to hand over to the next generation of *Hillviewers*.'

'You're right, you're always right.'

'True that.'

It was enough to break Rhiannon's sombre mood. She jumped down from the bench, her graceful agility impressing Mac as much as it always had.

'Last one to the house gets last shower!'

She took off before he'd even had time to move, and try as he might, it was impossible to catch her.

MAC STILL HADN'T gotten around to telling Rhiannon he'd been to Manilla and wasn't sure if this was the right time for it, with so much already in her head. He hated lying to her though.

Standing side by side sharing the bathroom sink brushing their teeth, playing the game they always did of trying to brush for the longest until toothpaste bubbles started escaping and dribbling down their chins, he knew he wanted to be doing the same thing in twenty, thirty, forty, fifty years and more.

'I've been waiting for the right moment, and I reckon there is no right moment to tell you this,' he said while she was gargling.

All she heard was 'right, reckon, tell you.'

'Huh?'

Sucking in his breath he pulled her around to face him.

'I went to Manilla to look at that farm.'

Her big blue-green eyes got bigger. She didn't move though, so he kept going.

'I wanted to tell you and I wanted you to be with me, but you have been so busy at work and then all this with selling *Hillview*, there never seemed to be a good time to discuss it, so I tried to stop thinking about it and forget it, but I couldn't. I just jumped in the ute one day and went there and back.'

'Right.'

'Anyway, it's an impossible dream, so that's that. I went, I saw, I left.'

Rhiannon leaned forward and kissed him gently on the lips.

'I love you as high as the moon. I do want to talk about it, but I'm not sure I can right now.'

She calmly walked to the kitchen to get them a glass of water for their bedside tables and stood at the sink for a long time. She was furious on the inside, but to be fair, she had been avoiding making any real commitment.

Was she ready to take this leap with Mac?

Did she really want to commit to going with him, going into business with him?

Should they do it as individuals or as a couple?

Did this mean they'd have to settle down and get married straight away?

Was his dream her dream also?

She stood on tippy toes and stretched her arms above her head as high as they would go, then let it all go and touched her toes, hanging like a rag doll. She didn't know, she didn't know.

SHE HELD MAC all night, close, and when she woke the next day, she knew.

'Morning cowboy.'

'Morning cowgirl.'

She leant over him to kiss him fully on the lips.

'When are you taking me to check out this joint of yours?'

Mac, who had hardly slept a wink all night, jumped out of bed and leapt back onto it, wrestling Rhiannon like they were four year olds on the back lawn.

'This joint of ours you mean!'

Eventually, though not without a tough battle, Mac had Rhiannon pinned on her back. He straddled her and leant down to kiss her lips, her neck, her breasts, her stomach. Going lower and lower, he used no words. He showed her, yet again, just how much he adored and loved her, every single part of her.

**FRITTERS for 3**

2 or 3 eggs

5 or 6 heaped tablespoons SR flour

Garlic salt, pepper, salt

Enough milk to make a batter

Chopped cold meat, onion, tomato, any leftovers

*Fry in butter until golden, serve hot or cold with tomato sauce*

# 32

Ayala got to work quickly, reconnecting herself with the world.

She did it all by phone, using a false name and false credit card organised through Kenneth in case of an absolute emergency, to hook up the internet. Kenneth buried her new identity so thoroughly that nobody, not even the most diligent detective, would ever trace it back to her or this location.

She subscribed to daily newspapers and plugged in the television Lucas bought which she hadn't allowed him to turn on.

The more she discovered about Clive, the angrier she became. She stalked Pat Richards from the ABC, studying his facial expressions, his earnest reporting style, his clear honest eyes. She obsessed so deeply it felt like Pat was looking straight at her, pleading with her to help him solve this mystery and bring Clive Philips to his knees.

'You pathetic excuse of a man!' She yelled at her silent walls. They didn't judge and copped every tirade she hurled at them.

'I fucking hate you, I hate you, I hate you, I hate you!!'
Silence.
'I should have killed you when I had the chance!'
Silence.
'I am a stupid, stupid woman for letting you manipulate me, again!'
More silence.

Once the anger simmered down, she fell into a depression so low she didn't think she could get up.

Some days the only movement she made was from her bed to the bathroom, then back to her bed again. She wasted away without the nourishment her body needed and spiralled deeper and deeper into despair.

Suicidal thoughts bounced off the ceiling before becoming a weighted blanket she couldn't move from under. 'Maybe I am better off dead,' she whispered to the walls, her voice hoarse from all her yelling. 'Maybe I should close my eyes and go to sleep, and never wake up.'

As she lay in her own filth, she analysed every minute of her life from the day she met Clive to the day she walked out the door. Her heart broke for her children. For the mess she had made of their lives, for the trauma they were going through. And for what? For Clive to use his power and money to walk the streets a free man?

Who knew what he was doing in between his designated police station check-ins. Who knew who he was entertaining in one of his many luxury apartments, behind closed doors.

What could she do? Who could she turn to?

Day turned to night, night turned to day. She was oblivious of the time, she didn't even have the strength to pull back the curtains.

She dreamed. She was flying across the Nullarbor Plain to her Bourke home, where Bianca and her boys were waiting for her. It was so real, she really did think she was flying.

She wasn't in a plane. Hundreds of tiny birds held a piece of her clothing, enough to easily lift her high into the air and glide peacefully over the wide brown landscapes of Central Australia. The whole trip they chattered and chittered, telling her she was good, she was kind, she was important.

She opened her eyes slowly and gradually adjusted to her surroundings, a tiny chink of light starting to show at the edge of the curtain. The birds were deafening.

During her darkest days she hadn't even noticed the morning birds, the happy, chattery, morning birds. She had always loved sneaking out of bed early, leaving Clive to snore like a road train, to greet the morning birds who rose with the sun.

Curious as to what all the fuss was about, in a half dream-like state, she kicked off her blankets and placed her feet on the cool, timber floor. She wriggled her toes, the floor felt fresh and refreshing, so she wriggled them some more.

Her legs shook as she walked to the window, and the sound of her growling stomach cut through the birdsong. It was like every single bird had come to her little white cottage by the sea and lined up outside her window to wake her.

They gave her an urge to be flamboyant and she threw back the curtain like a diva. The window faced away from the ocean, so she was blinded for a moment by the glare of the east-rising sun peeking through the trees.

The birds continued to chatter, and she fiddled with the stiff sash lock which she needed to twist to open the window to the world. She smelt her own body odour as she wiggled and fiddled, and the thought of how desperately she needed to shower scampered across the sill.

The birds got louder, the sun got brighter, and she sweated with exertion.

'Come on, you bloody thing!'

Eventually she won the battle with the lock and hooked her fingers underneath to lift the window. She didn't realise her own strength and the window opened with a bang, silencing the birds for a few seconds, before they settled and rearranged themselves.

Taking in big, gulping breaths of fresh morning air Ayala lifted. With birds for wings, there was no way she was going to let Clive get the better of her. He was in for the fight of his life. She would prove that the man does *not* always win.

# 33

'HI KENNETH.'

With a shaking hand he held Ayala's untraceable phone to his ear and walked outside into the back corner of the garden, well away from any eavesdroppers.

'How are you?' Kenneth asked with fatherly concern.

'I'm good. Fine. But we have a problem.'

'I know, I know. I've been reading the newspapers. It looks like he's going to get away with it, scot free.'

'It certainly does look that way. I have a plan.'

'Tell me.'

'I can't. It's going to work though. Just keep an eye on the kids for me, make sure they're okay.'

Larry would be turning in his grave to know how things had turned out for his only daughter. He would also be cheering her on, with full and complete faith she knew exactly what she was doing, even when it looked like she had no idea.

JOANNE HILL STEPPED off the Qantas plane into the stifling humidity of Phuket. Plain Joanne. An ordinary, unremarkable woman wearing denim shorts and a pale-yellow T-shirt from Kmart carrying a $20 handbag, also from Kmart, stuffed with ordinary, unremarkable essentials.

A small packet of baby wipes, tissues, a hot pink purse adorned by bling, bottled water, and a Danielle Steel novel with a bookmark sticking out the top. The bag of a woman whose children were all grown up and who'd left her boring husband at home for a solo getaway.

Sensible jewellery. A cheap watch with a black band, a plain wedding band, small hoop earrings. A plain silver necklace that disappeared underneath her crew-necked T-shirt. Plain brown hair with a long fringe covered the beautiful face hidden beneath.

Joanne Hill checked into a cheap motel on the poor side of town, well away from the glitzy resorts and women reclining poolside with a cocktail on the side table.

PAT ARRIVED A day after Joanne Hill, checking into a backpacker's hostel just three blocks from Joanne's cheap motel. He didn't notice her when they passed each other on the street, or hear her sudden intake of breath. Ayala's perfect plan might not be so perfect after all.

'WHAT HAVE YOU found?'

'Jeez, give me a break Detective, I only landed an hour ago.'

'Oh, okay, I should have at least given you two hours. There's no time to waste, Clive's lawyers are circling, we are trying to pull things together but having this would be the final nail in his coffin.'

'Right then, I'd better forget about the day spa I was planning to book into across town and get to work.'

Rhiannon rolled her eyes. 'Very funny Pat. Keep in touch.'

Pat pulled the notebook out of his bag and studied the names and places Rhiannon had given him. They hatched this perfect plan in Bourke, Rhiannon deciding to keep it just between them. Not even Andy knew.

First stop, the restaurant where Aawut, Rhiannon's key witness who had been cooperative from the beginning on helping her build the case to expose the paedophile ring Clive was part of. What Rhiannon wanted to establish was if Cive was the head of it, who else was involved, and how far its creepy tentacles reached.

She was worried though. Aawut started to speak more quickly on the phone, and was vague when she tried to finalise arrangements for him to come to Australia. Now she couldn't reach him at all.

'Is Aawut working here?' Pat asked. The blank looks from the waitress made it clear she didn't speak English.

He retrieved a photo from his backpack. If he wasn't so adept at watching people's facial changes, a small twitch, a sideways glance, a slight tightening of the jaw, he might have believed her when she shook her head side to side.

'When did you last see him?' She backed away, still shaking her head, then she was gone. Pat drummed his fingers loudly on the table to calm himself, then realised loud drumming wasn't calming at all.

Pat forgot about Aawut when a large man whose belly cascaded over his waistline in rounded concertina folds placed in front of him a steaming bowl of heavenly spicy coconut curry with fresh, plump prawns on a spirally bed of thin see-through noodles, covered generously with shallots and small shards of something dried and slightly fishy. He put his face closer and the laksa gave him a facial steam that went through his pores all the way to the pit of his stomach.

'Thanks man.'

'All good, tuck in.'

Pat looked up sharply, surprised by the recognisable Aussie twang. The large man eased himself into the chair opposite, leaned back and rested his folded arms on his comfortable stomach chair.

Pat slurped and slid his way through his laska, pausing only to wipe his chin from time to time with a bright orange napkin folded in the shape of a swan.

'That's what I like to see, a man who enjoys his food.'

Pat bit back the sneaky retort which came to mind as he rested his gaze on the stomach which looked from this angle like an Italian bundt cake, except it jiggled like jelly after its escape when Mum lifted off her Tupperware ring mould.

'Says a man who enjoys his food,' the man said it for him. 'Me name's Kev. Big Kev. Chunky Kev. Or just Kev.'

'Hey Kev, I'm Pat.'

'And which secret service do you work for Pat?'

'None. I'm not that sophisticated. I work for the ABC. Here on the hunt for a story.'

'Always on the hunt for a story. You're not the first and certainly won't be the last. There's no story here.'

'Really?' Pat wiped his mouth for the final time, his bowl empty apart from a small pile of prawn tails, and leaned back with his hands folded behind his head. 'Because I reckon I'm onto a pretty good story. And I also reckon it starts right here.'

'What, here? In this dive of a restaurant only the locals know?'

Pat looked around. Apart from Chunky Kev, he was the only white person in the whole restaurant. The babble of conversations in Thai, Vietnamese and other Asian dialects rose and fell as chopsticks fished around plates piled high with noodles, vegetables, meats and other delights. Many of them were young, full of energy and enthusiastic conversation.

'Yeah, I heard this was a bit of a hang-out for the locals. Probably why it's so popular with some, let's say, foreigners wanting a *taste* of the local culture.' Pat raised his right eyebrow, a trick learnt from his Grandma when he was a curious, copycat four-year-old.

'Don't know what you're talking about. Not many foreigners in here, as you can see.'

Pat pushed the photo across the table.

'Where's this local hang out these days?'

Big Kev shook his head. 'He's long gone. A dead loss that one. Hasn't turned up for a shift for…I don't know how long.'

'Why a dead loss?'

'Oh, you know. Stars in his eyes. Never satisfied with where he was. Always looking for where he wanted to be.'

'He didn't want to be a waiter?'

'No, absolutely not. He wanted to be waited on. And not here. Anyway, he's gone now. Probably got a better offer than $2.50 an hour serving Thai food.'

'You don't sound like there was any love lost between you two,' Pat probed.

'Like I said, no story here mate. This conversation ain't goin' nowhere interesting. You're barking up the wrong tree.'

Pat knew it wouldn't be long before Big Kev heaved himself out of his chair and disappeared into the depths of the kitchen where he obviously spent a lot of time.

'And what tree would that be?'

Kev laughed. 'Persistent little bugger aren't you? Just like that nosy young copper who keeps ringing here. I keep telling her he's not working here anymore but she keeps calling back. Bloody cops, hate the lot of them. Especially the women. Got no place in the police force. Send 'em back to the kitchen where they belong, I say.'

Pat found an in.

'I agree. She's a total pain in the arse that one. Typical nagging female. Nag, nag, nag. Just like my girlfriend. Had to jump on a plane to get away from the nagging,' Pat said. 'They need to leave these things to us blokes. We know how to keep a lid on things when they need a lid. We also know how to blow the lid off when that's what we need to do. I reckon it's time to blow the lid off.'

Big Kev, now intrigued, returned to the table.

'You reckon? And how do you suggest we do that without getting dragged into the muck. Because you know, Big Kev doesn't like being down in the muck. Otherwise Big Kev can't keep running the show.'

'Don't you worry Kev. Your secrets are safe with me. You can be my secret source, and I'll be yours.'

'DAMN IT, SO he's disappeared?' Rhiannon felt like ripping her neat work bun out.

'Yep, seems that way. Sorry McVee, I'll keep chipping away with Chunky Kev, but you might need to come up with a Plan C to catch Crafty Clive.'

'Righto then, thanks.'

Rhiannon stared at the phone, wishing she didn't always feel ten steps behind the people she was trying to find.

# 34

THE FOUR SIBLINGS sat around the dining table, the clatter of morning smoko adding volume to the animated story from the paddock about the thousands of goats Jack discovered while in the helicopter doing an aerial check.

'Thousands of the buggers and we didn't even know they were there. Never seen anything like it,' Jack said, shaking his head for emphasis.

'Did you get onto Robbo, does he want them?' Bianca passed Jack a piece of passionfruit cheesecake across the table, one of Ayala's Mum's recipes she'd written out for Ulla who'd been testing it for weeks with Red to try and get it exactly how he remembered as a child.

'Bloody oath he does. They're fetching a good price too – they love goat overseas. None of this lamb or beef, goats are where it's at. It's the most consumed meat in the world.'

Ulla appeared with a fresh pot of tea.

'I couldn't imagine eating a goat, they are so cute with their long eyelashes, big eyes and soft cuddly fur, how could you eat them?'

Ulla had been feeding a handful of kid goats Jack found abandoned by their mother, some only a few days old.

All four siblings laughed. Lachie, who'd been teaching Ulla how to mix up the formula and get the new goats to feed, knew how smitten she was.

'They might seem cute now Ulla but you just wait until they start climbing over everything. Destructive little buggers they are.'

As she leaned over Red to put the pot on the table, getting a whiff of sweat mixed with deodorant and dust, he smiled at her in a way which made her blush. She resisted the temptation to touch him on the shoulder and pat down his wild hat hair.

They'd become close. Ulla's fussing and feeding and straightforward nature had given Red the courage to go to Rhiannon to see if she could press charges against Clive for the awful things he'd done. But before he did, he needed to talk to his brothers, who as far as Red and Bianca knew, had no idea of Clive's bedroom visits.

Ulla hoped the smooth, creamy middle of the cheesecake, would help smooth out his nerves for the telling of his story. The sharp tartness of the passionfruit top would give him an energy rush, and the buttery base would hold him together so he wouldn't end up in a puddle on the plate.

Lachie lifted his piece in his hand and took the first bite from the pointed end. A few crumbs sat on his lips as he mumbled through his mouthful, 'Just like Mum's.'

Jack was next, he also ate with his hands. 'Yep, spot on Ulla.'

Bianca glanced at her brothers as she picked up a spoon with arched eyebrows to show them how Ayala had taught them to eat, 'with your best manners in case the Queen comes around for morning tea'. They ignored her as they shoved the rest of the deliciousness into their mouths.

Bianca took her time savouring her first bite. 'It's your best one yet, Ulla.'

Red was the final and most anticipated critic. He took his time and Ulla laughed nervously.

'Come on, you are killing me with your suspense,' she tested out one of the new Australian expressions she'd picked up.

'Well, um, mmmm.'

Ulla slapped him on the arm.

'Okay, okay. It's so close – Mum would be very impressed.'

Feeling happy yet sad, as quietly as Ulla appeared she disappeared, leaving the four of them to enjoy the tartness and sweetness of their memories of Ayala and what lay ahead.

RED WAITED FOR Bianca to pour the second cups of tea, wiped the crumbs and his sweaty palms on his riders and cleared his throat.

'I'm glad we managed to all get in the one place at the one time,' his voice cracked. Bianca smiled with her eyes.

'Coz, actually there's something I need to tell you.'

Ulla heard Jack's chair clatter to the floor and a clear, loud 'no fucking way!' before the slam of the gauze door and the stomp of his boots towards the garden gate. She thought the gate might come off its hinges after the strength in which he closed it.

Back at the table, Bianca was trying to comfort Lachie who was crying like a baby. The distress pulled Ulla back into the room where Red sat, white as a sheet, taking in the scene around him. He looked up at her and pulled her down to his lap, wrapping her tighter than an anaconda.

'It will work out,' she whispered over and over, so quietly only he could hear. He held her closer, and closer, knowing in that moment he never wanted to let Ulla go.

## PASSIONFRUIT DELIGHT (PASSIONFRUIT CHEESECAKE TART, BAKED)

### Base

*Shortcrust pastry*

1 ¼ cups plain flour

1/3 cup icing sugar

100 grams butter, chopped

1 egg

Blitz flour, icing sugar and butter in a mixing bowl (or food processor if you have one) until loosely combined. Add egg, mix/process until dough just comes together. Turn dough onto a lightly floured bench, knead lightly, shape into a flat disc. Wrap in plastic food wrap and chill for one hour. Lightly grease a 25cm round (base diameter) fluted tart pan with removable base. Roll pastry between sheets of baking paper large enough to line the prepared pan, ease into pan, trim excess pastry. Place pan onto a baking tray. Chill for 15 minutes.

Preheat oven to 180 degrees Celsius/160 fan forced. Line pastry with baking paper, cover base with dried beans, rice or pie weights. Bake 15 minutes. Cool.

### Middle

Mix 1 x tin condensed milk and the juice of 3 x lemons together and spoon over the cooled shortcrust base.

### Top

Mix the pulp of 3 x passionfruit, 1 teaspoon of sugar and 1 teaspoon of custard powder together in a saucepan, if it's not moist enough add small amount of water. Heat slowly until it's clear. Pour over the top of the condensed milk mixture and refrigerate until set.

# 35

'HEY MCVEE, GOT another call for ya.'

They really needed to get someone to train their new recruits on how to A, answer the phone properly and B, transfer calls.

'Put it through then, Constable Chesney, please.'

'I dunno how.'

'Well bloody learn!'

Rhiannon stomped to the reception desk, punched in a few buttons and the phone on her desk started ringing.

'See, not rocket science.'

Zoe flushed. She was still trying hard to fit in but Rhiannon didn't want a bar of her. She was torn, because after being at the station for a while, she realised it was Rhiannon she really wanted to impress, despite what the others said about her being an uptight pain in the neck.

'Hi Rhiannon, it's Red. Clive's son.'

'Red,' Rhiannon held her breath. 'How are you?'

'Not so good. Actually, pretty shit. But what do you do?'

Rhiannon didn't speak, waiting for him to continue.

'Anyway, I wondered if we could catch up, you know, somewhere private. Not the police station.'

'Sure, absolutely. Where are you?'

'Up the street, in the phone box.'

He hardly finished speaking before Rhiannon had her keys and was heading out the back door to her own car. She hardly stopped at the phone box before Red was in and they were driving off again, heading out of town away from prying eyes.

Red didn't speak until she pulled up under the shade of a river red gum arching over the drying Darling River with its giant limbs. Drought cycles were getting longer it seemed, just like it seemed to get hotter every summer, just like it seemed the frosts were more severe in the dead of winter.

'Bianca is in Sydney, off doing some training course on computers. We've got one on the farm now, it's a whole new world coming you know.'

'Yeah, I'm scared of the bloody things, give me a notepad and pen any day,' Rhiannon laughed. 'Bit of a dinosaur when it comes to things like that, I'd prefer the old-fashioned way.'

'Could probably make the cops job a whole lot easier when you think about it,' Red continued. 'Keep all the information stored somewhere, then you could put it on a floppy disc and post it to another police station and they could go through it all on their computer.'

'What, you mean instead of having to fax stuff through, or print it out and post it?'

'Yeah, safer too. Never know who's going to take something off the fax, or where your mail's going to end up.'

'This might be a stupid question, but what's a floppy disc?' Rhiannon couldn't stop the giggle.

Red smiled too. 'Yeah, it's a pretty funny name, the floppy bit. It's a square thing you insert into the computer and you can save things onto it. You know, documents, images, that kind of stuff. And then you can insert it into another computer somewhere else and all those same things will open up and they can see them at their end.'

'Fuck, really?'

Rhiannon was intrigued. Maybe computers weren't so scary after all. Imagine if she could put all her notes onto a computer where they wouldn't get lost, or accidentally thrown out, and then save the hundreds and hundreds of pages of evidence onto a *floppy* disc and post it to Andy in Sydney.

'That's blown my mind,' Rhiannon said. 'Maybe I need to stop being so old-fashioned and get with the times.'

'Yeah, maybe.'

The talk of computers broke the ice but once it stalled, Red's stiffness returned.

They'd been so caught up in the conversation they didn't realise how hot the car had become without the air conditioner running. Rhiannon wound down her window to let a breeze in and some tension out, Red did the same. She didn't probe, he was the one who'd called, so would talk when ready.

'Um, so, you're probably wondering why all the secrecy?'

'Not really, it's pretty tough being under so much public scrutiny, with the profile of your Dad in the community. I know how difficult it must be for people to be staring and wondering all the time.'

'Yeah, it sucks. Most don't really care, they're just nosy. They ask the stupidest questions and say the dumbest things. And the newspapers with all their theories and hidden agendas. We've been misquoted that many times, and they drag out all this old family stuff not even connected to Mum, or Clive.'

'We get that too. 'No comment' or 'nothing new to report' doesn't make a very good story so they pad it out with whatever they can find.'

'They'd probably get pretty excited if they found out what I'm about to tell you,' Red said wryly.

Rhiannon held her breath. She had an inkling what was coming but didn't want to jinx it. It was a full five minutes before Red spoke again. The only sound in the warm afternoon sun was the occasional bird and the buzz of the friendly flies who had discovered them.

'The first time I was only eleven. I didn't really understand what was happening at the time. Just that I hated it and wanted it to stop.'

Rhiannon felt tears prick in the corner of her eyes. No matter how many times she heard a story like this, she couldn't control her anger laced with devastation at what some parents do to their children. This was the worst, the absolute worst.

'Excuse me, I just need a bit of air,' she muttered as she clumsily opened the door and stumbled out. She walked around the giant tree trunk until she was out of view and sunk to the ground, scraping bark down the back of her sweat-soaked shirt. She took deep quiet gulps, knowing Red would hear her if she cried too loudly.

She wanted to scream her anger out so it could rise to the tops of the giant red gums and their leaves absorb and clean the filthy images she wanted to scrub from her mind. Instead she muttered, 'I hate you Clive you filthy piece of shit and I'm going to fucking bury you for what you've done. Hate you, hate you, hate you, hate you.'

'I hate him too,' Red said quietly as he joined her.

Rhiannon stood up quickly, turning her face away so Red couldn't see her shiny, tear-soaked cheeks.

'Sorry, I …' she wanted to explain. She didn't want him to see her as weak. She was meant to be here to protect him, not shatter and crumble under the weight of his father's sins.

'Don't apologise, Bianca told me you'd understand. She told me you'd probably cry, even though you're not supposed to cry in the cops, but you're different. You feel things the way we feel things.'

'She's got me worked out then!'

'She's pretty switched on, Big Sis, but she's devastated she never switched onto this.'

'Of course she would be, same as your Mum. He hid it so well, had everyone fooled. It's so obvious now but he got away with all the things he was doing for a very long time.'

They strolled along the shaded riverbank, going through different scenarios.

'I know someone, a reporter. He'll be sensitive. Still, you realise going public with this will be traumatic and humiliating for you? The media will have a field day, and although they'll be on your side, it's still a lot for you to have to live with. At your work, relationships, girlfriend?'

'I don't have a girlfriend, well, I am wondering if there is something with Ulla, but it's early days and is probably doomed to fail.'

Rhiannon turned to face him. 'Don't say that Red. This was not your fault, in any way. You did nothing, absolutely nothing wrong. It's all on Clive, all of it.'

Red stopped walking and hung his head low.

'But what if he's passed on his sickness to me? What if I end up having children and I get the same urges?'

'You won't. He can't pass it on. You're a good man Red and you have your whole life in front of you. It stops right here.

'You are dealing with this like a grown man should. Clive never dealt with anything that happened in his childhood, or his adulthood. He is a bad person. You're not. You have your Mum to thank for that.'

A flock of noisy corellas broke the silence, *crark crark crark*, as they flew overhead to strip the eucalypts on the other side of the river with their strong relentless beaks and insatiable desire to eat until there was nothing left.

'Do you think we'll ever find her? Dead? Alive?'

'I don't know Red, I really don't know. It's hard to say with certainty either way.'

Red looked into Rhiannon's beautiful big eyes for the first time since they'd started talking, distracted for a moment, unable to look away.

'I won't give up trying, I promise you.'

'CASSETTARI.'

'McVee.'

'I've got big news.'

'Is there any other kind?'

'This is real big.'

'Hit me with it, the suspense is killing me.' Andy's delivery was as dry as an unbuttered Salada.

Rhiannon couldn't keep up the cool, calm and collected act. She looked around to make sure she had the room to herself, then let it all go.

'We've fucking got him this time. We've got Clive, we've fucking got him!'

# 36

AAWUT HAD BEEN scared for his life for so long, and was as scared as ever by the strange smells and sounds of the Australian bush which greeted them last night.

It was late winter. The cold pushed him deeper under his doona, vastly different to the steamy nights under a mosquito net, until he couldn't resist the urge to see his new surroundings.

He pulled back the heavy curtains on his bedroom window. Foreign trees and bushes surrounded him on all sides, some covered in tiny bright yellow balls and others with vivid red long tubes of a million tiny strands and a fullstop on each end.

He always wondered what it would be like in Australia; Mr Clive promised him the streets were lined with gold, that one day he would take him there. He peered for gold along the pathways around the house. He couldn't see any.

By mid-morning the sun was sending warmth to a comfortable cane chair on the verandah, where he sat quietly in jeans and a T-shirt.

'Would you like another cup of tea?' Ayala asked through the open kitchen window.

'You have funny bird sounds here, what is that one?'

Ayala had been enjoying the warbling magpies as well.

'Those are magpies. They sing all day, every day.'

'Magpies? That's a funny name for a bird.'

Ayala retrieved a bird book Lucas had picked up in the op shop from the bookcase and took it out with Aawut's green tea. She kneeled down next to him, found the magpie page, and started reading slowly, her voice still gravelly from the long trip.

'There are few birds as familiar to Australians as the Australian magpie.

161

This striking black and white bird is a large species of butcherbird. Apart from its widespread distribution the species' familiarity is probably due equally to its pleasant carolling song, which is such an essential part of the Australian soundscape, and for its tendency to swoop at people during its springtime nesting season.'

Aawut ran his hand over the photo. 'Mag..pie. It swoops people?'

Ayala laughed.

'Yes it does, and can be quite ferocious! When the kids were little we had a very territorial magpie near the mailbox and they'd have to approach it like they were in a warfare situation, close to the ground. I made them protective helmets out of ice cream containers with long spikes made from sticks and big googly eyes drawn on the top to scare the magpies away.'

Ayala stood up abruptly and went inside, not wanting Aawut to see the tears her memory poured into her eyes. He put the book down and followed her inside.

'You miss your, what did you call them, kids?'

'Yes I do. I miss them terribly. I've got things into such a mess, I'm not sure how to fix it.'

'Did you know Mr Clive wanted to kill me?'

'No, but I guessed.'

'When my friend at the restaurant who's been hiding me told me you came, I knew I had to talk to you. I was scared. I had nowhere to go. I didn't know what to do. I needed to warn you.'

Ayala couldn't drag her eyes away from Aawut, a young innocent man born into a Third World existence sucked into the heartless promises and sins of a sick, sickening, wealthy white male.

She steeled herself against the waves of emotion that weakened her resolve and mentally counted to ten to regain her focus.

'Thank you for trusting me, even though I couldn't tell you anything much until now, I didn't know who was listening. He tried to kill me too. That's why I had to sneak you out of there, and to here.'

'Why is he trying to kill me?'

Ayala wasn't sure how much she should tell Aawut. He'd made himself disappear before, when he was the only one who could put Clive in jail, and he could easily disappear again.

'Because you know things about him the Australian police want you to say in court, so they can put him into jail and stop him doing what he does when he's in Thailand.'

Aawut sighed loudly.

'Do you mean with the young boys?'

Ayala's stomach turned on itself.

'Yes, that's exactly what I mean.'

Aawut backed out of the kitchen, he didn't want to be part of this, he didn't want to help the police.

'I don't want to speak to any police. They will lock me up too, for, for …' Aawut hung his head in shame. He didn't want to admit to Ayala the things he had done with Mr Clive, for Mr Clive, on behalf of Mr Clive.

'I don't think the police here will lock you up, they want to keep you safe, they will protect you.'

'I don't believe you. That's what they told me back home but then someone came to my house in the night. They, what you say? Break? Rip? I ran out the door where they couldn't see me. I run and run. I hided in a dark cellar where my friend would bring food, he steal from the restaurant. Sometimes he couldn't come for days so nobody suspicious. I get very hungry.'

Anger pumped blood around Ayala's body, she pushed down the fury ball threatening to push its way out of her mouth in a barrage of expletives.

'I saw a journalist there, who has done stories about Clive. I'm assuming he was looking for you too. Until I figure out what he's up to, what he knows, I had to get you out of there and hide you away.'

'Everyone wants Aawut,' he laughed to hide his fear.

'Yes they do. I will make sure nobody gets Aawut. I just need you to please give me some time to work out what I'm going to do. You're safe here, we're both safe here. Nobody knows we even exist.'

Aawut bowed his head. 'Okay Missus Aya. I trust you.'

# 37

AFTER HER CONVERSATION with Red, Rhiannon headed to Kings Cross so her and Andy could work on next steps to put Clive away.

While they were still keen to pin Ayala's disappearance and his involvement in an international paedophile ring onto him, they'd settle for his son putting him up on abuse charges. For now.

What Andy still didn't know was Pat was still in Phuket trying to track down Aawut, a card she only wanted to reveal if she pulled it off.

Rhiannon locked herself away in a small, poky interview room in the bowels of Kings Cross Police Station to go through recordings from a bug she had placed near Kenneth's garden seat. She got the idea when she visited for their very first conversation about Ayala and noticed the secluded back corner of the garden.

A wooden seat covered in Liberty Alicia Bell green botanical print cushions held court underneath the dense shade of a giant fig tree, at least nine metres tall. It was the perfect place for a private conversation. The perfect place to record a private conversation.

She spent the past several hours listening to Kenneth's past yachting adventures, high-level legal jargon that made little sense to her with the young lawyer, Michael, who he was gradually passing all his clients to, worrisome, earnest health discussions with his doctor whose health advice he was only selectively hearing and a few stilted, awkward conversations with someone unknown.

'She's alive Andy, I fucking felt it and now I fucking know it. Here, listen.'

Andy pulled up a chair and Rhiannon passed him her chunky black headset, police issue, which meant it was only working in one ear and the cord was held together with hundred mile an hour tape.

'I can't hear it,' he complained.

'It must only be working in your deaf ear, here.' Rhiannon switched them around for him and pressed play. The conversation contained long, drawn out pauses.

'*Are you sure?' Pause. 'Do you think that's wise?' Pause. 'We could find a way.'* Pause. '*They really miss you.'*

Andy's eyes widened, only slightly, but Rhiannon could interpret all his slight movements and gestures and knew it piqued his interest. He slowly and carefully pulled the headphones off.

'Bingo!' Rhiannon clapped her hands. '*They really miss you.* See? I knew it, I knew it, I knew it.'

'You do realise it doesn't prove anything don't you?'

'Bullshit, it proves Ayala is fucking alive. Alive, alive, alive!'

'Maybe, maybe not. It could be anyone, he could be talking to. Clive? Or someone else wrapped up in the family business he's helping that young lawyer untangle? There's a million and one ways you can interpret those words.'

'I've got a hunch though Andy, I really think she's alive!'

'There you go, two rookie mistakes right there. Hunch. Think. I admit a hunch can be a good thing, but a hunch isn't facts. And it's no good to think something – you need to know!'

Rhiannon slumped in her chair and stuck her chin out.

'Fine. You're right. I guess.'

Andy raised his eyebrows, ever so slightly.

'Okay, everything you say is true and that does make you right. But I reckon I'm more right. I reckon Ayala is alive and kicking and if I'm more right than you, well, that's the best fucking news I've had all year.'

Andy stood to leave, resisting the temptation to pat her shoulder in reassurance. She could be right. She could also be wrong.

'Keep at it, but just remember, don't get too far ahead of yourself.'

KENNETH WAS ENJOYING the Saturday Australian on his favourite seat under the fig tree in the back corner of his garden, the shade acting as an air-conditioning knob on this unusually warm August day.

Susan carried down a morning tea tray with a fresh pot of English Breakfast in his favourite Wedgwood jasperware tea set, plus a small slice of iced ginger cake, fresh from the oven with the lemon in the icing squeezed fresh from their thirty-year-old tree.

Next to the plate was a small container with heart pills, including a few extras his doctor prescribed a fortnight ago after his most recent 'turn'.

His secret phone was on the seat next to him; he'd been carrying it everywhere so he didn't miss Ayala's next call.

He imagined she was back in Australia by now with the young man named Aawut Saetang who he had arranged a passport and easy, no questions asked, entry into Australia for.

They had phase two of the plan all mapped out and he was just waiting for final instructions. He tried to press her on phase three, but she told him she couldn't think about that yet, as it involved her facing her children and the consequences of the elaborate tangle she had gotten herself into.

In their most recent conversation she hinted at not revealing to anyone she was still alive. This prospect horrified Kenneth, he didn't know if he could keep her 'missing persons' status a secret for much longer.

He hoped this would all be over sooner rather than later. He was tired, Susan too. She hated seeing him like this and almost wished he hadn't made a promise to his best friend Larry to look after Ayala once he was gone.

None of them anticipated a mess as chaotic as a group of four year olds after a birthday party where green cordial, food colouring and lollies were in endless supply.

'I love you my darling wife,' Kenneth turned his face up to accept the kiss she was initially planning for his forehead, so he could have it on his lips.

'I love you too my darling husband, love of my life, the most wonderful man I know.'

They kissed again.

'Want to sit with me awhile?' Kennett patted the cushion next to him.

'I'll come back soon, I'm not sure if I turned the oven off when I took the cake out. Silly old goose, I'm getting more forgetful every day.'

'You think you are!' Kenneth laughed. 'I'm still trying to remember what I had for breakfast.'

'Boiled egg on toast, cut into soldiers. Like you do every morning.'

He winked and they grinned like two young children at the secret conversation only they knew the real meaning of. He never forgot anything; his memory was as sharp as it always was, but this breakfast joke was to test her. She answered correctly most times, but not always.

It wasn't an unusual conversation compared to what Rhiannon heard repeatedly on the recordings from this private place where Kenneth took his newspaper and morning tea every day.

After a few moments Susan left to check the oven. It was off, like it always was. But one day she knew she'd leave it on. She stepped off the verandah onto the paved path which led to the garden seat, and saw Kenneth quickly grab the phone, hold it tight to his ear for a few minutes, then clutch his chest.

Susan watched the newspaper fall from his lap and the cup of tea bounce on the ground as he toppled off the seat. The scene unfolded in slow motion. As she ran on lead legs, he fell peacefully towards the soft green grass as tiny hands on the end of each blade reached up and lowered him gently to the ground.

By the time she got to him it was too late, and the tiny grass hands encircled them both into a hug that carried Kenneth from this life to the next.

'Kenneth! Are you there? Kenneth! Can you hear me?'

Susan picked up the phone, her words coming in soft sobs.

'He's gone, he's gone.'


AS THE SUN set over the ocean, something she still wasn't used to, Ayala sat on her verandah slowly sipping a glass of red. Everything around her was in perfect stillness and she wondered at the insignificance of herself compared to this wondrous nature.

Sip. The wine filtered through her body to warm it from the inside out. Despite the cool start, the day had warmed up to end with a balmy, humid evening. The setting sun illuminated fat clouds and she watched a light show dance across the ocean.

Aawut had gone for a walk and she tried not to worry as the evening dimmed the lights slowly until the trees became dark shapes. Her motherly instinct had kicked into overdrive with him around. Cluck, cluck like an old mother hen.

The last evening bird which had exited left of stage several minutes ago, returned for one final encore. Silence. Stillness. Sip.

'Kenneth,' she whispered. 'Cheers to you my dear old man.'

Sip.

Tears dripped off her chin and into the wine glass she hugged into her chest. Without her anchor, her rock, it was just her and this crazy world she landed herself in. She wondered if she should write this all into a book, but even in fiction it would sound too far-fetched.

She needed to rip off the bandaid. She needed to stop this craziness, the lies, the deceit. She had to return to her children, she had to go to the police. She couldn't send Aawut on his own, which had been her original plan.

Kenneth had been making all the arrangements for Aawut to get from Perth to Sydney, and he would take him direct to Kings Cross Detective Andy Cassettari.

When she spotted Pat Richards in Phuket, it cluttered up her plan, but as soon as she got back to her seaside cottage she stopped worrying about him.

Kenneth, oh Kenneth. What a wonderful, kind man. His family would miss him dearly. His colleagues, all the people he'd helped in his lifetime.

She hoped he would be by her side to cushion the blow when her children realised what she had done. Would they ever forgive her? Would they ever really understand her choices?

They say time heals all wounds, she wouldn't necessarily agree, but time had given her a new perspective.

She understood she had been caught in a whirlwind of drama and trauma. Discovering what Clive had been doing in Phuket flipped a switch in her brain she didn't know was there.

What she tried to do to Clive horrified her. She was embarrassed, sick with worry, and ashamed. If Bianca had already found the diary, she would know all the horrible things Ayala had done.

But if she hadn't, Ayala would have to face her and explain. She didn't know if she could face Red. She didn't want to look him in the eye knowing what she knew, knowing what she hadn't prevented.

Her two other boys, unique in their own ways, would take it differently. Four beautiful children who would all wear the scars their parents inflicted upon them.

She weighed up the different scenarios, the different ways out, as she shifted between staying 'missing' or returning to her children. She doubled over in pain. Red wine spilt like blood across the verandah as her body went limp and slumped forward.

AAWUT SAW THE red stain before he noticed Ayala's lifeless, still body in the chair.

Fear filled his heart. 'Missus Aya, Missus Aya!'

His mind immediately went to someone sneaking in on dusk looking for him, finding her instead…he couldn't finish the thought.

He gently sat her up, kicking the wine glass at her feet, checking her for an entry wound. Her body felt warm but in his panic he thought it was because it had just happened. With wild eyes he spun his head around, listening hard for strange sounds, quickly giving up because every sound was strange to his unaccustomed ears.

His nose was almost touching hers when her eyes slowly batted open, giving him the fright of his life.

He yelped, she yelped, and he fell backwards into the red wine stain.

'You might need some Napisan to get that out,' Ayala said dryly. Aawut had no idea what she was talking about but laughed anyway, which made her laugh.

'Missus Aya, you very funny lady. Strange also, and not make sense. Aawut thought you were killed.'

It felt so good to laugh they kept it going and going, until it gradually petered out into deep, dark silence.

'I thought the bad people had come. They could come, could they?'

Ayala's instinct was to reassure him but she didn't have the strength for it.

'Yes Aawut, they could come. I hope they don't, but they definitely could.'

# 38

DAYS LATER AYALA was still faffing about with her new plan, snatching only a few hours of deep, dream-filled sleep each night.

Her body ached from head to toe, even in her sleep, as she held herself in the permanent position of a rubber band stretched to its tightest point. A sharp pain in her lower back protested and prodded her awake.

She slowly uncurled, threw her legs off her bed and in a dream-like state pulled her yoga mat from the corner and unrolled it on the floor.

Once her feet felt the familiar rubber she slipped straight into her breathing. Lots of love in, lots of love out. She repeated the mantra of the yoga teacher from a Bali retreat she went on with her closest girlfriends, oh, what would her best friend Bee say when she saw her again? Would she want to be her friend anymore?

It took discipline to chase her thoughts away. Breathe in, breathe out.

She brought herself into the seated position and sat with a tall, straight back, chin slightly lifted, eyes closed. She counted to five on her breath in, and five on her breath out. One, two, three, four, five, pause. One, two, three, four, five for her breath out.

After ten minutes of simple breathing Ayala slowly unwrapped herself, went through some slow cat-cows, lifted gently into downward dog then jumped to the front of her mat to land, feet together, in a strong mountain pose.

Energy charged from the bottom of her feet through to the tips of her fingers.

This was the last time she was going to let Clive fuck up her life.

Rag doll. Plant the palms, left foot back, right foot back, plank. Vinyasa, meet you back in downward facing dog.

This was the last time Clive was going to make her feel weak and powerless. Just like he had to face the terrible things he had done, she had to face them too.

Jump to the top of your mat, feet together, really together. Uncurl and reach up. Palms together, elbows out.

The only way forward was forward.

Lots of love in, lots of love out.

Subconsciously her mantra changed from numbers to words.

Pat Richards.

Plant the palms, left foot back, right foot back. Plank pose. Lift your left hand to touch your right shoulder. Breathe. Right hand to left shoulder. Breath. Here for, five, don't forget to breathe, four.

Pat Richards.

Three, two. Her arms shook and her legs burned.

Pat Richards.

You can do it, down on the one. Rest in child's position. Lots of love in, lots of love out.

Pat Richards. She needed to make him part of the story only she could write.

Complex puzzles require extreme concentration and accuracy. She held the puzzle pieces nobody else would be able to find. She needed to fit all the pieces together to make sure Clive would never hurt any of them, herself included, ever again.

Finishing in corpse position, she tasted the salt of her sweat mixed with the flood of tears her yoga practice always released. With her palms on her heart she whispered, 'Okay Pat, I hear you. Let's finish this, and finish it for good.'

RHIANNON SAT ON Kenneth's garden seat with Susan, while Andy stood on the back verandah. Rhiannon couldn't help running her hand over the cushions – she was obsessed with Laura Ashley prints and had stitched numerous, including this Sherwood Forest pattern, into her patchwork quilts.

'I'm really sorry for your loss Susan, your husband was a lovely man.'

'Yes, he was, he lived a full, happy and rich life and helped many, many people along the way.'

Rhiannon and Andy played back the audio a couple of times; Rhiannon found it almost impossible to listen to as it reminded her of her dear Dad dying of a heart attack in his workshop.

Susan hadn't panicked in calling the ambulance. She knew no matter how fast they raced to get there, nothing more could be done.

'He had his first heart attack more than ten years ago; we knew he was on borrowed time. Eighty-one is a good innings, he was pleased to have lived so long to see his children and grandchildren grow up, and to welcome a great grandchild. He felt blessed his heart kept him alive for so long.'

'I'm sorry to be emotional,' Rhiannon explained. 'My Dad died a few years ago, heart attack, and I find myself tearing up at unexpected times. I still feel like he was taken from us too soon and he will never get to meet any grandchildren, or great grandchildren.'

She pulled herself together quickly; she had no business to be intruding on Kenneth's family's grief with her own. She was pleased Andy was too far away to see her crumble.

'I'm not here to talk about me though, I'm here to ask some questions, and I apologise in advance for intruding at this time.'

Susan's eyes were clear and accepting. She knew why they were here.

'I understand. You have an important job to do, and Kenneth holds crucial pieces of information which I'm sure you will appreciate having.'

Rhiannon raised one eyebrow. Maybe she didn't have to let on she'd been bugging the seat the whole time.

'You can start with this. It is the phone Kenneth used to call Ayala. He was worried our phones were bugged.'

Handing over the phone to Rhiannon, it was Susan's turn to raise one eyebrow.

'Are you saying Ayala is alive?'

'Yes, she is.'

Rhiannon's loud intake of breath turned into a gasp. She looked up at Andy, trying to give him a sign she was having a 'big news' moment.

'Kenneth knew I wasn't happy about getting entangled in all of this,' Susan continued, 'but he had a deep loyalty to Ayala's father going right back to when they were boys.

'I could tell he was in too deep. I wasn't privy to the details, but it seemed to me things were getting more and more complicated. He was an honest man his whole career, okay, so he might have been a bit creative with the law at times, but he was never a wheeler and dealer. I want you to know that, to believe that.'

'He always gave me the impression he had a strong belief in the justice system,' Rhiannon said, even though she knew she'd misjudged people before and probably would again.

'He did. Except when it came to Ayala. He didn't believe the justice system would look after her, he believed, he knew, it would look after Clive. He was a man with contacts in every corner and was never afraid of crooked deals or shady characters if it meant getting what he wanted.

'And the way he treated Ayala, well that was just not right. How could Kenneth turn away?'

Rhiannon cut in before Susan could continue.

'I'm wondering if you'd mind if I got my partner down here, he's been running the case against Clive down here while I've been working with Ayala's children back at Bourke, it would be really helpful if we could both talk to you.'

Susan stood up wearily, and Rhiannon noticed it took effort for her to straighten.

'Of course, and this is probably not the place to talk. How about I make us a pot of tea and we go into the drawing room.'

Rhiannon resisted the temptation to click her heels together as she followed Susan back to the house. Andy acknowledged her subtle thumbs up with an equally subtle nod. No words were needed, she knew what his nod meant: 'Good job, McVee. You've done good.'

'I COULD HEAR this voice from the grass after he died, and it was then I realised Ayala was still there.

'She said to me, 'I'm so sorry Susan, I really am. I know how worried

Kenneth has been and I'm sorry it has become such a terrible mess. I will miss him dreadfully; he was like a father to me my whole life. I owe him more than I could ever repay. He saved my life.'

'Then she hung up.

'I tried to call back after the fuss died down and they took Kenneth's body to the funeral home, but I couldn't get any response. Just an automatic message to say to check the number.'

Rhiannon knew Ayala was no fool; the woman had staged her own disappearance with the skill of an undercover agent. She figured as soon as Ayala hung up from Susan, she destroyed the phone and all its contents.

'I thought you might be able to do something to track where the calls originated from, or something,' Susan said, as she poured three cups of tea, followed by milk from a matching milk jug.

Rhiannon declined the sugar, Andy asked for three, then cut it back to one after he saw Rhiannon's expression.

He eyed off the perfectly symmetrical small yo-yos on the plate which he knew he could fit whole into his mouth and demolish without spilling a crumb, wondering if it was worth the roasting Rhiannon would give him.

She was still harping on about his sweet tooth, his girth, his fitness. Little Miss Goody Two Shoes who could eat what she wanted and still look youthful, plus outrun him by a mile.

'Do you have any idea where she is? Is she in Australia? Overseas?'

'I have no idea. Kenneth wouldn't tell me anything, he told me he had to protect me and the rest of the family from getting dragged into it, so all I knew was she would call every now and then. The calls were becoming more frequent lately though, and he was in the habit of carrying the phone with him wherever he went.'

Rhiannon flushed, deciding not to tell Susan they had been intruding into their conversations at the garden seat at this moment.

'Did he have any paperwork you know of which might give us some clues? A diary perhaps, or a contact book?'

Susan's face fell. 'No, unfortunately there is nothing. Kenneth was meticulous and careful.

'He had a turn a few weeks ago. After that I walked in on him early one morning and he was shredding some papers. He also burnt a few things in the small incinerator we have down the back that same day.

'He didn't say anything, and neither did I. We had our own way of understanding what each other was thinking, I trusted he was doing the right thing.'

Susan retrieved a small, embroidered handkerchief from her pocket to dab her eyes before delicately blowing her nose. Everything she did was graceful and classy, even blowing her nose.

Rhiannon and Andy exchanged glances.

'Thank you for your help, I know this is really hard for you.' Rhiannon took the final sip of her tea and made moves to leave.

'We will see what we can retrieve from the phone and will call you if we need anything else.'

Susan didn't get up to see them to the door. Rhiannon glanced back to see her sitting with back straight and shoulders back like she'd been taught by June Dally-Watkins, with her hands folded neatly and her ankles crossed.

Long after they left, she started clearing things away, wondering who had been drinking from the other two cups and why she'd laid out a full plate of yo-yos nobody had touched.


'WHAT NEXT?' RHIANNON could hardly contain herself. She could almost imagine the butterflies in her stomach go into panic mode and fly themselves into a frenzy.

'Easy. We find Ayala.'

'Right. Easy you say?'

'Or...' Andy raised an eyebrow, '...she finds us.'

# 39

PAT LANDED IN Sydney empty handed, tail between his legs, knowing he'd been within a bee's dick of getting what he and Rhiannon needed to move this case forward and the biggest scoop of his life.

He walked to his office with his bulging rucksack over his shoulder, crammed with full notebooks begging to be put on air, carrying a steaming brown paper bag bulging with his curry meat pie, and a cheese and bacon for his colleague.

The morning peak hour traffic seemed quiet compared to Phuket, although it wasn't the traffic that had altered, it was him. He always felt restless returning to Sydney after an overseas assignment. The city took on a dullness as he pined for the smells, colours and sounds of where he'd been.

He knew Rhiannon was in Sydney, but he hadn't told her he was coming back. She'd be so disappointed, he was so disappointed. Not for the first time, the thought her lifted his blood pressure. She was hot, those big eyes framed by long lashes, that smooth flawless skin. It took all his willpower not to put her up against a wall and show her how he really felt when she leaned in close for their private, secret conversations.

'Morning Pat the Rat,' his desk buddy Fergus greeted him. 'Got an extra one of those for me?'

Pat handed over the hot pie with the small square tomato sauce packet balanced on top. Fergus grinned from ear to ear, his pastel pink shirt straining its buttons to make way for another nutritious breakfast.

He was a good-looking fellow with floppy black hair with a natural curl and long dark lashes on pale green eyes, but he was a slob of the highest order. He would never change, unless he happened to land himself the perfect woman to whip him into shape.

'Where you been?'

'That's for me to know and you to find out.'

'Come on, your secret's safe with me.'

'No, can't divulge. Anyway, what have I missed?'

'Oh, you know, the usual. Underbelly stuff we can't report. Police corruption, political corruption, the occasional murder, a drug overdose or two in The Cross, car accidents, armed robberies. Like I said, the usual.'

Fergus talked through his pie, expertly containing the meat which threatened to spill out with every new bite. Pat watched with amusement, knowing this pie eating session would end with a smear of sauce or meat on Fergus's pale shirt.

'Just an ordinary day's work hey? Sounds like I've missed sweet fuck all.'

Fergus prepared for his final mouthful and right on cue, meat spilled over the end of his thumb and straight onto his shirt.

'Bingo,' Pat muttered as he handed him a napkin.

Undeterred, Fergus finished the pie, licked his fingers and swiped the remainder off his shirt before sucking it off the napkin.

'You're a grot Fergs, your mother would be so proud.'

Fergus grinned sheepishly.

'My best shirt too, stain free.'

'Now it will match the rest of the shirts in your wardrobe, you just don't look right without a pie smear down your front.'

Pat finished his pie neatly, not even spilling a crumb, and slam dunked the bag into Fergus's bin.

'Ten points!'

Fergus took aim at Pat's bin, missing by a mile.

'Ten for me, none for you.'

Fergus chuckled before ripping a giant fart. 'Welcome back Pat, good to have you back at the desk next door.

'Now breakfast is done, you need to tell me something exciting. Give us a scoop. Come on, I know you've got one tucked away in that grotty rucksack of yours which smells like…mmm…' Fergus came close and took a loud nose whiff. 'Let me guess…street food?'

Pat unpacked his notebooks onto his desk. 'Nothing to tell apart from dirty alleyways leading to dead ends.'

The newsroom phone rang, and everyone looked around to see who was going to answer.

'Probably some old lady whose cat is stuck up a tree,' someone yelled from the back corner, as they all went back to what they were doing. It was a game they played to see who would answer the phone and either get the story of a lifetime or someone boasting the biggest pumpkin ever grown.

Pat rolled his eyes. 'Fine, I'll get it.'

'Whoo, whoo, whoo.' Fergus started the newsroom chant which built in volume as everyone else joined in.

Pat gestured for quiet as he was about to lift the receiver.

'ABC Sydney, Pat Richards.'

'Hello Pat,' long pause, 'this is Ayala Philips,' longer pause, 'I believe you and I have a few things to talk about.'

PAT LOOKED AROUND the newsroom and wondered if anybody realised the scoop on the other end of the phone line.

'Is it really you?'

'Yes, it really is me.'

'How can I know for sure?'

'I saw you in Phuket.'

'When?'

'When you were looking for Aawut.'

Pat started packing up his notebooks back into his rucksack. Fergus raised an eyebrow from the next desk and Pat knew he was onto him.

'Do you have a number I could call?' Pat asked.

'No, I don't, not one I want to share.'

'It's just I have to race out the door for an interview,' Pat explained. 'I have another number you can reach me on, in, say, thirty minutes?'

He rattled off the number as he calculated how long it would take, if he ran faster than a leopard, to get back to his apartment building, up six flights of stairs and to his home phone.

'Fine, speak soon.'

Pat didn't hear her. He had already hung up and was halfway out the building.

# 40

HE ANSWERED ON the first ring. 'Hello, Ayala.'

'Hello, Pat Richards from the ABC.'

He selected his words thoughtfully.

'How can I help you?'

Ayala could have cried yet remained steely on the outside.

'I need to know if I can trust you.'

'Of course you can.'

'It's not just about getting a story?'

'You do understand, I'm in the business of telling stories?'

Ayala laughed wryly.

'Well naturally, I do. Before you tell my story, you need to listen. Carefully. When you do tell my story, you need to tell it in the right way.'

Ayala paused as soon as she felt a quiver in her voice, not wanting Pat to notice. He noticed.

'Okay. Sounds fair.'

Pat cradled his wall phone piece between his ear and shoulder and attempted to quietly unpack a notebook and pen from his rucksack.

He had the cord at full stretch, wishing it was longer as it almost pinged out of his shoulder cradle and back to the wall. The odour of the kitchen bin he forgot to empty before he went to Phuket distracted him, no amount of Glen 20 spray was shifting that smell anytime soon.

He bit his bottom lip, a trick he used, to stop him from breaking the silence which wasn't his to break.

'I will also tell you things I don't want in the public.'

Pat bit his lip again.

'When I say off the record that's exactly what I mean. But for you to really understand, you need to know the full story. From the very beginning.'

Pat's notebook had long been open, pen poised. 'Where would you like to start?'

# 41

RED DISCOVERED BIANCA in the office with her head on the desk, covered by her arms. He couldn't hear any noise and wondered if she'd fallen asleep, but her shoulders were shaking.

'Bee, what's happening?'

Biana, red-eyed, had trouble getting the words out.

'It's Mum's, Mum...'

'What? Mum? What's happened to Mum?'

'No, not Mum, Mum's Uncle Kenneth. He died.'

Red collapsed onto the office stool in the corner.

'Heart attack. In his garden. Aunty Susan only left him for a moment to check the oven, when she got back, he was gone.'

Red patted Bianca's arm, the best he could manage right now with the level of vulnerability he felt exposed to since sharing his childhood story so broadly.

'When's the funeral, can we go?'

'Yes, we should all go, the four of us. Mum would want that. It's next week, the girls are sending through all the details.'

The phone interrupted their trip down memory lane to summer holidays on the glittery north shore sailing on catamarans and small yachts with Kenneth and Susan's children.

Red answered then handed it to Bianca.

'It's Shiny Michael, The Lawyer.' Red's disdain for the suave young lawyer Kenneth had been gradually handing over all their legal work to was clear. Michael was far too much like Clive and his male business cronies with their shiny shoes, expensive cuff links and starched shirts. Bianca frowned in reprimand.

'Hey Michael, how are you going?'

'I'm very well Bianca, good as gold. Apart from being quite sad to hear the news about Kenneth. He was a top old man, taught me a lot.'

Bianca cringed. She shook it off, she had no reason not to like Michael. He'd been the upmost professional from day one and everything was in perfect order legal-wise. Maybe he just didn't do grief well. A lot of men didn't.

'I'm wondering if you are coming to the funeral, as it will be a good opportunity to go through some more paperwork. Susan asked me to help clear out his office and said she'd found a file with Philips on it we might like to look through.'

'Sure, sounds good. Maybe it is just something he hadn't gotten around to giving you just yet as part of the handover.'

'Yes, that is what I imagine it to be.'

'Okay, I'll keep in touch.

A COUPLE OF days after a loving tribute to the man Bianca and her brothers knew as their Mum's Uncle Kenneth, Bianca met Michael at the Marigold in Chinatown.

He initially suggested Golden Century, but it held too many memories. It was Clive and Ayala's special dinner treat when they took the children to the city. Bianca dearly loved the restaurant Eric and Linda Wong opened after moving from Hong Kong, where she sat in awe as a young girl when the nice-looking blonde man Clive introduced her to as Rod Stewart shook her hand. She knew she wouldn't step foot inside its doors, ever again.

Michael, only a couple of years older than Bianca, was a ladies' man of the highest order with his manicured nails, smooth shave, wavy dark hair cut in the latest 'lawyer' style and a masculine energy that could charm the pants of a Catholic nun.

Even Bianca, immune to the *men in suits* charms she'd grown up around at her family's numerous dinner parties and business events, couldn't help slipping in and out of a mesmerised state.

She lost the train of conversation every time he passed her something and brushed her hand, or when she got a slight hint of his understated aftershave.

It had been a long time since she'd been in the company of a young man who didn't smell like he'd just swum in a bath of sheep dip and red dirt.

It was also rare to dress nicely and not in denim jeans, boots, collared work shirt and Akubra. Today she chose a bottle green pencil skirt and white and pale green sleeveless shirt with a structured wide collar sitting in a perfect V shape. Simple bottle green patent leather pumps finished the outfit.

Her dark brown hair sat elegantly over her shoulders and framed her face like a loveheart. After the effervescent and completely over the top London hairdresser working in Vidal Sassoon recovered from the split ends her hat had hidden for the better part of the year, he told her she reminded him of Jennifer Aniston from the hit television series *Friends*.

With skill and snipping delivered at the same rapid rate of his conversation, Bianca's thick straight hair responded gratefully to being styled into a cut that would become the most popular of the nineties.

'As I was telling you,' Michael continued, jolting Bianca back to the here and now, 'I think the file was just incorrectly labelled on the outside as there was nothing in there about your family interests, just some completely unrelated property purchase in Western Australia for a woman named Joanne Hill, and a whole heap of stocks and shares. I thought he was handing them all over for me to manage, but he might have wanted to keep his hand in with a few clients. Worth squillions she is, you probably wish it was yours.'

Bianca didn't blink. Money talk didn't impress her. She had ambitions but financial wealth wasn't among them.

'It's unusual for Kenneth to mix up files but he did tell me on more than one occasion his health wasn't what it used to be.' Bianca bit into a steamed pork bun and thought she might orgasm. 'I haven't had food like this for a very long time, I forgot how incredible their Chinese is. It's as though I'm in Hong Kong right now.'

'Me too, I love this place. The food is first class. How long since your last meal of Chinese? Not many Chinese restaurants out your way.'

'No, there's not. I've been living on a more European menu lately, which has been quite an experience, thanks to the new live-in housekeeper who helps me feed the hungry cowboys and cowgirls who come and go on our place. She's a brilliant cook.

'Me, I'm more of a plain Jane in the kitchen. Meat and veg. Cooking has never really been my thing, as much as Mum tried to pass on her skills and love of preparing food.'

'I can't cook much either. One thing's for sure though, this is the kind of food I much prefer over grey boarding school vegetables, cheesy sauce covered everything, and junket.'

'Junket, does anyone actually make that anymore?'

They erupted into giggles, the mysterious file a passing blip in the long conversation of their long lunch.

BY THE TIME Michael sensed someone behind him as he approached his Potts Point apartment building in Tusculum Lane it was too late. There was not a single soul around; it was just on dark, and they timed their snatch and grab perfectly.

Someone covered him in a blanket and gruffly ordered him to lie on the floor in the back. Michael's mind raced through every misdemeanour and sideways step he'd taken to get where he was, scrambling to land on one that would place him in the back of a mob car with dark tinted windows and the smell of cheap men's cologne.

The car pulled over and the back door opened. The smell of the harbour was a welcome hit of fresh air, and whoever climbed into the back seat removed the blanket.

'Sit up, Michael.'

It took a few minutes to unfold and get himself onto the seat where he came face to face with a man he instantly recognised.

'Hope you enjoyed your long lunch with my precious daughter, you piece of scum,' Clive snarled. 'Don't even think about what you're thinking by the way, she's far too good for the likes of you.'

Michael chose to play it cool and pretend he wasn't intimidated one bit, as though this sort of thing happened regularly.

'It was a business lunch Clive. Now her family lawyer is no longer with us, she needs someone to look after her affairs, especially now both her parents are unavailable for support.'

Clive's hands formed into fists and Michael wondered if the next thing he'd remember would be waking up in cold water with dead weights tied to his feet dragging him to the bottom of the harbour.

'Going to be like that are you? No pushover I see.'

Michael didn't reply.

'Anyway, enough of all that, what I want is to find out if old sly fox Kenneth knew where Ayala was.'

'Why would he know where Ayala is? Nobody knows where she is, apart from you, according to the media and the police.'

'I didn't kill her if that's what you are thinking. She's not dead, she never was.'

'Why would I believe you? Do you have her as hostage or something?'

'I wish. No, I have no idea where she is. She's disappeared. But she didn't disappear so brilliantly on her own. Someone had to be helping her, and that someone had to be Kenneth.'

'I don't have any idea what you're talking about Clive, honestly. He never mentioned her to me apart from in relation to looking after your four children.'

'Speaking of that, I'm a little bit intrigued. What exactly are you looking after for my four children?

'Kenneth has been doing more than just playing the role of Uncle Kenneth to Alaya. Sly old fox too her father was, I bet he had something to do with all of this.'

Clive was rambling, Michael had no idea what he was talking about.

'It sounds like you have it all figured out Clive. There's probably not much more I can really shed light on, as you know more than I do. I'm just a caretaker, not a decision maker. All the decisions are in the hands of your children.'

'That's where you are wrong my boy,' Clive spat. 'I don't know everything. There is more to this story, and you are going to help me figure it out.'

'I really don't think I can help you Clive. It's a clear conflict of interest with your children. Plus, you are on parole awaiting serious charges. I can't be anywhere near you.'

'You have no choice.'

Michael tried to protest but the knowing look on Clive's face stopped him in his tracks.

'I know what you did when you were at law school Michael, you naughty boy.'

Michael's skin tingled as he tried to keep a straight face.

'I know you raped a girl and then your father paid off her father to keep her quiet. Wouldn't your current employer love to know their newest prodigy was in fact... a rapist. My Bianca wouldn't be impressed either.'

Michael's shoulders slumped and he hung his head in shame. He knew it would catch up with him one day.

A stupid, drunken, boyish act, egged on by his lifelong friends who all believed it was their right and privilege to have whatever girl they wanted, when they wanted, how they wanted. If she was drunk, even better.

Michael's father did what he believed was the right thing. Michael was so racked by guilt and so concerned about his career; he went along with it.

'No matter, we all make mistakes. I'm afraid you're going to have to pay for this one if you want me to keep it out of the papers. I know this girl's family, I used to get together every week after a tennis game for a drink with her father. She's a wreck, she'll never get over what you did to her.'

Clive paused for effect. 'What a small world we live in.'

'If that's not the pot calling the kettle black, I don't know what is.' Michael retorted. Clive didn't bat an eyelid.

'I've got my own set of troubles, yes for sure, but the bastards haven't got me yet and I don't believe they ever will. My priority now is to find Ayala and return her to her broken-hearted children. Surely you understand how important that is.'

Michael was confused. Clive the chameleon had changed from a spiteful, evil bully to a remorseful father who wanted to reunite his missing wife with their children.

'I'd love to help you Clive, I really would. But you're barking up the wrong tree.'

Clive moved towards him, and he scuttled backwards until the door rest dug deep into his back.

Like a jump scare scene in an American cop show, Michael was anticipating the king hit or shot to the skull around every dark turn of conversation.

'Don't do it, I won't breathe a word to anyone, just let me go. Please, you are in enough trouble, you don't need to make more.'

Michael's snivelling was getting on Clive's nerves. 'Shut up, just shut up!'

Michael didn't reach up to wipe Clive's spittle from his face, thinking if he maintained eye contact and projected goodness and honesty, he could change the electricity from a negative to a positive charge.

Clive was so close now Michael could see a dark hair curling upwards out of his left nostril. He closed his eyes in defeat and resignation.

A second later he was face first on a gravel road, wheels spinning and covering him in dust. The car disappeared into the darkness so fast he only caught a couple of letters and numbers from the number plate. F—Y – –2 and he wondered if he screamed it out loud or just in his head 'FUCK YOU 2!!'

# 42

RHIANNON WAS BACK in Bourke, in the storeroom, going through files. She hated the way police investigations were so stop, start.

Nothing ever fell into place in order, and she ended up twiddling her thumbs after she followed up on everything she could since her and Andy talked to Susan.

A visit to Keely's family when she had a few spare hours was a welcome distraction from the dead ends of Clive and Ayala. They had just finished a photography session with a photographer from the New Idea magazine who was helping them with a fresh appeal for information about Keely.

Rhiannon tried to appease their doubts about how intrusive the public exposure would be. 'You never know who will pick up a copy of the magazine and recognise her from somewhere. It could lead to the crucial piece of information we need to find her.'

The answers to Rhiannon's Keely and Ayala questions weren't in Sydney, and with the clearing sale at *Hillview* only a week away, she put herself closer to home and back in the head of S.K.Y., her mystery serial killer.

Dubbo police were looping her into their investigation into the two backpackers, but their wheels were also slow. They had mountains of detail to go through with the families, knowing everything they did from here had to be meticulous and to the standard which would satisfy the NSW Coroner in a future inquest. What they hoped Rhiannon could do for them was fill in the gaps and make connections to Lucy, Harriet and possibly more.

By mid-morning, two coffees in, the insurmountable task in front of her lost its glow. Empty files, half empty files, careless records, photos in files they didn't belong in, leading her down rabbit burrows and fox holes searching for the correct file.

'Fucking hell, what the fuck. Fucking idiots. Careless fucks. Fuck fuck fuck.'

A tentative knock on the door interrupted her tirade.

'Rhiannon, it's Zoe, I'm just checking, do you want a coffee?'

Rhiannon rolled her eyes. Her favourite. Constable Zoe Chesney. Still fresh from the academy, and the only other female police officer at the station.

Zoe was following Rhiannon around like a puppy. No, like a clingy toddler. No, like a leech. Rhiannon already had stern words with her about her sloppy phone answering technique and ocker attitude. Every now and then she thought she saw potential, but she'd been too busy to put any time into her.

'No thanks, thanks though.'

Rhiannon got back to her files, not noticing Zoe had opened the door until her shadow fell over the photograph of a fourteen-year-old Aboriginal girl who went missing five years ago and was filed with the case of an elderly man with severe dementia who escaped over the back fence of the nursing home while nobody was looking.

Annoyed, Rhiannon looked up into Zoe's cat-like eyes which were two different colours, one brown, one blue.

'Hah, well what do you know? Special eyes. Did you know some cultures believe you can see heaven and earth at the same time?'

'Or I was touched by a fairy.'

'Or you are a witch.'

Zoe laughed. 'My personal favourite is the witch. Because honestly, who doesn't want to be a witch?'

'True, being a witch is better than being a fairy. Especially in this game.'

Jokes over, Zoe stood awkwardly, fidgeting, tough girl exterior nowhere to be seen.

'Out with it, what do you need?'

'Well, I was just wondering, as I was sitting at my desk with nothing really to do I haven't done and redone ten times to make myself look busy and not useless, that I could, um, maybe I could help you. I'm pretty good with organising things, I won an award from my classmates at the academy for neatness. Which they call the OCD award, so I never really knew if it was an insult or a compliment.'

'I get it, I got that award too,' Rhiannon laughed. 'It is definitely an insult, but I like how you look at things from the glass half-full perspective.'

'Well, yes, I do tend to do that. It helps me not get too anxious, if I can look at the bright side, I don't have to deal with the dark side.'

'Mmm, interesting career choice. You'll be seeing more of the dark side than you'll ever imagine. Enough to last several lifetimes in fact. Look around here, this room has all the dark sides. But the biggest dark side is the fucking idiots who haven't taken the time to Investigate. Things. Properly.'

'Um, okay, well, I, um…'

'Here, don't be shy with me.' Rhiannon handed her a box. 'Find yourself a spot and get sorting. I'm looking for missing girls in eastern Australia, New South Wales, Queensland, Victoria, since 1988. Now we've found the two English backpackers, I'm looking at all overseas people reported missing in Australia.'

'Just girls?'

'Yes, just girls. That fits the MO.'

'It's just that, um, maybe, well, you know…'

'Oh my goodness Zoe, you're going to have to quit with the ums and the aaahs or I'm going to kick you out of here. One thing I've learnt is get to the point and get to it quickly before you get left behind.'

Zoe sat up straight.

'I was thinking maybe some young men might have gone missing too, you know like the backpacker who was working for your friends who disappeared and still hasn't shown up. Maybe the serial killer didn't just target girls?'

Rhiannon disagreed but remembered being young and earnest.

'Okay, should keep it open then. Any missing males that raise a red flag, put them in a new pile and I'll review them too.'

# 43

RHIANNON WAS MUSTERING sheep with Bill in Bore Paddock, following the familiar shape of his well-worn Akubra pulled low over his ears so it wouldn't blow off. The dust behind his bike started as a small red trail and gradually grew until she was in a blinding dust storm which coated her teeth and covered her sunglasses.

The wind snatched her voice as she chased her Dad blindly into the unknown. With a start she woke from her fitful, frustrating dream. Weak light pushed through the small gap around her curtain, and she gradually got the bearings of her childhood bedroom which she only had two more sleeps left to sleep in before it became little Rose's room.

She rolled into the wetness her dream tears left on the pillow to check her bedside clock, 4.45am.

As she was tossing up whether to wallow in her misery or face this day when people from all around the district and beyond would wander through her family memories and treasured possessions, she heard the sounds of machinery and barking dogs.

She hadn't heard Mac get up while she was busy chasing and yelling out to Bill on his disappearing motorbike.

Jane tapped lightly on the door, appearing with Rhiannon's favourite teapot and two cups on a tray. She was dressed, her hair done. The hallway light caught a tiny smear of pink lipgloss.

'Morning Mum,' Rhiannon sat up, adjusted her pillow and scooched over to make room so they could enjoy their tea in the position they drank the first cup of the day for years.

'Morning love.'

'I'm the last one up who's a rotten egg!'

'It's a wonder you didn't hear Mac clattering around the kitchen and walking on the floorboards like an elephant!'

'He's hopeless, he has no idea how to sneak around quietly in the mornings. He's like, 'well, I'm up, so everyone else needs to be up too!''

'Exactly, your Dad was the same. Took me a few years to adjust but then I started to appreciate the early starts, best time of the day.'

Rhiannon sipped her tea, white, no sugar.

'Nice brew Mum. You're definitely not putting this teapot in the clearing sale!'

Jane laughed, but it came out more like a cry-laugh, and she took a sip to cover it. Rhiannon threw her arm around Jane's shoulders and hugged her tight.

'We'll get through it Mum, it's the right thing, a whole new fresh start for you, the world is your oyster.'

Jane retrieved an ironed white handkerchief tucked inside her bra and delicately blew her nose.

'I know that. And I know your Dad wouldn't want me to continually feel overwhelmed like I do, trying to keep everything running here like he used to. Everyone's been such a great support, but they all have their own lives to live, I can't expect them to be giving up their time to help me out. But it's just the final moments ...'

'It was never going to be easy, we're nearly there though. Come on, let's face this day!'

Teacups drained, their feet hit the floor on opposite sides of the bed at the same time, they stood at the same time, and jinxed each other at the same time.

Rhiannon whistled as she made the bed, perfect hospital corners like Jane taught her, adrenalin and her strong cup of tea getting her firing. She neatened the boxes packed with all her childhood treasures sitting by the door, lifting the unsecured lid of the last one to place a precious photo of her in front of Bill on the motorbike.

Aged four, she looked up at him with complete adoration, both of them laughing with mouths open as the wind lifted her oversized Akubra. Two kelpies behind Bill peered around either side, ears pinned back in matching wind grins. Jane captured and froze the moment in time forever.

'You'll never leave us Dad. We mightn't be able to see you or talk to you like we want to, but I know you're always with me just as I'm always with you,' she whispered as she sealed the box with an expert flick of the packing tape dispenser.

She took one final look at her bare room before turning off the light and shutting the door, enveloping her memories in darkness as they waited patiently for her to relocate them and add new ones.

IN THE KITCHEN there was not a spare square on the benches or table.

'Bloody hell Mum, how long have you been at it, I swear there was only half this much food prepared when I went to bed last night.'

'I couldn't sleep, and I was worried about not having enough food.'

'Far out, there's enough here to feed all of Queensland, not just the southwest corner.'

Rhiannon admired the perfectly neat triangles of fresh sandwiches filled with plain egg and lettuce, curried egg and lettuce, roast beef, cheese and Ronnie's fruit chutney, corned beef and Jane's home-made yellow pickles, chicken and mayonnaise, plain tomato with pepper and salt, plain cucumber with pepper and salt and Rhiannon's personal favourite, roast lamb with Ronnie's fruit chutney.

Jane pulled a batch of fresh scones out of the oven and Rhiannon moved a few sandwich trays into the laundry and stacked them into the spare fridge.

'You do realise Ronnie will bring a similar quantity of food, and I organised for the Cunnamulla CWA ladies to cater so you wouldn't have to do all this, don't you?'

'You know how I am when I'm anxious. I like to prepare food.'

Rhiannon didn't hear her over the noise of the hand beater as Jane whipped cream for the scones.

'Oooh, I might have one of these for breakfast, want one?' Rhiannon cut a couple of steaming scones in half and generously loaded them with Jane's strawberry jam. Last summer had been a bumper harvest in the strawberry patch and Jane had enough jam to keep them going with scones, jam and cream for several years.

Jane lifted the beaters out of the cream, checking for the perfect peaks.

'No, I don't think I can, I've been munching all morning. Looks like you'll need to have two!'

'No problems there,' Rhiannon said through a mouthful of luscious cream, jam and pillowy scone.

'You are going to get a run for your money today on who's made the best scones, but I think these will be up there.'

'They're pretty good, but they'll pale in comparison to Kathy Richards's scones.'

'Of course, I had almost forgotten about hers, how's she going these days? Oh, it still breaks my heart when I think about Leesa.'

'She's okay, she's sturdy and picked up the pieces for all of them. The boys are at boarding school now, but she's still involved in everything, helps with everything, never sits still. Women like her are the backbone of small communities – the district would be lost without her.'

'I loved the *stitch and bitch* days with those ladies, lots of giggles.'

'Yes, same! Those of us who can't quilt to save ourselves mainly went for her scones! Are you working on something?'

'Not really, I've got a half-finished quilt in the spare room, I'm having a bit of trouble getting to it. I've got so many cases that are stop-start, and I can't get a decent run on any of them. Between the trips to Sydney and everywhere in between and way out of the way, I don't have the headspace for sitting still.'

'Then this.'

'Yes, this. Then Mac and his big dreams.'

Jane moved over to help Rhiannon cut the rest of the scones and arrange them on a platter to cool down before dressing them in their jam and cream hats.

'He told me about the chicken farming. He's got lots of ideas and seems to have his heart set on this one place down in New South.'

'Yeah, Manilla. I've never been there but I've been plenty of places nearby.

I took that trip to Coolah with Andy recently, it's in that general vicinity. Coolah was a pretty, pretty place, I am sure Manilla is just as beautiful. I know it will be greener than here!'

'That wouldn't be hard most years, haven't seen a good long wet for a while.'

Jane asked her next question gently. 'Where do you sit on the chicken farm front? Is it Mac's dream only, or yours as well?'

'It's Mac's dream. But wherever Mac goes I'm never going to be far away, so it can be my dream as well. Even if I don't move there straight away, I'll get my butt into gear for a transfer to somewhere not too far away.'

'Back to Kings Cross?'

'Maybe. If they'll have me. But don't tell Mac, we haven't gone into that level of detail just yet. We haven't even been to a bank to work out how we're going to afford it. Let alone how we're going to actually sort that side of things, given that we're boyfriend and girlfriend and nothing more than that.'

'Do you think it's worth having those conversations love? There is a big house there I think he's got his heart set on for the two of you. And he's made it no secret to anyone where he sees his future. With you.'

'I haven't seen the place yet, it's not a done deal by any means.' Rhiannon didn't want to let on how annoyed Jane was making her feel, not wanting to upset her today. But for pity's sake, she hated someone else trying to make plans and sort logistics for her.

'I love him, he's my best friend, and apart from Dad, he's the best man I know. Oh, and Andy, he's not too bad.'

Jane laughed. 'Andy's very fond of you Rhee, he is a good man.'

Rhiannon raised an inner eyebrow. She'd never heard Jane talk about Andy in this husky tone of voice and took a mental note to be more observant.

Keen to divert the conversation away from her and Mac, Rhiannon enquired about Jane's move. Sydney and Brisbane were the two cities Jane was looking at in newspaper real estate guides. Toowoomba was also an option, but she thought she wanted a complete change of scene, the polar opposite to her lifetime of outback isolation.

While Rhiannon was making suggestions about suburbs in both cities to avoid and where she thought Jane might be the most comfortable, and safest, the large cuckoo clock handed down through Bill's family's generations bonged six times.

'Mac will be in for his cooked breakfast any minute.' Rhiannon found the bacon in the fridge as Jane pulled the frying pan out of the cupboard and moved the full ceramic egg tray closer to the stove.

As Jane watched the bacon sizzle and cracked Mac's first egg into the pan she knew then and there where her future lay. She would look at apartments in Sydney so she could be close to Rhiannon.

Rhiannon was her future, and whether Rhiannon ended up in Sydney or on a chicken farm at Manilla, Jane didn't want to be too far away.

## KATHY RICHARDS' SCONES
4 cups SR flour
300 ml pouring cream
1 can of lemonade

METHOD: Sift flour (if you want), make a hole in the centre. Mix cream and lemonade together and pour into centre, combine gently with a wooden spoon until you have a dough. If mixture is too 'wet' add more SR flour.

Cook in hot oven (about 20 minutes) until golden.

*For new cooks, the missing steps most country cooks have in their heads include: Flour your bench and tip dough. Use your hands to flatten the scone dough about one inch thick. Use your scone cutter to cut out dough portions (or a floured small glass rim), then place portions onto a lined baking tray, with portions quite close together. They will all lean in together and join a little while cooking but are easy to pull apart once baked. When you have cut out all you can, re-roll out the dough, then press it back out flat to get the most scones out of your dough. That's it! During cooking time, you can whip some cream into soft peaks, and get the strawberry jam ready too.*

# 44

WITH RHIANNON OFF work for her family property's clearing sale, Zoe had even more time to spend in the storeroom. It was a quiet day in Bourke, and none of the other officers even noticed she wasn't at her desk.

Zoe had an incredible skill of making herself invisible in a room, something that would see her go a long way in her career. 'Observers' were highly sought after in strike force teams.

She knew she was only supposed to sort files into piles, but she had read through all of Keely's case files and the S.K.Y. investigation, feeling a strong pull from Rhiannon's dossier of meticulous notes.

She opened one of the remaining Bourke boxes and started flipping through to see if it contained any missing persons reports. Just the one. The file was slim. A Harold Smith was missing, reported at the Bourke Police Station by the road's maintenance manager at the Bourke Council in 1983.

Harold Smith, where had she read that name? She looked up at the butcher's paper on the wall entitled S.K.Y. The man everyone thought was Lucy's father was written as clear as day, Harold Smith.

Adrenalin coursed through Zoe's whole body, making her hands shake. The brief report said Harold moved into an old homestead on a property east of Bourke with his teenage daughter. After a week of reliable, enthusiastic work he failed to show up. The manager went out to the homestead looking for him a week after, but there was nobody there.

What happened to Harold Smith?

The more she read, the more Zoe believed there was more to Lucy than met the eye.

Something Jeremy said when Rhiannon interviewed him stuck out in the notes. He felt scared by Lucy, he said something 'just wasn't quite right'. He couldn't pinpoint anything specific but believed Keely was scared of her too.

Why were they scared of Lucy?

The timeline Rhiannon was building for S.K.Y. explored the possibility the EH Holden had been in the general vicinity of where the English backpackers went missing after police had found another backpacker who worked in a cotton-picking crew at Trangie around the time the girls disappeared and mentioned 'the golden couple in the EH Holden'.

Yes, Lucy was dead, but others were dead too, and Lucy had been there. Zoe's theory was wild and off the wall. What if the note was about Lucy? What if Lucy was S.K.Y. – serial killer, yes?

The thought sent fizzy bubbles up Zoe's nose that fired into her brain. Everyone was focussing on Lucy's male travelling companion as being the serial killer. They'd built him up in their minds as a good-looking version of Ivan Milat, who detectives arrested last year after seven bodies were discovered in Belanglo State Forest.

Although serial killers weren't new to Australia, with the likes of Derek Percy who murdered a child in 1969 and was linked to the death of eight other children in the sixties, and Paul Denyer, known as the Frankston Serial Killer for the murder of three women in 1993, they weren't a common occurrence.

Zoe wondered if Rhiannon was making too many assumptions that they were looking for a male serial killer, coloured by the more recent notoriety of Milat and Denyer.

Several hours later, exhausted and drained, she stood up and stretched after unpacking the final box. She had less than five minutes left of her shift and grinned internally at her efficiency. Rhiannon would be pleased to see her progress when she returned.

She felt a twinge in her lower back and bent down to touch her toes to loosen it up. Hanging upside down she moved her head from side to side, and noticed another box buried under a stack of toilet paper.

'Damn, not another one,' she muttered under her breath. She stood up straight and shrugged her shoulders a few times. Maybe she'd leave it until tomorrow, Rhiannon wouldn't be back for another few days, so she had plenty of time.

She flicked off the light as she left, slipping out of the station unnoticed after adding the time and her signature to the sign-out book. The late afternoon sun was like a hot iron to her head as she walked the four blocks to the cute, freshly painted rental cottage Rhiannon helped find for her.

Four hours later, unable to sleep thanks to the box under the toilet paper popping into her head whenever she closed her eyes, she dressed in civvies and headed back to the station.

At four strokes to midnight she opened a missing persons file labelled Lief Janssen. The school photo his parents posted to Eden Police Station, the town their last letter from him was post stamped in 1983, fell onto her lap. His neatly combed white-blond hair was cut short in what Zoe imagined was the school's required style judging from the smart blazer, white collared shirt and perfectly tied tie. A broad, open smile, piercing blue eyes and a square jawline to rival Brad Pitt's, made Lief the perfect package.

'Oooh, I'd love me a long, tall glass of that water,' Zoe muttered under her breath.

The penny dropped.

It had to be him.

She looked at the photo sketch based on Jeremy's description. Definitely. No doubt. Maybe that's why he'd been so hard to track down, he wasn't even an Australian citizen. Whatever record was available of him entering and still being in Australia hadn't been uncovered.

She made a note to ask Rhiannon if anyone had mentioned an accent, plus many more questions.

Did she dare write his name on the butcher's paper for S.K.Y.? Did she dare write up the theory that came to her like a lightning bolt from a summer outback storm?

She wrote it in a notebook first.

S.K.Y.

Lief killed Lucy.

But why? Did she know too much? Did she threaten to expose him? They knew Keely was with Lief and Lucy at that time, and Rhiannon and Andy thought it was highly likely she was dead too. Or did she escape?

Were Lief and Lucy a pair of serial killers?

'Whoa!'

Rhiannon's notes establish they had travelled together for several years before they picked up Keely in 1989, also that they'd been together when Harriet from Coolah disappeared in 1987. Also together when the backpackers disappeared near Trangie in 1988.

Surely Lief couldn't have hidden all these killings from his travelling companion? Who was the instigator? When you add the missing Harold Smith, reported in 1983, into the mix, with the missing Lief Janssen who last wrote to his parents from Eden in 1983, when did Lucy meet Lief? Her last high school was in Eden, that was in 1983. Did she meet him then? Before she moved to Bourke?

Had Lief been to Bourke and did he have something to do with Harold's disappearance? Or did she go back to Eden after Bourke and connect with him?

When did they start travelling together in the EH Holden? The police had traced it back to the recording studio in Eden, but didn't have a definitive date of when Lief drove it out of the long bush driveway.

'Whoa, what a trip!' Zoe said out loud as a wild idea popped into her head.

She got the glue out and pasted a copy of Lief's photo on her page, and drew a strong, red arrow from the word S.K.Y. to his beautiful, smiling face.

She glued the back of a photocopy of Lucy's photo and hesitated for a few seconds before resolutely placing it right beside Lief. Not below him with the row of other murdered and missing girls possibly linked to S.K.Y., but where Zoe felt in her bones Lucy belonged.

She drew a neat circle between Lucy and Lief, resisting the temptation to make it a love heart, and with a blue pen she wrote: *Lief killed Lucy and gouged her eyes out so she couldn't look at him anymore. This violent act was motivated by his desire to take back the control she held over him. Lief is trying to tell us Lucy is S.K.Y.*

An hour later she sat back and admired the handiwork she planned to give Rhiannon the minute she walked back in the door.

'If I'm on the right track, Keely had nothing to do with this, maybe he saw her as an escape from Lucy? Maybe, just maybe, there is a slight chance Keely is still alive.'

# 45

'THE WAY I see it is, you just need to come forward to the police, tell them you are alive, hand over Aawut so they can put him into protective custody, reunite with your family, and this will all be over.'

Ayala resisted the urge to hang up the phone in his ear. With calmness she didn't feel she quietly explained.

'You need to understand Pat, Clive has a lot of contacts. The underworld, the mafia, he's like the roots of a willow tree. He won't be sitting back feeling contented. He will be scheming, plotting and planning.'

'How could he ever find you? He hasn't yet.'

'No, that's true. That doesn't mean he isn't still looking. Once he figures out I have had a private nest egg since we were first married, which is the only file Kenneth hasn't handed over to the young lawyer Michael who's taking over his clients, but which I'm sure Susan has passed on by now as she would have cleaned out his office...' Ayala's voice shook as the dull pain of remembering Kenneth was gone washed over her, '...he's going to be furious.'

'How would he find that out?'

'He will, it's only a matter of time.'

'What about Susan? What does she know?'

Ayala's sharp intake of breath sent adrenalin straight through the phone to Pat.

'I spoke to her, briefly, when he died. I was on the phone with him when he had a heart attack, I heard her calling from a long way away, then closer, then closer. I stayed on the phone; I couldn't hang up...'

Pat waited patiently for Ayala to continue. When she didn't, he asked gently, 'Do you think she would have told the police?'

Ayala started sobbing. 'I don't know, I don't know!'

'Okay, it's okay. Maybe we should leave it for now, if you need a break.'

'No, no, I'm fine, I'll be fine. Just give me a minute.'

While he was waiting, Pat scribbled down a note, wanting to keep this clear thought in his mind which scurried like mice in a grain shed. *Rhiannon McVee can reunite you with your family.*

Aawut listened to the phone call from the verandah, where he spent most of his days poring over the extensive range of books Lucas stuffed every shelf, nook and cranny with. His favourite was *Every Australian Bird Illustrated*, first published in 1975. His next favourite was *Exploring Outback Australia* by Tobin Meryl Brown; Ayala had been using it to help him with his English. He also found a copy of the 1972 book by Garnet J. Ros, *Venomous Australian Animals Dangerous to Man,* which terrified and excited him at the same time. He spent his long bush walks jumping at every rustle in the leaves, wondering which dangerous animal was about to attack.

He couldn't pick up every word, but he didn't need to understand what she was saying to understand what she was feeling.

He'd only ever seen Ayala as completely in control, she'd hidden her weak moments from him well. Wringing his hands, he looked down at his feet, tapping feverishly in response to the sound of Ayala sobbing, wailing and speaking in a high-pitched voice he hadn't heard before.

He wanted to run. But where would he go? He knew from the outback stories he read he couldn't just walk out the gate and keep walking until he reached his destination. Not to mention the venomous Australian animals dangerous to man lurking behind every bush and under every rock.

Ayala appeared to gulp in some fresh air. She turned slowly to Aawut with tear-stained cheeks and red blotches around her eyes, taking a moment to notice the cause of the tapping sound on the verandah.

She walked over with gentle purpose and rested her hands on his knees, stilling them. With her face close she whispered. 'It will be okay. I promise, it will be okay.'

Her eyes were soon dry, and she winked as she walked back to the phone, Aawut's distress fuelling her mothering instinct and reminding her she had one chance to do this right.

'Hi Pat, where was I?'

For the next hour she outlined her plan. It was risky but he could make it work. If they managed to get Clive behind bars and blow up the paedophile ring he was part of, keeping vulnerable children out of harm's way, Pat didn't care if he never broke another story. This would be enough to last the rest of his life. Almost.

'Then what?' he pressed.

'Then nothing. That's the story I want you tell. I'm not your story. Putting Clive behind bars for good is enough.'

He looked down at his notes, the words jumping off the page: *Rhiannon McVee can reunite you with your family.*

He read them to Ayala.

She didn't want to hear them.

She couldn't come forward. After all the pain and suffering she knew she'd bestowed upon her children, she didn't think she ever would.

# 46

'HEY MCVEE,' PAT called from work, attempting cool and calm but only managing a squeaky, slightly false and insincere voice. Partly caused by the rush the sound of her voice gave him, mostly caused by the lies he was about to spin.

The sound of his voice was like a red rag to a bull. 'Where the fuck have you been? I've been worried sick something happened to you, far out, I thought someone killed you in a back alley and disposed of your body.'

'Don't be such a drama queen, I thought you were far better than that, Detective.'

'Bloody hell, Jesus, fuck. I'm so relieved to hear your voice.'

Pat blushed and the room seemed brighter. 'I missed you too McVee.'

'Don't be stupid, I didn't miss you, I just thought you'd gone missing.'

Pat felt stupid but recovered quickly.

'Well, it wasn't easy, but I've managed to do what you asked.'

'Get out! Really?'

'Yep, sure have. When can we meet? Too much for the phone.'

He and Rhiannon were open to the possibility his work phone was being tapped. His home phone was highly unlikely; he'd recently moved, his number was private, his building was secure.

'Got it. Understand. Considering we're nine hours apart, might be a while.'

Rhiannon raced through the things she had coming up. She was meant to go to Manilla with Mac tomorrow and look at the chicken farm, if it was a go they were making an appointment with the bank manager, with Jane, to discuss finance.

Mac would have to wait. This was big, huge.

*So is your future with Mac,* a little voice niggled in her conscience.

Yes, but this is bigger. This could just about be the biggest case of her career. If she could shut down a ring like this, her career would take off, there would be no stopping her. The doors it would open were beyond her wildest imagination. She'd have no trouble transferring back to Kings Cross Detectives. Ambition was fire in her belly.

*Mac will be so disappointed.* There was that annoying voice again.

'You still there McVee?'

'Yes, here. Figuring out a few logistics. I've got to be in Manilla for something. Maybe I could hook you up with Andy to start with, then I'll get there the day after tomorrow?'

Pat didn't hide the disappointment in his voice.

'Okay, but what's so important in Manilla that's more important than this?'

'Personal stuff.' Rhiannon was wavering; maybe she could ask Mac to postpone for a day? And go to Manilla on the way back?

She knew what would happen though, a quick trip to Sydney could just as easily turn into days and days, maybe weeks, depending on how it all panned out.

*This is the right thing.* Her conscience again.

'Sorry, can't change it. I know this is big. Huge. You either hook up with Andy or it waits a day.'

'Fine, I'll wait a day. Call me when you get here.'

Pat was mildly annoyed. He expected her to drop everything like she always did. He wanted her to come running, so he could see her again, look into her mesmerising eyes, soak up the brightness of her intellect, her energy, her enthusiasm. Pretend she was coming running for him, not for the information he held.

As quickly as the thought entered his mind, it was gone.

He had bigger fish to fry. He had Aawut, and soon they would have Clive.

# 47

CLIVE LOUNGED ON the deck of a small yacht, the one he borrowed from a friend when he wanted to go incognito. He was in a secluded spot at Clifton Gardens. Being a weekday, he had the whole bay to himself.

With his head buried in Wilbur Smith's latest novel *The Seventh Scroll,* adventuring through Egypt which was now on Clive's bucket list as soon as he became a free man, he didn't notice someone swimming out from the beach.

'Geez, you gave me the fright of my life,' he remarked as the toned, Greek Dimitris, whose tanned skin shimmered under the dazzle of Sydney harbour sunshine, appeared beside him.

'You did say to be discreet,' the young man replied with a wink, never missing an opportunity to show off the body God graced him with, especially to a man with more money than you could poke a stick at.

'Yes, discreet. My favourite word. Got something for me I assume?'

'Maybe. We think it's worth a follow up. We managed to get the tape from the restaurant that young lawyer took your girl to.'

'I'm impressed. You have a tape? How?'

'The how is for us to know. The what is for you to know. Here.'

Dimitris removed a small plastic package from a discreet pocket on the inside band of his short, tight swimming trunks, containing a tape.

'Have a listen and let me know what next.'

Clive didn't move from his deck chair; his book open on his chest. He discreetly took the plastic package and tucked it underneath the book.

'You never know who might be watching. You'd better get out of here.'

With a bright white smile, compliments of the teeth whitening his new job with Clive had paid for, Dimitris disappeared into the water in a graceful dive that hardly made a splash. Minutes later Clive saw him walk out of the water, like the Greek God he was, and disappear into the sand dunes.

Within minutes he was inside the cabin with earphones plugged in, listening to Michael tell Bianca about a file he mistakenly believed was filed under the Philips name by accident.

'Gotcha this time, bitch. Gotcha for good.'

# 48

'KEL, LOCK UP for me, will you?'

Keely, known to all in her winery in the picturesque Clare Valley as Kel, was carrying a box of riesling into the mail room, to join tomorrow's deliveries.

She sold it over the phone, sealing the deal with 'aromas of pear, white peach and frangipani' delivered in her warm, friendly, not-too-pushy sales voice Ange had been training her to use since she walked into the stately St Aloysius Church to ask for forgiveness.

She took a major detour from the trip Lief thought she was taking to Western Australia, switching buses as soon as she was able, changing her name to Kellie Johns, and going in search of salvation.

As her bus approached the green rolling hills of the Clare Valley, only an hour and a half from Adelaide yet feeling like a place she could easily get lost in, Keely went to the driver and asked if he could stop, immediately.

'We're only about ten minutes from the next stop, in Clare,' he said gruffly. 'I need to get off now,' she insisted. 'Please, please let me off.'

'Fine,' he conceded. 'There's a little place up ahead, Sevenhill, I'll stop there. I don't want to be the one who drops a young girl in the middle of nowhere, not supposed to.'

'No need to worry about me. I'm older than I look, and I can take care of myself.'

'That's what they all say.' The driver shook his head. 'You should be pretty safe out here amongst the Jesuits though.'

Keely wasn't listening, the beauty of the tiny town demanding her full attention. Roses climbed over rambling stone cottages, occasional clumps of ancient trees stood strong among paddocks of gnarly grapevines kept in long straight rows by old timber fence posts and wire.

She'd been here almost a year, welcomed with open arms by the Jesuits at Sevenhill Cellars, attached to the church. Tending to the vines in the vineyards, she discovered a passion for the winemaking process and was now in training to become a winemaker.

'You have the nose for it,' said the kind Brother Matthews who'd been at the winery for more than thirty years and needed help in the cellars as the business became an increasingly popular tourist destination.

Their mail order service was growing exponentially under the guidance of a new cellar door manager, Angela Ferguson, who believed passionately the Clare Valley was on the cusp of becoming Australia's premier wine destination.

'No worries, Ange, I'm almost done. Just got to label this one and I'll be done.'

Ange, who brought glamour and class to Seven Hill, the first winery built in the Clare Valley and one of the oldest in Australia, was gone before Keely could finish her sentence.

They were planning a long lunch in the cellars for a group of high-ranking officials Ange was wining and dining to expand distribution overseas and she had an important meeting with the chef she'd selected to cater.

Once finished in the mail room, Keely walked through the cellar door to make sure everything was put away and the lights turned off. As she was neatly placing the stools along the wine bar, she noticed a large handbag wedged between a stool and the bar. She shifted the stool and it fell with a loud thump, its contents spilling onto the stone floor.

She crouched down to put it all back in, looking for a purse amongst the magazines, lipsticks, pens and tourist brochures so she could call the owner. The New Idea magazine caught her eye. *Kylie's Grisly Murder* was the headline on the front. She couldn't help herself, she sat on the stone floor using the bar as a backrest for a quick read.

Twenty minutes later, absorbed, she flipped to a new page. In shock she stood up, her head hitting the overhang of the wine bar, knocking her out.

She lay face down on the cold stone floor beside a photo of a father surrounded by the Three Sisters, gripping a large, framed photograph of his missing daughter Keely Johnson, pleading desperately for his girl to come home.

# 49

'WHAT DO YOU think?'

'Oh, it's perfect. Just perfect. Look at how green and lush it is. And the hills all around, such a picture. The full dams. Even the trees look bigger here. It's paradise. It really is.'

Mac laughed and kissed her fully on the mouth.

'I guess you like it then?'

'I love it. When do we move in?'

Mac stood back, stunned. They still hadn't broached her work location but walking through the homestead which felt like home sealed the deal in Rhiannon's mind. Her heart completely dominated her logical brain.

'You mean it? We?'

'Of course, we. You don't think I'm going to let you live in paradise without me, do you?'

Mac lifted her off her feet and twirled her around and around. He put her down, took off his hat and threw it in the air.

Rhiannon roared with laughter, unable to resist a little jig. 'I haven't seen you get so excited since you were eight years old and ran to the lolly table at my birthday party to devour the Cheezels,' she said.

'I am a bit partial to Cheezels. We didn't have them very often as you could tell that day!'

He pulled her in close and kissed her again, and again.

'We'd better get a room,' she whispered into his mouth as he grabbed her around both buttocks and pulled their groins together so she could feel just how excited he really was. 'Or a shed. Or a big tree.'

Mac looked around to check the real estate agent had gone. The dust trail was barely visible on the drive, so he grabbed Rhiannon's hand and they ran into a stand of trees a few hundred metres from the sheds.

Nobody would be home for several hours; everyone clearing out to make way for this promising second inspection the agent confidently told the owners would 'seal the deal'.

Giant willow trees hugged a small creek, leaving a clear mat beneath where the roots had sucked the ground dry. Mac gently lay Rhiannon down after removing his shirt for a blanket. She reached up to touch his smooth chest, shifting her hands around to his back and pulling him onto her.

Within minutes she was naked from the waist down, Mac completely naked on top of her. Their boots and jeans lay in a tangle beside them.

'You are the most beautiful woman in the world,' he nuzzled into her neck, her ear, her mouth. She bit his lip gently while she undid the buttons on her white collared shirt, which wouldn't be so white after this. She arched her back so he could reach around and expertly unclasp her bra.

The wind whistled a quiet tune through the long willow strands as they explored each other, both marvelling that even though they were so familiar and at home, each time was a whole new thrill and experience.

A flock of noisy corellas flew overhead, drowning out Rhiannon's screams of pleasure as they christened what they both hoped would soon be their new home.

# 50

SHE DIDN'T HEAR the footsteps crunch through the sticks and dry leaves covering the path to the front gate. Or the small squeak of the gate as he carefully straddled it to leap over. A persistent *tap tap tap* on the stained-glass windowpane of her front door gradually drew her out of her deep exhausted sleep.

It had been a draining week shifting Aawut with the help of Pat. She was leaving it in his capable hands to contact the police and get the wheels in motion to get Clive behind bars.

Pat had continued to lobby her to come forward and reveal to her children she was still alive. She still couldn't. It would have to be enough to know she had kept her children, and all the other children and young people, safe from harm.

What Pat and Ayala didn't know was that Rhiannon and Andy already knew Ayala was alive. They just didn't know where to find her.

The adrenalin and stress her overactive mind put her through once her head hit the pillow meant she snatched two hours of sleep, at best, each night. Usually between four and six in the morning.

She rolled over to look at the clock on her bedside table. It glowed a dull blur, 4.36am.

*Tap tap tap, tap tap tap.*

Ayala imagined it was a bird, or some other bush creature, tapping on a window somewhere in this rambling house. The ocean roaring in the distance was the only other sound.

In her half asleep, half awake state, she pattered down the wide hallway past Aawut's room, noticing his door remained closed. Then she remembered he wasn't there.

It was a moonless, cloudy night and the house was darker than usual. She stumbled against the wall in her search for the sound.

*Tap tap tap, tap tap tap.*

She wandered from room to room.

*Tap tap tap, tap tap tap.*

Eventually she started towards the front door, solid timber apart from a stained-glass panel above head height. A hand shadow appeared, distorted by the rippled, coloured glass and Ayala's heartbeat filled her entire body.

Frozen in fear she saw a finger stretch out, *tap tap tap.*

She looked around for a weapon, something, anything. A large stick Aawut used while bushwalking lay beside her shoes near the door. She dropped to her knees to pick it up without making a sound, wondering if whoever was standing on her verandah tapping on her stained glass had heard her wander around blindly thinking the noise was one made by nature, not imagining anyone could ever find her tucked away out here.

The locked door handle rattled, and the tapping became more insistent. She knew she didn't have long until they moved around the verandah where they'd find the window she left open to catch the cooling coastal breezes through to her bedroom on these scorching summer nights.

She tried to be rational. Probably just someone lost and needing a bed for the night. Holding the stick firm, she unclicked the lock.

'Who's there?'

The tapping stopped. The ocean roared louder, and a gust of wind shifted a large branch across the roof to make a loud scraping sound.

Someone grabbed the door handle from the other side. In unison they turned it open.

Ayala pulled the door towards her, hiding the stick out of sight.

'Hello Ayala,' his big voice boomed through the house. 'Bet you never expected to see me here.'

Clive's perfect white teeth flashed in the darkness. Grinning like a maniac, he pushed the door harder and stepped over the threshold.

## TO BE CONTINUED

# Who's Who

Writing the fictional Missing Annabelle Brown Series and the Rhiannon Series between 2013 and 2017 carried me through a frantic five years culminating in Kings Cross Detectives discovering my missing cousin Ursula Dianne Barwick died in a car accident just a couple of weeks after she went missing in 1987.

The NSW Police 'system' fucked up more times than a tradie's apprentice, which meant two and two didn't make four for thirty years. It broke our hearts to learn Ursula lay in the Glebe morgue for fifteen months before a mystery woman identified her body as Jessica Pearce, 25, with a child, from New Zealand. What happened many years after that broke our hearts even more.

'After found' resulted in deep trauma, not only affecting my memory, but cutting Rhiannon, Mac, Andy, Keely, Ayala and the many other fictional characters in the Rhiannon Series from my life. I poured my grief into writing a memoir for Ursula, yet to be published, named *Yellow Sunbird*, and put this book, which I had started in 2017, aside.

A four-year break made it challenging to reacquaint myself with my fictional friends and finish this book.

Hair colour, eye colour, dates, locations – all the things I obsessed over while pushing for NSW Police to put fresh eyes on Ursula's case – swirled around and refused to settle neatly into place.

A conversation about this conundrum with my seventeen-year-old son helped me find the solution – a glossary, to help you (and myself) navigate through the complicated lives of my missing fictional friends and those who are trying to find them.

**Rhiannon McVee:** daughter of sheep station owners Bill and Jane, *Hillview,* Cunnamulla. Graduated from NSW Police Academy in April 1988.

First station post Kings Cross, Sydney, August 18, 1988. Currently at Bourke Police Station.

**Lachlan 'Mac' MacKenzie:** everyone's favourite outback cowboy. Son of Rhonda 'Ronnie' and Richard, *Leander Park*, two properties away from *Hillview*. Childhood friend of Rhiannon, first kiss in their final year of high school.

**Andy Cassettari:** Detective Sergeant at Kings Cross Police Station. Rhiannon's mentor throughout her career.

**Ayala Philips:** Wife of Clive and mother of Bianca, Jackson (Jack), Rodney (Red) and Lachlan (Lachie). Disappears October 1993, aged 40. Major suspect is husband Clive. Readers ask persistently, *Where the fuck is Ayala?*

**Lucy Wallace and Lief Janssen:** the golden couple who travel around eastern Australia fruit picking, corn tasseling (itinerant farm labourers). They pick up Keely when she hitchhikes out of Sydney in a green EH Holden.

**Keely Johnson:** From Sydney, disappears on September 22, 1988, aged 15. Linked to Kings Cross bikie gangs, Keely reappears in outback NSW near Brewarrina with Lucy and Lief before Rhiannon loses track of her again. In 1995 when this novel is set, she is still missing.

**Aawut Saetang:** informant from Phuket who Rhiannon is trying to track down in the case of Clive Philips, who is a major suspect in the disappearance of Ayala as well as part of an international paedophile ring which encompasses Thailand.

**Pat Richards:** Sydney-based ABC journalist, radio and television, at the forefront of digital online news reporting with the ABC embracing the digital age ahead of many other media companies, going online in August 1995 with the launch of www.abc.net.au. Rhiannon is one of his valuable police contacts, and he wants to break the Clive and Ayala Philips story. He is also secretly in love with Rhiannon.

**Alice and Duncan:** Alice's husband Toby goes missing in 1988, this is one of Rhiannon's first cases. Duncan is Mac's best mate, and owns *Charlotte Downs*, the property in the middle of Mac and Rhiannon's family properties. Alice, who has a child Rose with Toby, and Duncan marry in 1995.

# Acknowledgements

The biggest thank you, as always, goes to my husband and children, who do their best not to interrupt me while I'm attached to any book writing machine I can find during every spare moment of our busy lives.

My Mum Dianne and brother Luke have also carried their fair share of the stress load during the completion of this book, as have my friends Sarah Little and Jamie Klemm. Christine Kaine, who first taught me how to self-publish my books in 2013, remains a special and unwavering support person. Dennie 'Dee' Quintal has also been unwavering in her belief in my ability to finish this book, and many more to come. My mother-in-law Lyn Pouliot is as sharp as ever with her eagle editing eye, right down to missing commas and commas that shouldn't be there.

The recipes are from various places including Wendy Allen's Fritters and Tea Cake recipes that she, and then I, cooked many times while I was working as her governess in southwest Queensland many years ago.

The scones recipe is from our close friend Michelle Clark, whose scones are renowned far and wide in the Minyip community in the Wimmera in western Victoria.

The Passionfruit Delight is my Nanna Laura Hosking's recipe, passed down to my Aunty Trish. I filled in a few of the details as Aunty Trish makes this from memory and when I tried to recreate it, I got lost!

The Walnut Cake is a hand-written recipe from Rita Turnbull who served this up for morning smoko last year with the best cup of tea I've drunk for many years from large enamel teapot that sits in the centre of their table.

I would also like to extend a big thank you to Garrie and Rita Turnbull and their family who live in one of the most stunning places in the Australian outback. Their art of bush storytelling is beyond compare and I could listen to their oral history all day long.

During my four-year break from writing fiction which has included bushfires, COVID, moving house and dealing with thirty years of the ambiguous loss of Ursula, I have developed an added appreciation of the value of chasing your dreams, working hard and getting up with the sun every morning to do what you truly love.

Australian writer Melissa Pouliot, described by one of her children as a book writing machine, had her first story Santa's Elf published in her local newspaper when she was eight. In her first year of university she wrote her first book on a typewriter, based on her time as a governess in outback Queensland, then put it aside to pursue a media career. Two decades later she returned to her novel writing dream and in 2013 released her debut crime thriller *Write About Me*, which topped international bestseller lists and sparked a new investigation that solved the baffling cold case mystery of her teenage cousin Ursula Barwick. More books followed including *Found*, the sequel to *Write About Me*, and The Rhiannon Series, set in the contrasting yet eerily similar worlds of the Australian outback and inner-city streets of Sydney's Kings Cross. Drawing inspiration from the missing and the people left behind, Melissa writes every single day.

www.ingramcontent.com/pod-product-compliance
Lightning Source LLC
Chambersburg PA
CBHW022045240626
47154CB00007B/2569